For
GERARD W. VAN DER LEUN,
for time

CLIFF WALK

CLIFF WALK

MARGARET DICKSON

Houghton Mifflin Company

BOSTON

Copyright © 1987 by Margaret Dickson

All rights reserved. No part of this work may be reproduced or transmitted in any form or by any means, electronic or mechanical, including photocopying and recording, or by any information storage or retrieval system, except as may be expressly permitted by the 1976 Copyright Act or in writing from the publisher. Requests for permission should be addressed in writing to Houghton Mifflin Company, 2 Park Street, Boston, Massachusetts 02108.

Printed in the United States of America

Just lost when I was saved!
Just felt the world go by!
Just girt me for the onset of eternity,
When breath blew back,
And on the other side
I heard recede the disappointed tide!

Therefore, as one returned, I feel,
Odd secrets of the line to tell!
Some sailor, skirting foreign shores,
Some pale reporter from the awful doors
Before the seal!

Next time, to stay!
Next time, the things to see
By ear unheard,
Unscrutinized by eye.

Next time, to tarry,
While the ages steal,—
Slow tramp the centuries,
And the cycles wheel.

     EMILY DICKINSON
     "Called Back"

CLIFF WALK

PROLOGUE

Late in August, nights at the farm became cooler, and the morning grass, wet with diamonds of dew. Just past first light Crelly stood on the doorstep and shivered a little, listening for a bird song, hearing one or two wild notes. There was a soft lowing from the cows in the barn as Uncle Elder finished morning chores.

Over the eastern horizon, behind the distant river, a ribbon of light began to glow. The grass turned smoke-color, green. Crelly looked into the distant trees for a change of weather. Did the trees nod? Were they still?

This was, perhaps, the last moment of peace she would know in just this way, here. She had gotten up early, needing to spend some time in the search for a conviction she could put into words and remember, something to steady her. But the moment had passed; the light was ordinary. It was her wedding day.

Aunt Lois opened the door. "Going to be a good day, Crelly. You want some breakfast?"

The Aunt Lois of Crelly's childhood stood waiting for her to answer—if as a child, there would be no wedding, she would not be ready; if as an adult, they would go forward, all moments would go forward, never be the same again.

"I'll come and help you," Crelly said.

Two women worked in the kitchen, then. With the last of the blueberries, Aunt Lois made muffins. Butter, melting, soaked into every grain. The three—Crelly, Aunt Lois, and Uncle Elder—ate breakfast together. It was too late to be anything but casual, speak of cows, milk, the garden. There were pumpkins ripening; there would be no child on this farm to carve them or to stand in the dark, clinging to Uncle Elder's hand. There would be no child. This was in Uncle Elder's face as he pushed back his chair, winked at Crelly once, left to finish his work.

The two women went to the church, a square white building of two stories set on the rise of a hill in the middle of Edgar, Maine.

Wild grasses grew along the ancient stone foundation of the church. Aunt Lois twitched at them playfully, went to the front door and pulled it open. To either side stairs led to the sanctuary. She and Crelly went up, and with their own hands arranged baskets of flowers in the front, and fixed ribbons to the pews. The baskets flamed with garden gladiolus in rose, crimson, orange. Giving them a final glance, Crelly's face was suddenly on fire.

They went home. It was time to make last-minute arrangements of the long veil and the satin dress, which hung well on Crelly's slender form, its ivory color making her skin glow. She wore her dark hair curled about her shoulders as she always had. She was a blue-eyed bride, her features regular, lips curved up.

Aunt Lois nodded. "There," she said. "Now that's nice."

For an instant a child peered through Crelly's eyes. But Aunt Lois mustn't see—the time must go forward. "It fits beautifully," Crelly said. "Thank you."

Uncle Elder came down the stairs, moving his shoulders back nattily in his unaccustomed suit jacket. When Uncle Elder dressed up he grumbled, but he did have style. And, Aunt Lois always said, he knew it, too. Catching sight of Crelly he paused in the doorway, and dark color rose upward over his face, to the top of his shining, bald head.

He looked at Aunt Lois. "Lois, that is one of your better jobs," he said. "Crelly, you are beautiful."

"Thank you, Uncle Elder."

A sheet had been put on the seat and floor of the truck to protect her dress. Another was laid over her lap. With quiet courtliness Uncle Elder held her skirt up for her to take, so that he could shut the truck door.

Too soon they were at the church. Crelly managed her gown, whispered her thanks to Aunt Lois, felt the last clasp of those firm fingers, the laying of her cheek, smooth and flushed, on Crelly's own. Uncle Elder gave her a final hug. She took his arm. Upstairs at the back of the sanctuary, he patted her hand with his bunged-up clean one. Once, as a child, she had asked him about those scarred, bent fingers. "An argument with a ripsaw," he'd said. "A disagreement with a load of lumber."

"I don't know," she whispered to him desperately. "I don't know."

Then they had no particular station, he older or she younger. They examined together the monkey puzzle of life, trying with their grave regard to fathom it. These looks had the power of intention only, the best they could do. The best they could do was to approve of each other, and they did.

"This is as straight as I can build," Crelly whispered.

Uncle Elder's face reddened. "It'll be as good then, Crelly, as any of us could do."

Her hand clasped firmly in his, they waited for a nod from the organist, began the short, informal walk among friends and neighbors, and John's family and friends, down the aisle to the front.

Crelly was afraid she had forgotten who John was. No. His eyes locked with hers. She saw in his expression humility, love, admiration. She was beautiful; he thought so. She was lovable; it was in his eyes. No matter what happened, he had woven himself forward and back in her heart, in some design she could not yet describe. Surely, she thought, if there were mistakes made on earth, this was not one of them. She strained to hold her love, prove it to herself. She took his hand; his fingers were cold.

"Her Aunt Lois and I do," rumbled Uncle Elder in answer to the minister's question. He sat down next to Aunt Lois. The short marriage service began.

For these moments, John thought, I will forget what came before, what might come after. He looked down, saw Crelly's smile. This was between him and her, no other. His mother's endless telephone apologies to her friends for the "small rural wedding" didn't exist. His father's restive snort of laughter as they stepped to the front of the church—"Couple of brass-tailed monkeys, aren't we?" —that was gone. Beside him stood a small-shouldered, blue-eyed new life, in a dress the light turned from ivory to gold. They would be something new, have something different. They would be blessed. Her hand was in his; he didn't let go.

In the pew behind him sat his mother, her manicured hand toying with a necklace of opals. Her elegant face with its down-turned lips seemed to say I will pretend I like this place. It will all be over soon, this rustic, romantic excursion, and then we will carry on with real life.

Behind her were friends and relations, dressed in weekend-in-the-country seersucker, with low-heeled, sensible shoes. On Crelly's side of the church the women wore more colorful polyester jersey, with white shoes and large white clip earrings to match. Their consensus was that John's side, for a fancy crowd, didn't dress up much. John's side knew just how expensive an understatement could be.

"Oh, the beautiful ocean, Maine's beautiful ocean, that's where they live . . ." This, too, was thought on Crelly's side. "If I didn't live here, I'd take a fling at the ocean."

On John's side, faces as craggy as the coastline examined the interior of this little church, smelled the late summer grassland smells, and thought, Have we chosen wrong? We remember in our bones this place, and places like it, and we love them.

At the back were Marta Davis, and Emil and Gretta Brunholtz, from the university. They, too, sat on opposite sides of the aisle, but they smiled and waved.

At the front, John stood. He was tall and blond, his face hollow below the cheekbones, his forehead high. For these moments, he thought, we have brought them all together. We have dared to do so. God help us.

"What God has joined together," said the minister half apologetically, but with the surety of the ancient warning in his voice, "let no person put asunder." He smiled at John. "You may kiss the bride."

Crelly turned to John. Their kiss reminded them of the first butterfly touch of lips between them, of all the kinds of kisses they had shared since, and which tempted them into the future. Then they broke away, a little embarrassed to have shared so much with all of these people.

There was a friendly chuckling. As Crelly's arms fell away from John's shoulders, some women in the back of the church saw with admiration that Lois Leavitt had appliquéd fine lace on the sleeves of the wedding dress. These women had waited for the kiss—which was a good solid one, they were happy to see, none of your sweaty little pecks—and now they hurried downstairs to bring out the platters of finger sandwiches, homemade goodies. They were thinking that a kiss sealed a promise, and this had been a good strong seal.

These women were the town Women's Association. They hurried about. Lois Leavitt had always helped them with their own family weddings, reunions, funerals, so they didn't stint. Feeding a crowd was their special skill. Someone made deviled eggs, someone else tiny popovers filled with lobster meat. Someone made inch-wide cupcakes and decorated each painstakingly with tiny silver candies, and someone, of course, made the traditional bride's cake, filled with cherries and walnuts, set in tiers of white frosting, with marvelous roped decorations at every edge and delicately tinted frosting flowers on every flat surface. These women would have scorned to set the usual bakery-white bride's cake in the place of honor at this laden table. No, here was a cake of character and stature, rich, chocolate, and delicious.

John clasped Crelly's hand in his and they moved quickly back down the aisle. He would not lose her now, they would never again be separated. In his joy, he didn't feel her hesitate or hear her gasp. He hurried along and Crelly went with him, hanging on tightly. She had seen across all the smiling faces one face, a form prowling at the back of the church. Gene.

Gene looked at her, caught her eye. His was brown and cold, ice in a brown glass.

Crelly hurried on. This is only Gene, she told herself. My brother.

There was again no time to think but a reception, handshaking, much kissing, the opening of gifts, eating. John's father, Jack Werner, went to his wife with a paper plate full of food. "You should try these lobster puffs, Helen. They're really very good. Cook might like this recipe."

"Cook is not here today," Helen Werner said, "although I'm sure she would have felt right at home."

"Oh, I'll get the recipe for you and send it along," said Aunt Lois, who was standing by. She knew Helen Werner. They had locked horns before. Quite sweetly, she said, "You could make it yourself, Helen. It's not hard."

Helen Werner had never lifted a hand to cook in her life. She inclined her head. "What a good friend you are, Lois."

"The bride cuts the cake," someone began to sing. More and more voices took up the refrain.

"Isn't that 'Farmer in the Dell'?" Helen Werner rattled her necklace at her husband. "At our son's wedding?"

"The tune?" said Aunt Lois. "Yes, I believe it is."

Flashbulbs popped; there was laughter. Crelly's knife opened a small cut in the cake. "It's chocolate," she whispered, eyes large. "Oh, John. I can't."

"You'll have to," he whispered back. "Look at them. They're counting on it."

Crelly took a breath, nodded. More pictures were taken as, over grave cellular aversion, she ate the cake.

Once again Crelly caught sight of Gene, standing a little to one side. The crowd sang and laughed. Gene appeared to smile with them. All was well, Crelly told herself. Here was John's hand in hers. To everyone's delight she lifted her lips. He kissed them. There was applause; cries of "Encore!" filled the vestry. There was even champagne, a gift of Jack Werner's, to wash away, ever away, the ugly sweet taste of chocolate.

On the way back to Portland, John and Crelly were not sure what to say, whether to laugh or cry. There would be no honeymoon: John's mathematical projects and Crelly's upcoming theater roles awaited them. Also, a honeymoon had not been planned into Helen Werner's budget. They did have this weekend, however, these few nights.

Once back at the condominium, it was possible to ignore its cruel decorator lights, Helen Werner's orange touches, the steely little dining room, the blazing orange, silver-shot bedspread. When you stepped from the shower, the mirrored panels in the bathroom reflected fragments of your body, bounced them among the fluorescents, a shoulder here, a navel, a breast.

Here was John, his face in mirrors, and, farther down, the nest from which his penis sprang. This was John Ashley Werner; there his forehead, his dusty-blue eyes. She stood on tiptoe. He leaned toward her so she could lay her lips gently on those eyelids, touch her tongue to their soft outer creases.

The blankets were pink wool, gold wool; the sheets smelled of some unfamiliar scent, of no laundry soap Crelly had ever used. The bed was not of her choosing, the pillows unfamiliar. Naked, she shivered. John pulled her down beside him and covered her. She could feel the still-damp length of him.

Crelly was scared, not of the sex, but of the irrevocable quality of the decision they had made. Of course, this was not a leap for her and John, only the next logical step. They had to be together; as John would have said, that was the given.

John reached up, shut off the white globe of light, a baleful eye that pulsed over his head—he had long since learned to ignore his mother's decorating. The wedding ceremony was over; he wanted to begin. Still, something in the way Crelly lay stopped him. "Would you mind if I pulled up the shade and opened a window?" she said.

The shade went up, the sash. Evening air bloomed like a flower. "What do you see?"

"The ocean." Casco Bay, and far out upon it, islands where lights twinkled. "The street. Streetlights. There's a car parked across the way."

John waited. "Time to come to bed?"

Far below a man, quite tall, dark-haired, got out of his car. Did he look up at her? Crelly drew back. His face was a pale coin on its flat, on its edge. In a moment his car pulled away.

"You okay?" said John.

She turned to him. "Do I know you?" she said lightly, a joke a performer might make.

"I believe we've met." His tone matched hers. "John Werner. Remember me?"

"John Werner," she murmured, eyes cast demurely down. "Oh, yes. I do remember now." She looked at him and laughed so as not to acknowledge an old fear: why should she see a traveler on the street and think it was Gene? Why should she be afraid? My brother, she told herself. Only my brother.

And who are you? she wanted to say to her new husband, his dark head and shoulders silhouetted against the pillows. Tell me your name again.

The interior of Gene's car, as he pulled into the street, smelled like chewing gum, old shoes, crankcase oil. He knew where Crelly was. He had a fair idea of what she was up to. Let her sizzle in her own juices for a while, he thought. She won't be able to forget us forever.

The dashboard was furred with greasy dust which reflected red in the lights from the controls. Gene turned on the radio as he headed back up Forest Avenue. The lights from the back end of his jitney dragged dangerously near the pavement. The car's front end was wide and flat, so he had to pull half into any cross street in order to see. His signal lights were out; he hoped he could get through town without being stopped.

All the car windows were open, but the smells never left this interior. They were like his own, he thought with a grin. Secreted by the creases of seats, holes in the upholstery.

The radio flicked, flicked again. He thumbed the knob, whirling it into a wild mishmash of static. It had been a long wait in the dark car until Crelly's lights in that fancy building went out. On the way home he would have to think through his plans, have them all ready for Alice.

The car whizzed. Gene's hands slipped in sweat over the steering wheel, slipped forward then back over its black, ridged surface, gripping and releasing.

Gene

1

A farmhouse, Aunt Alice said in the summer of 1973. With country all around. Fresh air. They would fix the place up; it would be a fine example of Victorian architecture. They would have to get some linseed oil, Aunt Alice murmured.

As the car bumped along, Gene heard Aunt Alice telling Uncle Bib that the proper contacts had been made. "Don't worry," she said. "This is all just temporary."

Now and then Uncle Bib pulled the car to the side of the road, fit two fingers to his wrist, took his pulse. The car, a low-browed old Ford, coughed as it started up again.

"The first thing we've got to do is get a new car," Uncle Bib said. "Put that in your budget right now."

Aunt Alice's lips pulled back as if she had been asked to smile for one too many pictures.

They turned a bend, another, then onto a dirt road. The back of the car was piled with bedding, dishes, clothes. They had left their furniture behind to be sold. The children, Crelly, eight, Jimmy, five, and Gene, almost thirteen, were tucked into the corners of the pile.

There were only two houses on this dirt road in Edgar, Maine. The first belonged to another relative, Aunt Alice's brother Uncle Elder, and his wife, Lois. Seeing their neat little farm gave Gene hope: the next would be just as well kept, neat. They would be comfortable. They would be okay.

Both farms were part of Grandfather Leavitt's legacy, the third part of which had been a large sum of money that Gene's mother, the third Leavitt child, had long ago received and banked. Gene's mother, Ann Leavitt Kemp, was dead, as was his father; both had been killed in an auto accident. The Leavitt money had been put in a bank trust, along with the money from the Kemps' accident and the sale of their home.

The total, Gene had heard Aunt Alice say, was a whopping big sum. It was to be paid out according to the Kemps' will, in a ten-year annuity to the children, with Aunt Alice and Uncle Bib Herrick named as their guardians. This wasn't as good as getting the money in a lump sum, Gene had heard Aunt Alice tell Uncle Bib. Still, in ten years they could work their way out of anything.

The Ford joggled along. Gene looked over at Jimmy, whose damp, blond head swayed at each bump. Jimmy's sweaty body was grimy. It had collected dust from the car interior and seemed to have been drizzled with blacking.

All Gene could see of Crelly, over the pile of junk, was the top of her brown head. Crelly would be clean. She would sit still so as to stay clean. Her eyes, large and deep blue, would be taking in everything. Aunt Alice and Uncle Bib had a running joke with Gene and Jimmy about how a little dirt was a lot of fun, but Crelly never smiled at this. In her eyes was such perception that she was sometimes disconcerting. Gene thought Aunt Alice and Uncle Bib might be a little afraid of what Crelly saw.

Gene dreamed of cold water, of beaches, remembered suddenly a walk along a beach in Portland, Maine. He had been with his father on that day, the day after Crelly was born. The water was cold and shining. Far up in the sky, as Gene watched, a big black bird swooped out, fell dizzily toward the surface, into the water, out again. Up the bird went, leaving a rippled airplane shadow, and then again, down.

"A crash?" said Gene, age five, pointing at the bird.

"Oh, no," said his father. "Just eating, see? He always comes up again."

"Is he black?" said Gene, shading his eyes.

"Not really. He just looks that way. A tern, maybe. A big one, though. Look, up he goes again."

Gene watched. The bird soared away. "Well," said Bill Kemp, "I got to get going. I got to see that new little sister of yours. All right?"

Gene nodded. He was still staring up into the sky, but the bird had disappeared. All he could see was his father's head, blocking out the sun, and around it a corona of light.

Crelly, they had named her. After the wife of a mathematician to please Gene's father, who taught math. Crelly Kemp. Crelly wore soft clothing in light colors. When Gene's father came home from work, he always picked the baby up, carried her on his arm.

Gene thought he himself had never been so special. He was just one more kid in the gangs of children who swept like skirls of suds, forward and back over a tarred Portland playground.

You had to be tough among those kids. You had to take care of yourself. Nobody else would do it. Gene had learned to wage a rock fight when he had to, spit if he needed, come home dirty.

A boy named Matthew had been his friend. Matthew didn't take care of Gene, but bawled him out for not taking better care of Crelly. Matthew named himself Crelly's protector while she played outside, or looked at books, or watched the other children with those solemn eyes.

Crelly had never had to learn to fight, she'd never had to lift a finger. Once she and some other kids had been attacked on the street by a bunch of rowdies. Matthew had stood his ground, fighting with such noble energy that Gene joined him, hollering to Crelly and the little ones to run! Run! He and Matthew had lost that fight, chased home from the park with bloody noses in a hailstorm of rocks.

Occasionally the Kemps traveled up to Lewiston, to visit Gene's mother's sister, Alice, and her husband, Robert Herrick, called Uncle Bib. The Herricks owned a store, a small, triangular place built into a corner of a weathered building on a side street. Each wooden step tread was made of two damp, weathered boards, and the risers were of scarred white wood. The screen in the door was black; the interior of the store smelled of old, roach-riddled wood and new cellophane wrappers, of tobacco, stacked newspapers, Fritos, cupcakes and long strings of red licorice.

Uncle Bib and Aunt Alice lived in the apartment directly over the store. It smelled like old toast and empty spaghetti cans, like chocolates, which Uncle Bib brought upstairs in ten-pound boxes and left open on a table beside the divan. Some of the chocolates were as large as eggs.

Uncle Bib was all stomach, his head a round ball rolling atop a globe. He wore wide black suspenders and baggy wool pants. Uncle Bib always looked at a boy as if he knew that the boy might be thinking of some low joke. Gene ate Uncle Bib's chocolates, but he stayed away from that dusty knee.

Aunt Alice's face was long, with dark eyebrows, full lips. Their apartment was not where they lived, she told Gene; they lived in the store. That was why the old divan had an olive green chenille bedspread flung over it. Puffs of olive cotton had been pulled out of it long since, leaving lines of little holes. It also explained why, when you stood by the window, the curtains made a powdery choke in your throat.

Once Gene had peeked into the bedroom, fascinated by the empty soda bottles in a case at one side of the bed, by long rows of paperback books in boxes. He had started to look at the books, but Aunt Alice had come and led him out.

"See anything?" she'd said.

"You—you don't have any sheets on your bed," Gene ventured.

Aunt Alice gave him a humorous look. "There are worse things than no sheets."

Crelly was a little girl then. Gene remembered her in a red plaid dress with a clean white collar. Her shoes were white, with a design of holes at the toes and little gold buckles. She was always leaning against their mother's knee.

Jimmy, not quite a toddler, would be set on a blanket, its clean pastel softness laid out carefully on the dusty machine-braided rug beneath.

Their mother Gene thought of as an attitude, of accepting innocence, a kind of virginal decency. When she knelt on the floor to change the baby's diaper, Uncle Bib leaned over in his chair to watch. Aunt Alice kept saying, in a high caressing voice with a soft Maine *ah* to make the word into two syllables, "There. There."

Gene's mother looked up at those two dark forms and her expression was simply pretty, reminding Gene of baby powder and white ruffles.

Gene's father was restless on these visits. He stood in doorways with his hat on, waiting for his wife. One side of his overcoat would be pulled back, his hand placed sportily in the pocket of his suit jacket. "Ann, let's go home," he would say. "Come on. It's time."

But Bill Kemp could deny his innocent kindergarten teacher of a wife nothing. When it came time, as a formality required by his insurance company, for them to make wills, he had allowed his wife to name Uncle Bib and Aunt Alice guardians of the children. They were good with kids. He didn't expect to die.

In September of 1972, Gene's parents went on their annual day trip to see the foliage in the White Mountains. They would be back by evening, his mother assured the sitter. They weren't quite ready to go off and leave the children overnight.

"Come on, come on," said Bill Kemp, smiling at his wife. "Got to hurry and get there, so we can hurry and get back."

Ann Kemp gave out kisses. On her face was that secret, haunted look good mothers get when they leave their young children. She and Bill sped off to the Presidential Range, spent the day wandering, shopping, eating. The foliage was still brilliant, its color almost audible, a train on rusty tracks. The leaves were brown curled over red. "We've got to hurry," said Bill Kemp. "We'll be late getting back."

They rounded a curve, headed toward another. Bill Kemp stiffened, pushed back, let go the steering wheel. Ann Kemp saw only the sharply veering landscape, the hasty pudding of their fall.

"A heart attack," Uncle Bib said later. "Holes in that windshield the size of softballs."

"Bib, please," said Aunt Alice. "The children."

Uncle Bib was in the process of losing his store then, but no one knew that. Gene remembered the last months there in a blur of misery. He had missed his parents. Aunt Alice expected him to take care of Jimmy. Once a week it was also his job to take everyone's wash to the Laundromat, an unclean place with yesterday's soap gritted on the fronts of machines and driers that smelled of someone else's sweat.

Crelly was too young to help, Aunt Alice said.

In living with Aunt Alice, self-respect demanded that some things you learned not to see. Dirt was one. Aunt Alice's life was busy; cleanliness must catch up as best it could, she often said. Another was food. They ate boiled potatoes and canned spinach, a little spinach juice on the potatoes to take the place of oleo. Late at night, Uncle Bib stole down to the store, brought up other food for him and Alice. Gene would find the wrappers in the morning, of cupcakes, candy. These, too, he learned not to see.

One day he came down the street, the laundry in sacks on a cart behind him, and noticed what appeared to be birds flying out of the apartment window. The birds were actually books, tossed out one after another, fluttering to the ground.

Passersby stopped to look. Automobiles slowed down. One stopped; a man reached out, picked up a book, drove off with a squeal of tires. Aunt Alice dashed out of the store, rushed inside. Uncle Bib tore out, began gathering up the books, dusting them off, hiding them against him.

Gene ran up the back stairs in time to see Aunt Alice pull Crelly away from the window, shake her hard.

"If this ever happens again, I will throw you out the window!" Aunt Alice swooped Crelly up, held her near the ceiling. The little girl's face was dark red, her eyes wide with fear. She didn't cry out. "There will be no one to catch you! No one! Do you understand?"

Crelly nodded, her long hair flapping.

"All right then." Aunt Alice's hands had big, square knuckles. She held Crelly as if she were a twig to be snapped, then set the little girl down and looked at Gene. "Watch out for your sister," Aunt Alice told him. "You take care of her, now."

For other things Gene had learned: don't see.

Don't see Uncle Bib giving chocolates to children. Don't see his taking Jimmy with him into the bath. Don't see the men who came at night with tightly closed boxes, stamped in red on one side. *Pink Lady,* 25 copies, $1.95, September release. Stored in a back room on one wall, those books towered to the ceiling. Don't see the men's tight, quiet faces. Don't see special customers.

The expression had gradually become hyphenated in Gene's mind, an attitude. Don't-see.

Some indiscretion of Uncle Bib's cost him the store. Gene wasn't sure about this. A parent had come, threatened him. Men had visited at night. Uncle Bib got sick. He stayed in bed, trembled on his way to the bathroom, went back to bed again; to compensate he ordered Alice and Gene around more than ever. Jimmy bounced on his bed, climbed in with him. Crelly disappeared around doorframes.

She always escaped, Gene thought as the car joggled. He stared at the white parting of her hair.

The Ford trundled farther and farther into the woods, climbed a long hill. At the top they pulled into what once must have been a dooryard but was now overgrown with pigweed. Gene stared. The house and barn before them sagged into scallops at the roof and foundation. The shingles were black, ridged with weather. All the windows seemed to be broken. There was no path to the door, no doorstep. The front entrance had once been painted blue. The door was nicked and scarred. Where the doorknob should have been was only a hole, stuffed with a rain-stiff rag.

Everyone in the car was staring.

"I told Elder never to touch it," Aunt Alice muttered. "I told him, 'Let it fall in, for all I care.'"

Gene had never met Uncle Elder. Edgar was too far northwest of Lewiston, out—as he now felt—in the middle of nowhere.

From the ground to the threshold was one big step, like heaving oneself up into a hole. Inside, the plaster walls were grimy, webbed with cracks. The furnishings were covered with mouse droppings, gnawed by small animals. The wide painted-board floors had rotted in places you had to test, walk gingerly around.

A wide doorway separated living room from kitchen. Aunt Alice led the way into the kitchen part. A rusted woodstove sagged in one corner, naked cherubs picked out in orange fuzz on its black oven door. In another corner was a long sink, its drainpipe running straight out the wall. Strips of old newspapers were stuck to the wall for wallpaper, pieces of old catalogues and magazines. May 1933 was the date on one. Aunt Alice made a sound in her teeth.

"I remember when Father bought this place—house, barn and land, whole thing—for one hundred dollars. I told him I didn't want it!"

"The old man's revenge." Uncle Bib clung to the doorframe. "You should have been more like Ann, or Elder."

Aunt Alice sent him a scathing look.

Beside the stove was a door. They all climbed down wavering steps into a mud-floored cellar. Light came from one basement casing. Streams and slopes of high ground marked the floor, like a relief map of some river valley.

"Gene," said Aunt Alice, "the furnace looks good."

Gingerly he stepped over to look. The furnace was a woodburner, rusted, dank. The handle of its woodbox squealed as he turned it and peered in.

"Now there," said Uncle Bib. "A good job for a boy your size." He clung to a post. "Do you think he can handle it alone, Alice?"

"Course he can."

The stairs shook. Up they all went. On a table in the living room was a lamp, a round Victorian commodity with a shade trimmed in fluffs of cotton. Alice turned it on. "At least we have electricity. I called them." Hairs of thick dust swung from the lampshade. Gene thought they looked like worms.

Another set of stairs, twisted like a half-open accordion, led crazily up. On the second floor were two bedrooms. One of the rooms was fairly clean, its plaster quite whole. In the ceiling was a fixture holding a bare, old-fashioned light bulb. There were spiderwebs everywhere, but the room smelled sweeter than the rest of the house, perhaps because of strong sunlight that poured in through its one window. Gene was drawn to this sweet smell. Surely this room could be his.

Across the hall was a larger room, quite dark, square shingling nails bristling through its boarded walls. Gene thought, Give this room to the little kids. I'll take the other one. I'm the oldest.

Crelly had followed them up. She stood in the doorway taking it all in.

She didn't say a word, but Gene knew. Crelly would have to have the sunny room.

2

Winters they shivered.

They had covered the windows with plastic sheeting, but it was little help. They could have got hold of new glass, but that was no good, since the sashes themselves were old. Every wind made the sashes tremble, drop glass. Before the glass, the sashes would have to be repaired, but that was no good either. The window frames were also crooked; no straightened sash would fit them. The house would have to be jacked up, the foundation fixed, the shingles replaced, the window frames and sashes rebuilt. All to replace a pane of glass.

As a little kid Gene had believed it was possible to see a whole world through a window, but at fourteen he knew better. After they moved in here he had borrowed shamefully, sometimes without asking, from Uncle Elder, who lived down the road, trying to rebuild. Boards and whole kegs of nails were swallowed, gone. Possibly Uncle Bib, with his chest pains, stomach pains, dizziness, weakness in the legs, and headaches, convenient whenever there was work to be done, sold them.

It didn't matter now. It didn't matter what Gene did, whether he stayed or ran.

He knew he was going to be caught.

His hands quivered. They were sore from endless afternoons on hillsides, dragging down fallen trees to feed the open maw of the furnace. Winters, he thought, you could slip on that black ice in the cellar, fall right into the mud.

At school last year one teacher had tried to scrub pitch-stained scars off his hands with boiling water, so frustrated was she by the boy who sat in her classroom too tired to study, too troubled to care. His hands had puffed up on that day, turned a strange orangish red.

Gene had learned to look for nods of approval from Aunt Alice as a termination of abject misery. "We all know you can read," she had said, looking at his hands. "To spite that goddamn teacher."

At this moment Gene's hands dug into the stuffed arms of his chair. Don't-see, he thought. From don't-see it was only a step to black.

Black was like hunger; Gene was always hungry. Alice said that what she fed them was wholesome: cereal, potatoes, bread and peanut butter. But the diet was dull, incomplete. Sometimes, when Uncle Bib left his room to go to the outhouse, Gene stole in, found what he really craved—sweets, chocolate, cupcakes; all the wrappers would be empty or half empty, and the smell like a pain in the gullet. Gene would pick up the wrappers and lick out the crumbs, helplessly plastering the cellophane to his face.

The relationship between want and satisfaction was, to Gene's mind, black. It couldn't be denied, no matter what, and rose out of don't-see.

Whenever Uncle Bib had left his room over the last two years, Gene had gotten up, gone to search. Once the don't-see was in place, there was no reasoning. Surroundings meant nothing, there were no niceties, except perhaps the urge not to be caught. His mind was black.

By his fifteenth year Gene had begun to realize that treats could be found not only in Bib's room but in other places in the house. He had learned to wait until a room was empty and then, in black, unable to stop himself or help himself or think, he would begin to search. It became a habit.

He had begun to find such things as a cupcake and a magazine beside a pile of boards. A foil-wrapped chocolate and a book, underneath the sink. Fudge and pictures.

At fourteen Gene knew Uncle Bib had left these things in these places to hide them from the children. He knew he shouldn't touch them, but he was in black. He was tongue-to-cellophane, gut-to-chocolate. He took the sweets, wolfed them down, waited for Bib to protest, but the man never did. Gene looked at the pictures, the magazines. He opened the books, read.

Whim wham.

Gene had never lost his craving for sugar, but, besides the other things he found that year, sugar became the mild drug. Black called him, but for a more potent medicine, the puny white matter urged from a penis the size of a peapod.

This fall, particularly, the space between Gene's legs heated automatically at the thought of a search. His head was full of black. He wasn't able to enter a room without thinking: behind that stack of boards is a woman's body. In that chair is another, hidden in the cushions.

The smell was of old newsprint and chocolate; the grainy pages of the books were rumpled, sometimes damp. The pictures were always of women and children, their faces blacked out. Gene had learned to flick the pages forward and back, to go at last to the most potent picture he could find, of the open space and dark lily between a woman's legs. Gripping himself, he imagined the page was slick, deep, open. Finally, he spouted.

He was not the only one in the household who was hooked. Walking down off the hill late one night the summer before, Gene had come upon Uncle Bib hunched like a spider, his eye to a hole in the barn wall. Uncle Bib was rubbing himself, his hands busy under the curve of his belly, his head pulled to one side, his mouth open in a silent scream.

Gene, half hidden, had pulled back. There was a fumble of clothing; Bib lumbered away. When he was gone Gene put his own eye to the hole. Inside the barn sat Jimmy, age six. He was looking at a magazine, then down at himself and giggling. His pants and underwear were bunched around his ankles.

Gene didn't know about Aunt Alice. "We are real pioneers here," she would say. "We have to invent everything again, start over in the world by ourselves."

"Take care of your sister," she told Gene.

This fall Gene had found books about sex and sisters. Finding them, he had grown so careless or so obsessed, it seemed to him that people in the household must know, must be watching, but when he looked along the surfaces of doorways, or of windows where it seemed to him Alice or Bib might lurk, he saw nothing.

Only sisters. The sisters in these stories begged for the penis, screamed when they got it. For Gene this fall, sisters had become the sibilant lock that slid open at a touch: whim wham.

Crelly went to school clean. Days went by in which he watched her walk from the bus to the school building and thought of thin, clean thighs rubbing together.

Aunt Alice watched them both. It showed on her face, in the half-humorous way her dark eyebrows drew together. No ethic. Only black. Whim wham.

Gene sat in a living room chair, shivering. It was early morning; he was dead scared. Where was Crelly now?

The day before, as he and she had sat together on the school bus, Gene had noticed that a bit of Crelly's hair was stuck in her collar, leaving an attractive white triangle at the back of her neck. Unable to stop himself, he had reached over and pulled the hair out, but then he had had to shift in his seat, blushing.

Crelly had given him one tense, blue-eyed look, pulled away. Later she had avoided him, giving him quick glances, sidestepping. She knew. Crelly, it's easy, he had wanted to whisper to her. Just let go. Don't-see.

After school Gene had worked on the hills, come in, eaten his supper. Crelly had gone upstairs when the dishes were done, climbed into her bed. Waiting in the living room, Gene had known every move she made. He had watched her many times.

There was no door on Crelly's room.

Eventually little Jimmy and Uncle Bib and Aunt Alice all turned in. The living room was empty. Gene began to search. In a corner he found a magazine; under a chair, another. But he had seen both before; they were no good to him. Then, between the cushions of the sagging sofa, he found a book that answered.

It was small, cheap. On the cover was a picture of a naked girl child in bondage and a young boy with a leather whip. The pages of the book were thick and yellowish with a red rim, the dye of which had seeped downward in tearlike drizzles. The outhouse smell of the pages was enough to arouse him; Gene searched through them with damp fingers. Here was the young man touching the little girl, opening her legs, entering. The girl was the young man's sister.

Black. Blood throbbing, Gene made his way up the stairs to the room with no door.

Where was Crelly now? Gene's guts slid. He had scoured the fields around the house, stumbling in the dark, half sobbing her name, but either she was lost or she would tell. His stomach was froggish. What would they do to him if she told? The embarrassment alone was more than he could think of. There would be no one to stick up for him. Alice and Bib would not want to be dragged into it. This would be his fault.

The morning light grew. He felt sick. At the first real sign of sun he heaved himself from his chair, went to stir up the furnace fire, the kitchen stove, as he was expected to do. Standing over the flame in the stove, he couldn't get warm. A little while later Alice found him lying on the sofa, wrapped in a blanket. "Sick, are you?" She was dressed, but her face was shiny from sleep.

"N-no. Crelly's r-run away."

"Oh?" Alice's eyebrows drew together.

"I was just up there," Gene lied. "There's no sign of her. Her w-window is open, the plastic is torn."

"Jesus," Alice said. "Jesus Christ." She ran a hand through her hair, pushing it back.

"I looked." Gene quivered. "N-no sign."

"Well, then, there's a little girl that can go straight to hell." Alice slammed outside, came back in. "Nothing ever quite good enough for that child! I better talk to Bib." Then she stood still. From outside, still far in the distance, came the rumble of a motor.

"Elder. What do you bet?" Swiftly she went back through the kitchen and into the bedroom. The truck approached. If Gene had had anything in his stomach, he would have thrown it up. There was the slam of a truck door; footsteps on stiff grass.

Uncle Bib and Aunt Alice came from the bedroom. Bib stood by the stove; Alice went to the door, opening it before the knock.

"Alice, Crelly is with us," Elder Leavitt said. "I need to speak to you and Bib."

"She is?" Aunt Alice exhaled a sound like relief. "Now, what ails that child, for heaven's sake? We just realized she was missing, Elder!"

Elder came in. His usually fair face was a dull red. He planted his feet far apart on the kitchen floor.

Gene, under his blanket, planned rapidly: if anyone blamed him for anything, he would say Crelly was overexcitable.

"Well, Elder!" Bib said. "Glad to hear Crelly's with you! Look, cup of coffee? Let me take your jacket, it's warm enough in here. Sometimes I don't get the fires started as I should, but I did all right today."

"Bib, I wasn't born yesterday. Middle of the night, bare feet and in a nightgown and sweater, that's how that little girl arrived at our house, and I want to tell you, she was cold."

"I don't know what could've got into her," Aunt Alice said. "That child is an awful handful sometimes, Elder."

"We got her warm. We questioned her. She won't say a word. Lois and I aren't fools." Elder's hands opened, shut. "Bib, a man stays in the house all day, time begins to hang heavy on his hands. Maybe he isn't as well as he could be, maybe he's got some other kinds of ailments but just physical, I don't know. He might even frighten a little girl with some of the thoughts he was thinking."

"Elder!" said Aunt Alice. "How can you say that?"

Gene stole a look outside the blanket. Bib raised his hands, held them palm up. The motion drew strings of blurred dark with it. Sweet and salt mingled on Gene's tongue.

"I never laid a finger on that child, Elder," said Bib.

"No?"

"Elder, that child is just too good to live with, has been since we got here," said Alice. "Has to have things just so. Always turning up her nose. She doesn't say a word, all she has to do is look. I, for one, have gotten damn sick of it. I don't know how you could say such things to Bib. I think you ought to be ashamed."

Elder looked down and away, then back. "Bib, we know you've been sick. Lois and I, we think you need help. We're going to keep Crelly safe with us."

"You think you'll get a share of the insurance money, Elder? Is that it?" Alice gave him a knowing glance.

"To hell with that. You keep the insurance money, Alice. We'll keep Crelly with us. I'll even come up here and help you fix this house up, do whatever I can. But Bib has got to get some help. He's a veteran, the VA will do something. There are hospitals."

Under the blanket Gene hardly dared to breathe, for fear of changing the course of things.

"Goddamn it, Elder." Bib swayed, grabbed the edge of the table.

"If you refuse, Bib, expect that we won't bring that little girl up here again. I'm going home to start making arrangements with the VA over at Togus. I'll let you know what's needed." Elder Leavitt slammed out.

Inside the house there was silence. Elder's truck rumbled away. There came an odd sound, of breath drawn through noses. Gene, looking out, saw that Bib and Alice were bent over the stove, snickering. "Shot his bolt, didn't he?" Bib gasped.

Alice's mouth worked. "One less kid to feed. Nothing wrong with that."

Uncle Bib looked in toward Gene, huddled on the sofa. Alice

nodded. Still snuffling, the man headed back to his bedroom. In a moment there came the whine of bedsprings.

As Aunt Alice moved, the unsteady living room rattled. "Looks like Crelly's gone for good," she told Gene.

"I want you to know that no matter what lies Crelly tells about us, we'll be all right. She knows that, too. Hell, Gene, she'll be fine down there. Have whatever she wants, live in the lap of luxury. Don't worry about your sister anymore. Whatever she says, we can always deny it. Right?"

Gene thought of the white triangle at the back of Crelly's neck. "Right," he said, managing a weak grin. Alice turned away.

Gene got up from the sofa and went, still shivering, back up the stairs, to sleep the day through.

In forty-eight hours Elder was back with Aunt Lois, but Alice had been expecting them. She had tumbled the living room and the kitchen into a kind of breathless order and had dragged a seldom-rinsed washcloth over Jimmy's face, abrading forehead and cheeks, nose, even lips, as if to clean his face of features, leave it blank.

"Interfering," Alice muttered as she moved about. "Goddamn nosiness." When Alice muttered, Uncle Bib moaned from the bedroom, "I'm sick, Alice, I'm sick." Alice would sigh and go to him.

On one of these trips she put on a dress and stockings, came to stand over the cast-iron kitchen sink, looked in the little square mirror above it. She brushed back her hair, which was prematurely gray, and fastened it at the back of her head with a string. On each high cheekbone she rubbed a flame of rouge. Gene thought the rouge made her look crazy.

When Aunt Lois and Uncle Elder pulled in, Alice plastered a dark red smile on her face, opened the door for their visitors.

Aunt Lois was a plump woman with a gentle, troubled look. She smelled good. Clean suds, Gene thought. Fresh linen in a cedar chest.

Behind her Uncle Elder stood in his work clothes, which were carefully patched, creased by the iron at the sides of the arms and down each leg, front and back.

"Alice," said Elder, "get Bib. He has an appointment with a doctor this morning."

Aunt Alice hesitated, made an effort to seem reasonable. "By rights, Elder, I should take care of Bib, you know. After all, he's been my responsibility so long."

Gene looked up across Alice's thick earlobe and the pale planes of her cheek. Just in front of her ear a muscle tensed, let go. Watching it Gene knew: Bib had Alice trapped, and Alice, Bib. They were partners in crime, never to be split up for fear of what one alone might say.

Uncle Elder must have sensed something; he cleared his throat. "You have to realize, Alice," he said, working hard to speak gently, "that the problem is Bib's, not yours."

"Alice!" It was a call from Uncle Bib. Aunt Alice lowered her head in what was to Gene's eye an uncharacteristically submissive way and excused herself. When she was gone, Aunt Lois gave Uncle Elder a prescient glance.

"Perhaps you children should run outside," she said.

Jimmy got up and went out, but Gene was too scared, too fascinated, to leave. This was like watching a black flower open.

"How can she keep him here?" Aunt Lois whispered. "How can she, Elder? Doesn't she want him to get better?"

Uncle Elder shook his head.

From the bedroom came Alice's low-pitched voice: "Ayeh, Bib. Ayeh."

"Sleep," said Bib, loud enough so that they all heard it.

"I told you," whispered Aunt Lois. "I knew she wouldn't do it."

Elder didn't reply. Aunt Alice towered in the doorway, and he tried to smile at her, failed.

"He's decided not to go," said Aunt Alice abruptly. "He says he can get better on his own." She flung her head up, looked at her brother, a challenge.

"Oh, Alice," Aunt Lois said.

"He's not going to be buried alive in a loony bin because of some rabbity little kid. Here, I can take care of him."

"But they can treat him," said Uncle Elder.

"No." Aunt Alice's lips moved like a red flag. "Don't think we don't appreciate your concern, Elder. But this time it is all out of proportion."

"Where is he? Let me talk to him."

Aunt Alice drew back. "His mind is made up. He's resting. He says, Elder, he doesn't want to see you."

Uncle Elder's shoulders sloped; nobody said anything.

Aunt Lois stood up. "We'll keep Crelly with us," she said. "We'll keep her away."

"Well," said Aunt Alice, "you don't want to believe everything you hear."

Aunt Lois gave her sister-in-law a look, turned. "Elder, it's time to go home."

There was a long pause. Elder Leavitt nodded. His voice rumbled into the room with an ancient depth, like that of a prophet, or perhaps only of a decent man. "So be it," he rumbled, and then again, "So be it."

They left.

Gene followed them out, stood in the grass, watching, as their pickup pulled away. He felt extreme relief, sudden loss. Stumbling to the middle of the dirt road, he waved at the back of the truck until it disappeared.

3

Crelly had run out and left him. With what? An itch. Black without the whim wham. He had been abandoned, and for weeks he had had to live with the fear that she might tell. Day after day he had had to sit by while fear turned his bowels to water.

It was months before Gene realized that Crelly was not going to tell. She was too damn busy pretending she lived on the other side of the world. A decent, churchgoing, self-righteous little prig, in every damn skinny inch of her, was what Crelly had become. Like all the rest of that misguided bunch with their threadbare, lip-service morals. Gene, when he thought of Crelly, spat.

"Gene?" Bib cried the summer after Crelly left. "Come in here! I want you!" But when Gene went in, only Aunt Alice was there, wearing some soft, peach-colored thing that gaped open in the front. He had walked right in on her. He was sorry, it was his fault; he began to back out of the room.

"No!" she said in a voice that made him mind, pulling her robe shut. "What did you do in school today?"

Coming down the stairs for a drink of water, when there had been nothing to drink at supper, he found Alice at a sponge bath in the sink, her long white legs open so the darkness between them was visible, while she toweled her hair dry. She rushed away, only half covered.

Directed to put away the washing, he found her bent over changing her slacks, the cheeks of her buttocks white and firm in ragged underwear. She paused there waiting for him to touch her, and he reached out. One light touch and she turned on him in a fury, pushed him out of the room, her bare breasts like teardrops.

Giggling, Bib pulled him aside in odd moments to whisper, to drag from bedspring or bureau drawer magazines without names. "We men have to stick together." His breath would stink of chocolate. One look at the magazines was like a sickness in your blood, Bib's world; buttocks and breasts, on pages smelling like old comic books.

Gene began to look at Alice and wait his chance. He tried to control himself in this, a pitiful last shudder before capitulation. But for a while he also believed in a father, a manlike creature he half remembered from before the crash—tall as a building his father had been, with a corona of light around his head.

In watching Alice, Gene grew to hate the act he performed on himself with the help of Bib's magazines. He was tired of black, which, except for a few mindless pulsing moments, was predictable. He grew to dread the depression following the whim-wham.

He needed something with more power.

Nothing mattered, he thought. If you took a good look at the world, at, for example, how many different kinds of copulations took place in it at any given moment, you had to come to that conclusion. There had to be a new world order. They had to get rid of the worn-out ones that existed, construct something a little closer to home truth.

He sat on the dusty sofa and waited for Alice. He would do whatever Alice wanted, but in waiting, heat hurt like the cold. In summer he and she tore the plastic off all the windows and found themselves suddenly like animals too loosely herded to care anymore who mated with whom.

One summer day Alice sat across the room from Gene, wearing a pair of shorts and a short-waisted top, so that he could see the pale skin of her midriff. To him, at fifteen, she looked old, perhaps as much as forty-five or fifty; the skin of her face was beginning to be covered with fine lines. But he didn't care about that. The skin of her neck looked soft, with a sheen upon it. The breasts below would be soft.

They were discussing a new world order. "The bigots who think they can define prurient!" Alice was laughing. "When art itself is pornographic! But that could be changed if people were honest enough."

Gene, sitting on the sofa, shifted repeatedly as the soft words went on. How could he admit to her what it was he wanted?

Bib had taken Jimmy and gone to the store. Alice looked at him, down at the magazine page she held in her hand. Gene sat very still. The ridge of his jeans across his abdomen poked upward. Did she know?

"Now look at this, just look at it. Innocent!" Aunt Alice held up a print of an old-fashioned painting of plump, naked cherubs. She had torn it from some women's magazine. "Not a stitch on any of them. Look, Gene." She laughed fondly. "There they dangle."

Gene rose, walked toward her, his legs slightly splayed, his need and his apology naked on his face.

Alice met him halfway. Her hands went to his zipper, to release him. He moaned with relief.

His penis was pale, heavy for its length. It stood out between them. Her hand closed over it. "I'm sorry," Gene muttered, close to tears. "Be—be careful. I can get a woman pregnant with this."

She shook her head. "Barren. It doesn't matter." She bent. Her lips closed over him. Inside her mouth was delicious black. At the end, he wept tears of release.

During the winter of 1976, Alice showed him, as a mark of her special favor, a plan of their finances. He was moved by her confidence in him, and felt love for the simple marks she had made on paper, her financial kingdom.

"Spring, 1973–Spring, 1977," she had written on a small piece of paper. "Monthly Income."

The children's annuity was what they lived on. "$550 per mo.—food," Aunt Alice had written. "$60—electricity. $90—auto." Uncle Bib had bought a secondhand car, a monster; Gene had learned to drive on it. "$100—miscellaneous." There were other small essentials. Then she had written, "$300—mat. and hush." The grand total was $1,100 per month, the amount of the Kemp annuity.

Gene pointed to the $300. "What's this?"

"Well, fifty dollars is materials, our—reading matter," she said and lowered her eyes. He knew immediately: the books, magazines, the large glossies, faces in black. "The rest," Alice said, "is insurance."

"Is what?"

"Yes. The same people who sell us materials know Bib from way back. Some of the things Bib has done, they could get him into trouble. The money insures that that will never happen. Bib's connections keep us safe for so much a month. It's an organization, really, from all over—out of state, in state. In this area they work through Maine Lyne Grocerie. Bib makes his payment once a month. You know Red Potter? His son, Nick? Drives up the road sometimes, looks around?"

Gene nodded, but with distaste.

"Well, Nick knows. It's his job."

"He's a drunk," said Gene.

"Yes," said Alice, "but there are worse things."

Looking into her face, Gene saw that she had told him everything, but in a way that would protect his youth, his inexperience. There are tough guys out there, her eyes told him. We have to be careful. Desperately he wanted to prove himself capable enough to handle all this.

"Doesn't leave us much to live on," he said in his most adult way. "Maybe we should, I don't know, get food stamps. A lot of people do. It would help."

"Well, it would," said Alice. "We thought of that. Bib even talked to some people. But with Crelly gone, it turns out, we could get into quite a legal tangle, lose part of the annuity. If they sent out investigators"—Aunt Alice gave Gene a veiled look—"there's no telling what Crelly might say."

"No," said Gene. "No."

Alice nodded. "Bib and I might get assistance if he could prove disability, and heaven knows he hasn't worked in a long time, and probably won't now. But to get disability, he has to talk to doctors."

Alice said no more. Gene suspected that the "hush" category in her budget included things she and Bib had done together, which held them together, one unable to function separately from the other.

"Exposed," Gene muttered, with a clinch of the fear he had felt since Crelly's leaving and its attendant hatred. "So. It's Crelly's fault, then."

"Yes," said Alice, brightening. "Her and her damn comfortable little life. But, Gene, just look here." She handed him a second piece of paper. "1977—Spring," she had written. "Monthly income including Gene's job (at first). $500 per month (approx., Gene), $1,100 —annuity. Total, $1,600 per month."

Gene read this. "Job?"

"We could save!" Alice said excitedly. "Thanks to you, Gene!

We'll fix this house up and sell it, then maybe, I don't know, buy another little store somewhere. If we're careful, we can!"

She looked at him and he saw her hope. "All right," he said. "I'll work for that."

On his sixteenth birthday, Gene quit school and got a job, with the help of Nick Potter and Alice, at a nearby henhouse.

Two years later Gene knew: nothing really mattered to Alice. Bodies were ordinary in all their functions, and none of that fazed her, although she was an artist at creating the arching back, the groan, the height of passion that made your own hand lift and grasp, finish yourself off, too soon. Every ultimate act was his fault.

But what Alice liked was the look in the eye. Innocence, she needed. Ashamed innocence made her legs ripple and her hips move; the damp, perspiring forehead, the clouded eyes that almost, but not quite, made a judgment—those brought Alice her best climaxes.

Over the past two years Alice had become more and more open with Gene. When she came upstairs in the dark to his room, his body arched automatically. Instantly turgid, conditioned to be so, and managing to avoid, with her nearness, the old blank aftermath of whim wham, Gene did whatever she wanted.

He didn't care. He was Alice's man. And he had gradually come to realize one thing: they were going to have to get rid of Bib.

The man lived in some little world of his own. He ate twice as much as anyone else and he never worked, not at the smallest household task. He cashed the annuity checks, spent them on treats for himself. The house reeked of Bib's cologne.

"Gene'll take up the slack with the money" was what Bib said, but Gene was angry. He worked for Alice. Too often building materials, pipes, bags of cement, other things that they managed to save up for, Bib sold. The things would simply disappear.

Alice got an extinguished look when something she needed was missing. She was angry. One night she showed Gene a revised budget with the heading "Budget, A.B." Food money on it was much reduced. "A.B.?" Gene questioned.

Alice nodded. "After Bib," she said. "We could free up a lot of things around here. I'm tired of his little dictatorship. And he thinks that boy is his."

When Alice cashed the annuity checks herself, Bib used Jimmy as a sniper. The boy was under his thumb and would do whatever he said. Jimmy was eleven this spring; he dodged about the house, deliberately fey, malicious.

"Jim, go put salt in the sugar bowl," Bib would order, and it was done, a little practical joke for Alice to discover later. "Jimmy, go balance the glasses." The glasses would be balanced so that opening any cupboard would set off an avalanche of dishware. The household, consequently, was slightly off balance while Bib reigned from his bed.

"It's that child that really gets me," Alice sputtered. "This can't be good for him." Her eyebrows drew together. Gene saw the same look that came when Alice pawed through piles of photographs, frantic for one that would give her the fix she needed, whim wham.

"We'll have to see what we can do," he told her.

During the day Alice worked on the house, if she could find materials, or sat in a corner of the living room close to the stove, a cup of coffee in one hand, a decorating magazine on her lap. In a room with walls that spit plaster and floors heaped with clothes, old boards, and mess, she would very often leaf through shiny pages of walls painted pink, furniture painted white, of calico and chintz in pastel shades. When Gene came in from work and she looked up at him, he thought her eyes were two small, colorful pastel swirls.

"Read this," she said one day in the spring of 1979.

It looked and smelled like the other materials. Gene took the little book, sat down to read.

First, a woman was forced to have sex with her husband in unnatural positions. Then she was raped by each of her three half-grown sons and shut naked in a room, so much anomalous flesh to be used for the parties her husband and sons threw. She was cut with knives, forced to eat excrement, raped with a broken bottle, and finally left, impaled on a bedpost, to die.

The whole book was eighty-three pages long. The print was large enough for a child to read, the words often misspelled. There were no margins, and the paragraphs sloped upward and down. By the time he had finished reading Gene felt seasick, yet filled with such a deep sexual urge that he turned to Alice as she stood in the doorway and began fumbling with her clothing.

Her face was unmoving as he took her, and although he saw this he couldn't wait, shoving at her savagely, grunting at the image he saw of a ravaged, bleeding, open woman. He had never been so hotly engorged, but the liquid he spent was like a crooked pencil of acid, driving upward, burning its way.

He lay with his face against Alice's neck, ashamed.

"It's Bib's book, Gene," Alice said softly. "I found him making Jimmy read it." She paused. He could understand it was a sharp, political alignment she was calling for. She felt herself endangered. "Bib has got to go," she said.

The words meant nothing to Gene. They were like an interrupted beacon, falling on the dark shapes of buildings.

"I'm sick of taking care of him. Who knows what Jimmy might do under his influence?" Alice's voice was cutting. "A filthy old man, with children on his breath."

She waited. Gene said nothing.

"You'll have to borrow a shovel." Alice's tough voice admitted no refusal. "I haven't even got one of those anymore, thanks to Bib. And Gene, if anyone asks, we'll call the disappearance Togus."

"Won't someone want to visit him, though? Won't they wonder?"

"Who? No one in town knows Bib but Elder and Lois. Togus is far enough away so they'll never ask. They stopped caring about Bib a while back."

Gene was quivering, mortally frightened. He lay his face against her, waited. She waited. What came to him at last was don't-see.

The next morning he went down to Uncle Elder's to borrow a shovel.

Bang! Bang! Bang! Three hard knocks, his signature. Aunt Lois turned to Crelly. "One of these days he'll just break it down," she said. "Easier on everybody."

At Uncle Elder's holler of invitation, Gene went inside. There the three of them sat, Elder, Lois and Crelly, in a kitchen smelling of eggs and coffee. The smell turned his stomach over: he was hungry. Crelly sat in a far corner, with a whole round, wooden table for protection, but she didn't look frightened—only clean, well fed, comfortable.

"Pull up a chair, Gene," said Uncle Elder. "Cup of coffee?"

The sun shone on Uncle Elder's bald head. At breakfast, straight from his shaving in the bathroom, was the only time you saw this. The rest of the day Elder Leavitt wore a hat, lightweight in summer, heavy felt in winter. The hat was dark blue with a brim in front and a red "B" on it, for the Boston Red Sox.

"No. I thank you anyway." Gene spoke slowly, as a man of

fifty might. "We just ate a big breakfast up to home." Unable to stop himself, he turned to his sister. "Crelly."

She nodded, her eyes completely unaware of any past between them, her lips pressed together in a polite smile.

"Not even a muffin, Gene?" Aunt Lois persisted. When Lois Leavitt concentrated, a little vertical line appeared between her eyebrows. Did she think he didn't know the talk she sometimes made to Crelly? How she worried about the nutrition, up the road? How she'd seen Jimmy out in the fields, looking peaked?

"No, thanks," he said, waiting.

Uncle Elder leaned over his plate and sopped up the last of his egg with the last bit of his muffin and ate it. He leaned back. "Gene, what can I do for you?"

"I need to borrow a spade."

"Oh? What you up to?"

"Nothing much. Little project for Aunt Alice. I'll bring it right back, don't worry." Bastard, Gene thought. Didn't Elder know that this kind of asking could be a way of expressing contempt?

"Well, I got a spade you can take." Uncle Elder looked at Aunt Lois. When he spoke again, the words hurt. "I got to have it back, though, Gene."

"You think I won't bring it back?"

Uncle Elder held up a hand. "Just, it's hard. Cash is tight, as you know." In the man's steady glance at Gene was history: years of borrowed, unreturned money, tools, motors, tires, seed, milk, wood, apples from the trees, boards from the pile, nails, hammers, window glass.

It was not that Aunt Lois and Uncle Elder had so much. Homemade underwear on the clothesline; mended boots in a box by the door; sweaters unraveled and the rotten parts of the yarn cut out, the yarn knotted and knit up in mittens and hats of odd colors, stripes in circus-wild combinations, which they wore. They had to use everything, waste nothing. That was how they got by at Elder's farm.

Uncle Elder wasn't a pious man. A point of honor for him, however, was the seventy times seven of forgiveness, which he tried to give to this nephew of his without being asked, as if forgiveness were something owed in every case, at all costs.

Gene knew his power for setting Uncle Elder against Uncle Elder, a morality test. "Well," he said, "is the shovel out in the barn? Do you want me to get it?"

"I'll come along." Elder Leavitt rose. He had lost things before without being able to explain just how. It wasn't in him to think of Gene, his dead sister's son, as a thief, but it was in him to help the boy understand ownership when he could.

Gene turned to Aunt Lois. "By the way," he said, "Uncle Bib's thinking of going over to Togus."

"He is?" said Aunt Lois. "Well, good. A load off Alice's shoulders, I shouldn't think, after all the care she's given. How does she feel?"

" 'Bout as you do. We've all tried. Yesterday she said to me she'd be glad when he was gone." Somewhere in Gene a high, wild laughter rose. He squelched it.

"Well, course she would. I don't know how she's managed. A mental hospital is the place for a man who can't get over imaginary sicknesses. They'll take care of him, there."

"Yep," said Gene. His eyes widened, his lip quivered humorously. "Time for him to go, I guess."

"Decide on his own, did he?" said Uncle Elder.

Gene swallowed horror and humor simultaneously, waggled a hand in the air. "Oh, yes."

Elder turned toward the barn.

"Well, tell him we wish him luck," said Aunt Lois.

Gene followed Elder out.

That evening he lay on his bed fully clothed, the long-handled spade upright against a wall. He didn't think about himself, because when he did his pant legs began a low slow shiver, and he could see the outlines of his shoes, waggling a little at what seemed a great distance from him, with little connection to his body.

He thought about truck driving, about calling in sick this late afternoon. He thought about Alice. As he did he heard her climbing the stairs. Automatic gears in his body began to slide as at a switch, metal disk against greased metal disk. A clot of phlegm uncoiled itself at the base of his trunk.

She came to stand against the window. Gene saw not only the caress of light on chosen places in the folds of her clothes but also the black flick of endless pages of blanked-out faces, bare flesh.

"You ready?" she said.

"Yeah."

He wasn't, but he swung his legs over the side of the bed. There was a bad smell in the room, of something cold and fetid, of unwashed feet in leather shoes. Gene felt the sticking of his shirt at his armpits, his pants at the groin.

He and Alice didn't speak to each other. Shovel in hand, he followed her down the crooked stairs and through the black house. He was breathing through his mouth. He could feel her presence, sense just where her feet fell and how her body moved inside her clothes, her flesh white, her belly long and smooth, her breasts wide-placed, brown-nippled.

They stopped at the threshold to Bib's room, looked in.

There was a small light suspended from the head of the bed. Gene could see Bib's yellowed long underwear top, the chocolate smudges down its front.

Alice's eyes turned on Gene.

His feet felt like chunks of wood; with difficulty he set them into the room. Inches from the bed he stared into Bib's sleep-befuddled face.

Bib hauled himself upright, half awake. As he did, the light above the bed began to roll, casting odd shadows. "Alice?"

Gene couldn't move.

"What is it?" Bib rubbed his eyes, squinted at the shovel.

Alice pulled it from Gene's hands, raised it over her head. "Bats!" she cried.

Bib's face cleared: once there had been bats in the house, and Alice had driven them out with a broom. The shovel whirred in her hands, droned. Bib fell sideways, no blood on his face, only surprise.

"There," said Alice, turning to Gene. "Now."

Gene grasped the shovel handle, raised it high, as he knew she wanted him to, but could not bring it down.

"I won't have you scared!" Alice grasped his hands. Together they brought the shovel down. The blade made a mashing noise.

Hearing it, Gene realized how much he had hated Bib's laziness, his assumption of power. Pulling the shovel from Alice and standing by himself, he slammed it into Bib again. This is for us, he told Bib silently. This is for me.

Again Gene smashed the shovel down onto the bed in such a frenzy that Alice could not have interfered. Some rational part of him knew he was murdering a corpse. He swayed. Alice caught the shovel as it dropped.

"There," she said gently, a word in two syllables. "That's all it is."

She was breathing heavily, her face shiny white, her eyebrows pulled together like the wings of a large black bird. She sank down on the bed beside Bib's body. "Easy," she said, gesturing at the bloodstained bedding. "Right?" She patted a place beside her.

"Right." Gene was quivering all over. He sat down beside her, his back to Bib.

"It doesn't happen in this business very often anymore," Alice said in that surprised, gentle voice. "But now and then I hear through Nick that somebody has gone. Somebody has got too big for the organization and has had to be taken care of."

"They'll ask?" Gene drew a breath, working toward calm.

"Oh, yes. No use lying to them, our necks if we do. We'll have to make arrangements through Nick, pay. But we'll save that in the food budget alone. The rest will be ours. A chance." Alice pulled back hair that stuck out about her face. "Bib wasn't giving us a chance. We're free, Gene. We did it."

She flicked out the light. There were moonbeams on her shoulders, upon the bed. Bib's body looked like no more than wavelets on the water. In a little while they were gathering him up, winding him in all the bloodstained bedding.

They had always been kind to Bib, Gene thought, scarcely daring to touch the limp bedclothes, clumsy about it, so that Alice had to take over. They'd brought Bib his food. When Bib took his infrequent baths in the tin tub in the kitchen and took Jimmy right in with him, so that Jimmy climbed and splashed about trying to get away, naked, Gene and Alice had always left the room.

Bib's body was a week-old wash when they'd finished, clothy and lumpy. They dragged the bundle up the hill and dumped it. Alice looked about her.

"Odd spring," she said. "One minute the ground's soaking wet, the next cold as ice. Spongy right now. Shouldn't be too bad."

"No." Gene was exhausted. "Not too bad."

"Holler if you need help."

She looked at him. He felt small, skinny, inadequate. "I will." She nodded, turned away.

Gene picked the shovel up, sank it into the earth. The dirt was heavy and damp, but it crumpled like chocolate. He sweated, dug. Grunting, he pushed the sack of laundry over and over until finally it fell into the deep, tipsy cleft he had made.

But the body didn't stay wrapped. Gene wrestled with coverings, pulled away helplessly. There Bib sat, immovable, exposed, his lifted hand the color of sky at the rim of the hill, a cold night blue.

His face was blacked, its darkness dripping onto the swaddled bedclothes.

Gene fought not to cry out, saw that Alice had come back again. She bent over Bib in the hole, straightened.

"We were young once," Alice said. "We thought it was all . . . good." She stared down into Bib's smashed face. "I dunno. Nobody's fault. Should have been a better world." Her hands made fists. She turned to Gene. "You're gonna cover him all right up?"

"Oh, yes."

"Ayeh." It was a word like two notes on top of each other, minor, ironic. "Ayeh." She went back toward the house, each foot falling flat to the ground.

He was nineteen; he'd never seen a dead person before. He wanted to cry, he wouldn't cry. He returned to his shoveling, in his heart an aching jealousy that Alice should care, even that much, for Bib.

He was grateful that the dark still held in some places in the sky. This was don't-see: little damp stones falling into blood, worms fighting for equilibrium as they fell against the sheets.

Lois and Elder and Crelly, Gene thought suddenly, would have insisted on a coffin; that would have been decent. But it all came to the same thing, didn't it? He thought of Crelly with sudden anguish: was this digging what he got, his world, while Crelly had so much more? Gene clobbered the dirt with the back of his shovel, smoothed it, stepped on it to tamp it, sank to his ankles.

"Ahh!" he cried. Fingers: could they sift up through the dirt, wrap around his feet like blue bands?

He leaped away, looked up. Jimmy, a scat little hill wanderer, was standing in some bushes.

"Well?" Gene said roughly.

Jimmy turned, darted away.

Gene banged the shovel into the empty brown sockets he'd made in the top of the grave. He banged until his hands were bleeding, the shovel handle was split, the grave was flat, and Bib was dead.

Later he returned Elder's shovel to the place he'd found it. He left it shining clean, but the handle was badly broken. From the woods across the way he watched. Elder came out of the barn, turning the spade over and over in his hands. At last he sat down on his doorstep and splinted the handle, wrapping it with black electrical tape.

4

The summer after Bib left, Nick Potter, organization man, came by. Nick had wavy black hair and womanizing eyes too often glazed over with drink to do him much good.

"Bib isn't here?" he asked, speaking through the open window of his car.

"We took care of him," Alice said. "We had to."

Nick looked out onto the hill.

"I asked you to warn them," Alice said. "You didn't do it?"

The man leaned his head back onto the seat. Gene saw he was playing a game for his own drunk amusement.

"Alice, I always like it when the little woman gets riled up." Nick looked her up and down. Alice would have made two of him.

"How much?" she said.

Nick laughed. "Two hundred dollars. Now that's not so bad, is it?"

Alice relaxed. "No. Not so bad."

Holding his neck stiff, robot-like, to steady himself, Nick backed out, pulled away.

"Two hundred dollars," said Gene. "Is that a lot?"

Back inside the house, Alice figured. "We're going to be able to save some money, Gene. We could finish up this house, sell it. Or mortgage it, maybe, for materials to—no." She looked as if she had been slapped.

"What?"

"We can never mortgage this house or sell it," she muttered.

"It's in my name and Bib's, together. We'll just have to work and save like mad until the annuity runs out. Then, I don't know what we'll do."

"Alice, I'm always going to take care of you."

Her face softened. "I know you will."

This was Gene's work. He was up at six every morning, putting on yesterday's shirt and jacket and leaving his frigid bedroom while Alice still slept in her own. Down two flights of steps he went to empty the ashes in the furnace, rake the coals, stoke it. The wide mouth of that furnace was never satisfied. Up again to the woodstove. He started this fire, filling woodboxes with wood he must provide by borrowing, steadily, off Elder's hills, in places his uncle would not detect.

He put on a kettle, made instant coffee, drank it while the granules still floated on top. He left the hot water for Alice, was quiet so as not to disturb her when he rattled in the cupboard among cold jars and boxes and shoved some bread in a bag for his lunch.

When the kitchen had warmed up he left it, got into the cold car, rumbled off down the rutted road past Elder's house, which lay straight and tight to the ground. Warm inside day or night. Gene tried to keep Alice as warm as that.

On to work he went, backing the cold truck they assigned him. He waved his arms for a signal. Chicken dung schussed down through a tube.

There was a town ordinance against dumping hen manure out back at the farm. The manure tainted streams, drew hordes of insects to houses in the neighborhood. The firm Gene worked for wasn't a quaint little egg farm with one sagging barn; it was a small branch of a mega-industry, nationwide eggs. The by-products had to be carted off to state-designated landfills. That was Gene's work.

There was a world of difference between a small farm's spring spreading of cow manure on greening fields for fertilizer and the constant wet production of a million hens trapped in tiny cages. Trucks like Gene's rumbled in and out all day. The dust decorated the corrugated sides of the long low buildings that housed the hens and coated the nostrils, tongues, and lungs of the men and women who worked for minimum wage inside. It lay against the windows of the overseers' offices and went home on their shoes at night. Nothing fresh or clean could defend itself, but green pushed forward each spring, tainted from its first uncurling.

Gene got back into his truck for the first run, hawking and spitting brown goo onto the road as he pulled out and began the first fifteen-mile trip of the day to Breaks Mills. Once there, he dumped his load, turned back, got in line for another. He did this for eight hours, then marked his time card, went home. He would pass Elder's farm once again. It lay neatly against the landscape and, inside, Aunt Lois would be making supper for Crelly.

Not for him. He would go into the drafty house Alice had not cleaned, drop on the counter a couple of store-made Italian sandwiches, onions and oil, olives and pickles and cold cuts. The sandwiches would leave spots of oil on the counter. Gene might draw pictures in the oil with one split, toughened finger.

For Alice, repeated contact flattened whim-wham no matter how hard Gene worked. By the fall of 1982, he knew he would not be able, even in fantasy, to supply what Alice really needed. Either he would have to fill completely the place created and left vacant by Bib or he would be discarded somehow.

Alice knew his innocence was gone. These days she had begun to bring pictures of children, sometimes of babies innocent in snowsuits, up to his room. She would lie on her stomach and look at them while he caressed her buttocks, entered her from the rear. In coming, he would pitch forward, breathing in the smell of newsprint.

A wall in the living room was a series of beams and boards perhaps a hundred years old, black with age. One fall day Gene came home from work to find that Alice had torn the plaster and laths off the other walls as well, in case sometime they might get hold of some insulation. Her eyes were shiny. They could use the laths for kindling, she said. Gene nodded, broke the thin lengths of wood in pieces for her with one leather foot. Plaster dust rose. His clothing grew stiff with it.

Alice worked beside him. She was watching him. He didn't look at her. They both knew the time for a change had come.

"Get cleaned up," he told her when the laths were shuffled over by the door of the kitchen. "We'll go for a hamburger." It was a command.

Alice shook her head, went to her room.

Gene watched her go. He was angry. What right did she have? She should do what he said. Soon he would be supporting their family. And what did he ever ask for? Nothing.

He sat down in Alice's own chair, leaned so far back that the front view was mostly of jeans and leather shoes. Beyond was his tiny face, the eyes in it dark. His hair fell over his brow and down into his grease-stained collar. His chin was sunk in his chest. The chin was bristly, the shoulders, arms and body, those of a man.

On the table nearby was the round Victorian lamp, its fluted shade dipping crazily. In this room, Gene thought, a lot of child's illusions were hidden, cheap print with the smell of the outhouse on it. Somewhere in this room was his lost childhood, and a little girl in a white nightgown. Crelly.

His hands clenched. If he got near Crelly now he would take her by the shoulders, shake her until her neck snapped.

The murky room waited. He was tired of its hidden agenda. What he wanted at this moment was to own real buttocks, take possession of breasts with long, hard nipples. He would teach them how to lie, nubbled and salty, in his mouth. To stay there until he was done with them.

Gene stood up, made his way through the kitchen into Alice's room. She lay in the center of her big bed, a box of chocolates on one side, magazines strewn about.

"It's time," he said.

"You have to know what I need," she said, not as loudly as she meant to.

Gene shook his head. He had come for what, by rights, was his. "Move over," he commanded. "I know you."

Alice opened his clothing, allowed his penis to spring out. Her lips fell to him; he gasped. Behind his eyelids, the bedroom light went from red to black. A hot, liquid time. He pulsed, spilled, climbed in beside her.

He reached for her. She offered a breast to his lips. He fastened on it.

"Jimmy," she breathed.

Gene heard. He knew he would soon have to turn, as any victorious general might, to the fields of a new campaign.

With Jimmy, Alice went slow. He was wilder than Gene had been, quite apt to take off through the fields and be gone for hours.

Jimmy was slender, rackety, all elbows and knees. Poor nutrition made him look much younger than his fourteen years. His hair was a dirt color once blond; his deep blue eyes started from his face in a strange way. There were times when Jimmy's head seemed too large for his body and his start-eyed glance to see unimagined horrors.

"Jimmy!" Gene would holler that fall. "Come here! I need you!"

"Jimmy!" he hollered, cleared out, doubled around the house to the back bedroom window, to watch.

Jimmy's eyes, when he came into the bedroom, were innocent. Alice's face was tight, intent. She rose up on the bed, shielding her bare breasts from his view. The boy fled. Later, in Gene's arms, Alice climaxed with hard, shuddering heaves.

Bib's work on Jimmy had been done, however. On successive nights the boy fled too quickly, terrified. One night in late fall Alice reached up, hauled Jimmy into her bed, undressed him, touched him. Jimmy's little spout lay limp. Watching it roll on a belly rippling with nerves, Gene felt himself grow hard.

Alice leaned over Jimmy, moved this way, that. The light on the bedpost swung. Nothing worked. Finally she got out a magazine full of young boys, opened it, turned Jimmy on his side so he could see it.

But when she tried to flip him onto his back, she couldn't climb on him fast enough.

Jimmy's horror became a permanent presence in the house. He began to refuse to eat. He vomited. In a few weeks he looked like an old man, spent his days wandering.

Alice complained. "I can't get him to settle down. He won't stay still long enough."

Gene took Jimmy aside.

"Where the hell do you go?" he asked, as the boy pulled into the house after a long trek in the fields. "What do you do?"

"Nowhere." Jimmy was sullen. "I do nothing."

Off the dark lip of a pitcher of Gene's anger, the tiniest drop spilled. "Yeah?" he said. "You could be helping Alice, you know."

Jimmy threw himself on the sofa, all appendages, no body. "Oh, sure," he said. "We all know what she wants."

"Oh?"

"Sure. But boys are better." Defiantly, he caught the expression on Gene's face.

"Maybe," said Gene softly, "you should go up on the hill, Jimmy. Maybe we should see if Bib would like some company."

Jimmy's eyes popped out. His head twisted on its narrow stem. Uttering an unearthly cry, the boy fell over on the sofa, began to shake, rolled from sofa to floor, lay there hitting with head, fists and heels until the room rattled. Alice came running, but in a few seconds the seizure was over. Jimmy fell into a deep sleep. When he awoke, he remembered nothing.

From then on, if Gene came near or Alice touched him, Jimmy's head would begin to twist.

"I'm afraid, Gene," Alice said. "You can't tell me a normal child would act this way. Normal kids used to come into our store all the time. Jimmy is sick." She looked at Gene with pastel eyes. "What are we going to do?"

"Let him rest," said Gene. "Let him stay home from school. If he misses a grade he can make it up later. His health is the most important thing."

Alice had no eyelashes anymore, but her pale lids lowered flirtatiously. "He needs rest," she said. "Needs good home care. I don't know what they do, down to that school. Make kids sick, I guess."

Money was tight.

The annuity the Kemp children had received for ten years paid one final time in October. Gene sat down with Alice, tried to work out finances. He was earning $700 a month, take-home, with occasionally some overtime, but they were spending $500 a month in hush money and materials. Once a month Gene parked at a certain spot and left the cash in an envelope on the seat of the car while he went in to buy groceries. When he came out, the money was gone.

Money was one problem, kids were another, Alice said. They needed kids who were fresh, who suspected nothing. Those kinds of kids would begin to think it was all their fault. Scared kids generated money.

In his company truck Gene followed school buses on their way home with children. "Little ginks think they own the world," he would mutter, tapping his hand in a tight rhythm on the dashboard.

Often he thought of Crelly. Comfortable in college. Perhaps, he thought one day in early November, he should pay old Crelly a little call. See how she passed his morality test. See how much money she had, how much she thought she could spend.

It was a good idea. He didn't tell Alice.

"Well, Gene," Crelly said when she walked into the sitting room at her dormitory and found him standing there. "Come in. You came to visit me? How nice of you! Sit down, why don't you?"

She had turned into quite the young lady, Gene saw. Her brown hair shone in the light. Her hands were clean. He was conscious of his own dirt-rimmed fingernails.

He felt uneasy with her rightness in this place, the smile she wore.

He studied Crelly's competent person, her intelligent face.

He didn't sit down. She too stood watching, waiting for him to speak.

Gene thought, Does she take all this for granted? The white woodwork, the comfortable sitting room with its low couches and nice little lamps. Upstairs, he supposed, all these college people slept. There must be three, four bathrooms in a house this size; he was conscious of his counting of wealth in bathrooms.

"I see you're doing pretty well," he said.

Crelly nodded, frowned. "Is there—is there a problem, Gene?"

"You think that would be my only reason to come?" He shambled around the room, put his knuckles on a windowsill, against the frame. "Not much cold air leakage here."

Crelly tried to smile.

Gene rocked up, sank his leather heels into the carpet.

"Up there to home, Crelly," he said in his fifty-year-old voice, "Aunt Alice is having an awful hard time making ends meet. Got some bills to pay, got to fix up the house before another winter. It's hard, Crelly. I happened to be driving by and I thought of you. Oh, and something's wrong with Jimmy, he's developed some kind of fit, needs medicine. Crelly, I don't know how we'll make ends meet. We could use some of that money, that scholarship money I hear you have. As much as you could give us, Crelly. You understand."

"Gene," Crelly blurted, "how can I? It wouldn't be—honest. Besides, I never even see the scholarship money. It all goes right to the school, to their bookkeeping. Uncle Elder sends me five dollars now and then. I can loan you a dollar or two." She met his eyes, looked away.

Selfish, he thought. "So you're untouchable? I didn't realize that." In his mind a door slammed, hard. Carefully he opened it.

"Guess you'll grow up to be a teacher or something," he said. "Live in a nice house, be comfortable. Hey? And it won't matter to you, little Crelly, never matter to you who's in need, right outside your door. Your own brother won't matter to you."

Crelly flushed. "Gene, please, don't be angry. I can call Uncle

Elder, he'll know what to do for Jimmy. If a doctor is needed, Uncle Elder won't refuse you."

"I hear you're pretty good on the stage," Gene said abruptly.

"Y-yes. I guess so."

He nodded. "Then you just keep right on acting, little Crelly. Stay right in the theater, where it's safe. Better that way, right?"

He walked out, slammed the front door behind him so that its etched-glass panels jiggled in their ancient frames.

By the time he got to his own road up in Edgar, he found he was following Elder's pickup truck. They both turned into Alice's driveway. Alice came out.

"Alice. Gene." Elder Leavitt's eyes were icy. "Crelly called. Said there was something wrong with Jimmy, said you needed help."

Alice's spangled glance saw everything Gene had done. Quickly she covered it all. "Elder, Jimmy's been an awful sick boy," she said. "Taken with seizures."

"They got agencies with money for this stuff!" Elder stopped. "I'm sorry about Jimmy, Alice," he said more quietly. "Poor kid."

"I'm afraid," Alice said, "that if he doesn't get some help, he's going to go like Bib. We've got to have some money."

Elder Leavitt wasn't a heartless man when he was angry. "Okay," he said. "Gene, get in. We'll go see what to do about the medical. If money's tight, there's agencies."

Gene hesitated.

"Get in!" Elder snapped. "Because I'm telling you this, mister: you're never going to ask Crelly for money that isn't hers again."

Gene looked at Alice.

"Elder, you don't need to bother with this," she said. "All the paperwork. You're right. We should sign up. Gene and I can go down tomorrow morning. Sorry we bothered Crelly—we got a little desperate. We just weren't thinking, that's all."

Elder huffed, but he was calming down. "Down to the Department of Human Services," he said. "These days it doesn't take them long to check. Got computer hookups right to the VA, to Togus, for Bib, to Social Security for disability. You just have to go, that's all. And not to scruple about it, it's your right."

"We will," said Alice. "Look, sorry again about Crelly."

"Well, you sign up. Best place to go." Elder drove off.

They went back to the house. Alice sat in her chair by the stove. Around the chair, on the floor, were dirty cups more or less filled with coffee, light brown coffee drizzles down the sides.

Gene sat on the sofa, staring at her. Something had to be done around here. He didn't know just what. "Jimmy!" he hollered. "Get down those stairs!"

Footsteps on the ceiling, down the side wall. Jimmy appeared in the doorway. He was thin as a drifting wisp.

Gene's voice was sympathetic. "Only trouble with you is, you never quite got over Bib, right?"

Jimmy's face reddened.

"Come in here." Gene spoke tenderly. Jimmy came. "You think too much, right? That isn't healthy, Jim. Makes people see things."

Jimmy choked back a sob. "Blood," he whispered.

"See?" said Gene. "That isn't healthy, is it?"

Jimmy shook his head.

"Exercise," Gene said. "Got to get out of the house more, old pal. Why, you could run up onto the hill and back."

Jimmy didn't move. "Lay off," he said. His eyes popped.

"Right now, Jimmy," Gene ordered. "Run! Go on! Or do I have to carry you?"

The seizure came upon Jimmy like a vast black cloud. The room took on an aura, Alice's eyes shone with rainbows, his head twisted. "Get away from me," the boy said, swishing one hand, but it was too late. He cried out, fell to the floor where his body rattled, spittle frothing from his mouth.

Gene looked at Alice. "I doubt those doctors would do anything for him."

Alice shook her head. "The problem is in Jimmy himself. By rights, he should be able to cooperate."

Gene nodded. "I don't know how you manage sometimes, Alice," he said slowly. "Was he bad today?"

"Awful."

Jimmy stopped rattling, slept. They left him where he lay. But in the middle of the night he woke them up.

"It's cold," he muttered, standing beside their bed. The light was on. Gene kept it on at night so as not to be reminded of Bib. He blinked.

"'When these lines you see,'" said the boy suddenly, "'remember you must follow me.'"

"What?" Gene shook his head to clear it.

"Don't mind him," said Alice. "He's been all over these hills, found an old graveyard somewhere."

Jimmy spoke: " 'With nerve and sails unfurled, she steered her bark for yonder world.' "

"Jimmy, go to bed," said Gene.

The boy went on reciting: " 'May this my Glory be, that Christ is not ashamed of me.' "

To warn Alice, Gene said, "I think he's going to have one. Jimmy, go to bed. Unless you want to crawl in here, Jim. With us."

But Jimmy didn't have his usual seizure. Instead he went to the black window. "I can see you all!" he roared, turned, pulled back, slammed his fist into a wall, then again. Gene had to get up to subdue him, lead him to his own bed.

Bang! Bang! Bang! Gene's signature was on Uncle Elder's door the next day. He made inconsequential conversation, then said, "Oh, by the way, Jimmy's going to live with some cousins of Uncle Bib's, up to Bath."

"Well, isn't that nice," said Aunt Lois. "Which cousins are those?"

"I don't know as you'd know them."

"Isn't it good Jimmy's seeing some new places?" Aunt Lois smiled. She had done her duty pleasantly, as best she could.

"Yes. What I came for was to borrow an ax."

Elder shook his head. "Look right through the sink window, Gene. See that load there?" Elder called it a "lud." In a small heap to one side of the barn entrance were two cords of wood, oak and birch, waiting to be split and stacked. "Been trying to get at that for three days, and this afternoon, by God, I intend to."

Gene lay one dark hand against Aunt Lois's white porcelain sink, looked out the window, nodded. The door vibrated in its frame when he went out.

He drove off, snaked back through the woods, waited while Elder disappeared into the far regions of his fields. Then Gene melted around a back corner of the house, crept into the barn. He picked out the shovel he would need. Elder had long since fitted the blade with a new handle; the initials E.L. were burnt into the blond wood of it. The ax was what Gene had had in mind, but this would do.

In the afternoon he dug, to be ready. When he had finished he went back down to the house to sit on the living room sofa. Alice was in the yard. After a while she came into the house and leaned over the stove, her toe up on the fender. Her form against the dark wall behind was a question mark.

Gene said nothing. If he moved his heels back just a little, he could feel the shovel under the sofa.

Alice turned away, went to the kitchen. Gene knelt, pulled the shovel out, went up the creaky stairs. Jimmy was not in school, so weak with a chest cold that he'd spent all day in bed.

Jimmy was not in his bed. What looked like a scarecrow was slung limply from a rope. It hung by the neck, below a rafter.

With shaking fingers Gene cut the body down, concealed it in bedclothes, carried it out onto the back hill with distaste, as one might rid a house of a used tissue or a small dead animal. In the grave he had already prepared he buried Jimmy, a little quiet funeral, all that was needed. "Because by rights," Gene muttered, "he's been dead a long time."

Later Gene climbed into bed beside Alice, bringing his grit with him to her cold mound of raggle-taggle patchwork. "Got to have children who cooperate" was all she said. "Ayeh."

5

There were two general stores in Edgar, the larger a long building that housed, at the back behind a wrought-iron window grating, the town post office; the second had a Budweiser sign in pink neon, lit night and day.

The first, the Edgar General Store, was family-run. Three generations could be seen behind the wooden counter or at the back of the store, heating corn chowder on a hot plate for lunch. The board floor was uneven but spotless, the selection of food basic and adequate. Behind a glass were meats beautifully trimmed. You could buy food or nails or rubber boots or motor oil or sewing supplies. At noon you could get home made sandwiches and pie. The air of established quality about this place made Gene's shoulders itchy. He only went there when he had to.

The second store was on the Edgar–Breaks Mills line and was named the Maine Lyne Grocerie. It was set up on posts and painted pink. The wooden steps shook as you went up to the door. Inside was a lunch counter and a grill behind it that smoked when it was heated. An egg fried there would taste of hot dogs, onion, pepper steak. Beside the counter was a case of candy and, beyond that, packaged cookies, pastries, doughnuts. To one side were laundry detergents, Crisco, Campbell's soup. Along the fourth wall were cases of beer and wine.

Gene parked his car in back of the Maine Lyne, the money in a special yellow envelope left strategically on the seat.

Maine Lyne, too, was owned by a family, the Potters, an old man and his two sons. One son had married extraordinarily well, into the family who owned the egg operation where Gene worked. You never saw this son in the store anymore. He worked in the carpeted central office at the egg farm. The second son, Nick, an organization man like his father, worked here. Nick, his wavy black hair combed slickly back, parked outside the store at night, winter or summer, in a beat-up car, the radio on loud as he emptied cans, crushed them, tossed them out the window.

For years it had been Nick's job to keep tabs for the organization and to collect what payments he could from the front seats of cars that had been strategically parked out of sight, in back of the store. Gene distrusted him; he distrusted any man who couldn't control an addiction. But on this day in January, he knew, he was going to have to talk to Nick.

It was cold. The snow lay in the parking area in a tough sheet of slick white. Gene slipped a little as he walked toward the store. Snow was heaped in dirty slags at the sides of the road; icicles dripped from the store's sagging roof. Gene kicked at a frozen fist of snow, looked around for Nick, went inside.

The store smelled greasy; it was dark. The oak candy counter was old-fashioned, with glassed-in shelves above to a height of five feet. Below were heavy drawers with cupped brass handles that cut at your fingers.

The old man who owned the place, Red Potter, saw Gene come in, went to his window. He looked around, motioned with his head.

Gene was always amused by Red's wariness; there was rarely more than one customer in the store. He went behind the counter, knelt. His fingers strained at those little upside-down cups. The drawer came open. Inside were boxes of various types. Red stood by his window and watched while Gene looked. He would have to pay extra for the things in this drawer. One box held plastic penises of a wobbly rubber type, with double heads and double erections; these were $3.95 each. Another held inflatable female torsos, faces painted on the fronts of the bodies, breasts for eyes, large red-lipped open mouths painted at crotches. Inside each mouth was a small reusable plastic sac. These were $6.95. Gene pushed aside boxes containing imitation ivory deflowering tools, fake fur leopardskin penis covers, slammed the drawer shut, tried the next.

Here were magazines, the faces blanked out on the covers, the bodies bare. Below these were copier pages stapled together, pictures of women or children, faces blacked out. To one side was a plain envelope with ALICE written on it. This Gene picked up, sliding it beneath his jacket.

When he got back to the car, the payoff envelope would be gone, as always. There was a protocol to these things. Nod at Red, leave, don't speak. Gene knew that this time he must break protocol. It felt odd to walk up to Red. "Need to talk to Nick."

The old man's yellowish eyes raked Gene's face. "Wait in the car."

Gene went to his car, turned it on to have the benefit of the heater, rolled down the window a crack. A few minutes later Nick drove around, parked. Nick in the daytime was a quiet drunk, competent, dangerous.

He got in on the passenger side, a man of forty, his skin sagging at the jowls. He held a cigarette; the tips of his fingers and his fingernails were yellow.

"Something the matter?" Nick's teeth were yellowed, too, Gene saw. Close to, the man smelled of tobacco and incense.

"Nick, I'm sorry to bother you," Gene said. "Alice and I got trouble. We're not just sure what to do."

"Trouble?"

"Money," said Gene abruptly. "I bring home take-home seven-fifty, eight hundred a month tops. I've looked around for other jobs, and they just aren't there. No training, never finished high school."

Nick nodded.

"I pay out to the organization five hundred a month insurance," said Gene. "Some of it for stuff that I don't even know about, that Bib did. What I'm getting at is, couldn't the organization give me a break? I can't get assistance of any kind because of Bib."

"What about Alice?" said Nick. "She could get a job."

"She hasn't worked in years. She just sits—no kids, no hope. I don't know which way to turn."

Nick puffed on his cigarette. "I thought she didn't look so hot, last time I was there. Gene, there is a major misconception you have." He tamped his cigarette on the knee of his twill pants, rubbed out the spot. "See, we're not set up that way. I'm surprised to hear you pay so little, but I guess that's Maine for you. See, those big-city guys, they look at what you're paying, and to them it's just a drop in the bucket. If I take what you say to them, they'll say, 'Who's this guy trying to kid? Nobody works for wages like that. Christ.'"

Nick touched a yellowed finger to his tongue, removed a wisp of tobacco, silently rubbed it between his fingers.

"Then I don't know what we're going to do," Gene said.

"Course"—Nick stretched out his legs, leaned far back—"you could work some of it off, maybe. They'd probably let you do that."

"Doing what?"

"Procurement or something, I shouldn't think. Look, stop in here tomorrow, keep stopping. I'll let you know. Getting kids. For the business." He leaned on the door handle, got out.

Two days later, parked in the same spot, Gene rolled down his window for Nick, who stood beside the car, hands in his pockets against the cold. "Procurement," Nick said. "They say you could earn maybe four hundred a month, two trips. Picking up kids, working with me. Take them to Lewiston. Photography, quality business, artistic. But I can't drive, you got to drive." The man wove on his feet, pulled his hands out of his pockets in time to clutch at the car for support.

Gene nodded. Nick stumbled away.

Arriving home Gene paused for a moment, sitting in his car, to stare at the property. The barn had fallen in. He had spent hours ranging over the hills for fuel, at last bringing in barn boards to feed the furnace, keep Alice warm. There wasn't much left of the barn. These days he was working on the shed.

Nothing seemed to help Alice. Day after day she sat, her face still as a totem, her eyes fixed on nothing.

"Bib, he got me into this," she would mutter, "and I blamed it on the navy. All the little foreign children, you know, they'd do anything for money. But no, there was something wrong with Bib before he went. 'Alice,' he would say, 'watch me charm this little dolly.' It was like having power, for him. He had charm, too." She tilted her head. "In the early days. He needed it. So did I." Once again her face would become as still as the face on a coin. " 'Whatever works,' Bib would say. 'Whatever works.' "

At this moment, with last year's plastic fluttering at the windows, the house looked more tumble-down, more hopeless than ever. Sighing, Gene went inside, told Alice the news. "A quality business," he said. "Artistic. Better, maybe, than the stuff we've been getting. None of that shit is good for anything." He and Alice hadn't touched each other since Jimmy's death. They had been blaming this on poor materials.

Alice's eyes widened. "Well, good," she said. "Good. Then we won't be dipping into savings."

She had managed to save a few hundred dollars, a nest egg for emergencies, which she kept hidden somewhere in the house. They'd been living on that since the annuity ran out. Every time they took some of it, Gene felt how much he had failed.

"But you'll have to be careful," she said. "Especially these days. Damn ordinances. Damn judges."

"Hey, we're talking art here. I promise. They won't be able to touch us." He held out his arms.

"Quality," she murmured against his shoulder. "That's what I always tried to tell Bib."

Gene pulled her close. "You know, we're going to have to fatten you up," he said.

In carpeted rooms at the egg farm, administrative decisions were made that affected the lives of the lowliest employees. Security deposits on company mobile homes in which some workers lived were doubled, wages withheld over disputes. Some worked without wages until the disputes were settled. There was no union. The hardest hit were those who didn't know how to fight, only how to work.

Subsistence was what people needed at these times. They earned it one way or another, as did their counterparts all over the country.

The next Friday evening, Gene and Nick drove toward the egg farm, pulled off into a dimly lit area of mobile homes, went down a rutted road. "Now remember," Nick said, "first on the list is, you got to be nice to them. They got to think you're their friend, you're doing them a favor."

They climbed shaky metal steps, pulled a door open. It clamored on rusty metal hinges. Inside was one light, a bare bulb over a tiny sink. The people inside, a mother, father, and two children, were small and thin, perhaps Oriental. The children, age eight and ten, had wide black eyes; their coats were already on. The mother nodded once at them.

Money was pressed into her hand. The children followed the men out. At another trailer a boy and a girl, both towheaded under the trailer lights, followed Gene to the car. He and Nick drove the children to Lewiston to an old warehouse, where all the pictures for the materials were taken.

Dennis was the only name Gene knew for the man who did the photography, an organization man. Nick knew Dennis well, and the two talked, joked back and forth. Dennis was young, with a grayish complexion and many acne scars, his hair combed straight back. He always wore the same outfit: brown pants, bell-bottomed, a white shirt, a light-colored scratched leather suit jacket, an aqua tie held in place with a small clasp that was supposed to be silver, but something coppery showed at the edges.

In March, Nick told Gene privately that he'd like not to have to work with Dennis too much longer. Dennis was big-city, Nick said, while he and Gene were country boys at heart.

"We wouldn't scare those kids so much, or huddle 'em in and out of their clothes so fast, would we?" Nick would say.

Gene would agree. Nick wanted his father to sell Maine Lyne Grocerie to him and Gene, if they could get some money together. Red could then retire to Florida, and Nick and Gene could be partners. They would set up part of the store for kids, Nick said, maybe even show cartoons on a big screen, sell some popcorn. Hell, Alice could work there, tend counter if she wanted. If they could get a little money ahead.

He himself had a little. How much did Gene have?

Gene went to Alice. "We could pay off Red Potter and he'd go to Florida," he told her, hardly able to contain his excitement. "We could put in a little carousel, Nick says, paint things, maybe even build a playroom on back."

Alice was cautious. He asked a question to catch her: "I wonder how much you'd need to carpet a room, say, ten by ten?"

"Carpet?" she said, took out a stub of a pencil, asked for his new black-handled knife, sharpened the pencil in four crude cuts. "You have to figure." She looked at him. "Say you were really going to do this."

"We'll take in money at that store, Alice. I'll keep on with my job, too, at least until we get it all going."

She was quiet. A blush rose to the roots of her hair. "I thought we'd be buried here," she said.

"No. That'll never happen."

Alice's face blazed. "Yellow is always good. Gene, could we make the playroom yellow? Or, if we had stencils, couldn't we make a border of red and blue designs, little merry-go-rounds, maybe?"

"Sure," he said grandly. "We could set that store up like you never saw. You and I'll have to run it, course. Nick doesn't care. He just wants someplace he can stay drunk in."

Alice found a women's magazine, opened it. "You'd have to figure," she said. She found a page of decorating ideas, sat back down in her chair. Using the pencil stub, she made notes in the margin.

Gene swaggered to the sofa, sat. Soon he and Alice and Nick would be running their own business. Just as well; these rooms were falling apart. When Alice was low in her mind, she didn't feel like pulling out boards from the barn or shed to burn. She would take framing from the walls or boards from the upstairs floor. "I just don't have what it takes to care," she would say.

Gene's eye caught at the round shape of the base of the Victorian lamp on the table to one side. The lampshade had deteriorated. A bare light bulb swelled with many patches of color before his eyes. "That lamp's still good," he said. "Just needs a shade. We could take it to the store with us."

Alice nodded, her face made of patched color. "Nothing like a lamp on a table for creating a soft glow."

"How much money do you have, Alice?"

"Fifteen hundred dollars," she muttered, still figuring. "Will that be enough?"

"I'll ask."

Not quite, Nick said. They would have to be patient. Two months at the outside.

Gene decided he could be patient for that long. This was March. By May they would be fine. Meanwhile, he could put up with the warehouse. There, he and Nick separated the kids, told them to undress, leave their clothes on boxes of old invoices. But the place was filthy. One mother complained that her kid's clothes came home dirty; she couldn't get them clean.

One night in April, Gene and Nick went to a new trailer, brightly lit, clean inside. The woman welcomed them in as if they were long-lost relatives. She had a pointed face, high color in her cheeks. "This is May Lynn," she said, introducing a short, plump girl, perhaps ten or eleven. As May Lynn looked up at them, something in Gene moved and answered: Dennis would like this one. In this kid's eyes was real quarry, absolute innocence.

The mother gave her daughter a little push forward. "Isn't this nice, May Lynn? These are your uncles. They'll take you for a nice ride."

May Lynn nodded obediently, followed them out the door.

"What ails the woman?" Gene muttered.

"She's buried it," said Nick. "She thinks this is a tea party."

May Lynn sat in the back seat with two little boys she knew from the school bus. One of them reached out, put his hand on her knee. She pushed it off. No little kid was going to monkey with her. She could just make out the kid's eyes, which were moist, like a little animal's. The back seat seemed warm to her, sticky.

May Lynn watched everything. The place they went to was in the city. It was chilly and dark, with many steep stairs you fell against because you couldn't see. There was the smell of tires, wet rubber, grease, motor parts. "Here," said one of the men. "Take off your clothes, leave them here. We'll call you."

It was too cold for stripping; May Lynn knew enough not to say so. It was dirty, too. The whole atmosphere was dirty, as if you had been dared to do something dangerous at a carnival. Her eyes went everywhere; she was on guard without knowing why. She waited for a little while, then stole closer to where the men sat. She was careful to stay out of sight.

"Here's my knife, boys," one of the men was saying. "I'm going to lay it right here. Nothing to be afraid of but just to remember, so you'll cooperate. Pretend it's not even here if you want." She looked. She'd seen little boys without clothes before—that was nothing. What she hadn't seen was a knife like this one, its hasp narrow and black, its blade long, thin and pointed.

As quietly as she could she went to the stairs, then down them one by one. Someone called her name from above. A saving impulse told her to open the door to the warehouse and leave it open, then double back inside the building.

All three men called out, raced down the stairs, ran outside. Quickly May Lynn went back up into another part of the warehouse and sank out of sight among boxes of papers. After a long time the men came back, playing flashlights into every corner. She didn't move. Finally they packed up, took the boys, and left.

Alone, she didn't cry. She shivered and waited until daylight, thinking. Then she walked until she found a school, sat on the doorstep wearily.

There she was found by a teacher, who took her in kindly. She was fed, questioned, at last turned over to the proper authorities.

She was filthy; her clothes were torn. There were no records of fingerprints, since her family had moved around so much. She looked like the child of a street wanderer, and eventually it was decided that that was the case. To all questions about her parents, she shook her head. Finally she was put in a good foster home, found herself at last safe among strangers.

"This is gonna cost you!" Dennis screamed at Gene and Nick. "You dumb hicks! Who knows where that kid went? She could be at the police right now. Jesus Christ, if she talks—" He thrust his scarred face into theirs. "This is gonna cost you," he said. "The mother's going to want money. My people are going to want money. You're going to owe us."

There wasn't a thing to do or say. Gene and Nick went home. They lay low. They waited. Nothing happened.

The extra payments began, and since they no longer worked with Dennis, there was no extra income.

Alice said nothing. She gave Gene all of her savings—a little more than $1,400, it turned out. Then she went into the living room and sat.

In the daily April terror of losing everything, of falling once and for all over the edge and drowning in a black sea of his own making, Gene's mind began to make extraordinary leaps. Surely there was an answer somewhere. There had to be a way for them to live!

His truck bumped over the roads, his hands beat on the steering wheel. Money. He had to have it. Dead tired from miles and miles of illegal extra shifts of driving, he knew he would have to have enough to buy out not only Red Potter but Nick. Then he and Alice could be on their own. They'd be away clean, no funny business after that.

With this dream Gene grew desperate. He began to look into every face he saw with the same hidden question: Are you the one to help me now? In his need, he spent more and more time at Elder's, the most prosperous place he knew. And he was there one day at the end of April when the mailman came.

"There he is." Aunt Lois stepped out onto the doorstep to see, waved. The mailman waved her letters at her, then slid them into the box; it was a long walk up across the lawn to the head of the driveway. Aunt Lois ducked inside for a sweater and then went out. By the time she was back, Uncle Elder had come up from the barn. The three of them, Elder, Lois and Gene, sat at the kitchen table while she sorted. "Damn light bill, damn phone bill," the newspaper, and there—a letter from Crelly.

Aunt Lois read the letter, passed it over without a word to Elder, who read it, sat back.

"Mentioned that what's-his-name again."

"Elder," said Aunt Lois. "We mustn't jump the gun."

Elder grunted. Aunt Lois smoothed the letter flat as it lay on the table and bent over it, rereading.

Gene sat back, his face humorous, but he was angry. Did it matter to them so much what Crelly wrote? They cared about every word she sent them.

"Oh, Lord, they're coming out. Did you hear that, Elder?"

"Now don't worry," said Uncle Elder. "We'll look him over."

Gene laughed, a short bark. "Crelly and a man?"

"I wouldn't put it quite like that." Aunt Lois spoke more sharply than usual. She didn't bother to look up at him, her eyes fixed on the letter.

Gene stood. He spoke formally, to punish her. "I'll be going, Aunt Lois."

She didn't seem to notice; neither did Uncle Elder, who waggled a hand in the air, erasing Gene from it.

Damn them, Gene thought. He got into his car, drove home, braked, went straight inside. "Alice?"

She sat by the stove. He might, he saw, have to rupture that depression she was in, infect her with a little life.

"Ayeh?" she said.

"Alice, stand up! We've got to get you going!"

He pulled her out of her chair, but she was hunched over a bit, her blue plaid flannel shirt flapping about her men's pants. "What are you up to?" she said.

"Do you know who I am?" He snapped at her playfully with his teeth. Her chin pulled back.

"It's only afternoon, Gene."

"Hell." He led her into the bedroom. "Lay down!" Obediently she climbed onto the bed, lay under him. His teeth flashed as he fastened them lightly on the skin of her neck, leaving a trail of little red marks. She fought him, he held her down. "That's the way," he said. "Fight."

Alice struggled until one arm was loose, slipped a hand between them, grabbed Gene in a slick place.

"Now, you cooperate," she said.

"No, you cooperate." Gene loosed her hand, held both of them over her head with one of his. Muscles rippled flabbily under her breasts, down her sides to her belly. He kneed her open, entered.

"You know me," he groaned as he tensed, laid himself against her. "Alice, you know me."

Crelly and John

1

Crelly never said a word to Aunt Lois or Uncle Elder about why she had run away to them. After a while they stopped asking. These days, in the summer of 1978, Crelly couldn't remember much about it, either.

Forgetting was easy. All you had to do was concentrate on whatever you were doing and push all the bad things to a dark drop-off in your mind. This exercise had become easier and easier for Crelly: concentrate on making beds at Aunt Lois's, on the clean patchwork coverlets, the shiny white cotton sheets.

Go to the kitchen and walk through it. Smell the smells, of breakfast coffee or evening soup. See the shining dishes, the plants growing on the windowsills. Make a pudding—butterscotch, not chocolate; her continued abhorrence to chocolate she'd never been quite able to send over the rim—and watch the butterscotch froth as it heated, smell its fragrance, pour it into custard dishes, their fluted sides rising from the counter like six crystal flowers.

And if, just for an instant, the steam rising from those flowers smelled of chocolate, or if the dishes reminded her of dime store candy in fluted wrappers—well, then one had to push that over the edge, too. Here are six fluted pudding dishes, clouded with steam.

Suds, bubbles—swish the soap saver under running hot water. Crelly loved all surfaces to be clean. The soap saver was of metal, a clever contraption. When you squeezed the handles, a perforated soap dish opened, and you could put inside any slivers of soap you happened to have. If the suds went down in the dishpan you swished the soap through again, then hung the saver back on its hook. Sun shone through the window over the sink. The bubbles rose high from Crelly's energetic swishing.

And if sometimes a black form seemed to hover over her, a form as large as a man's, its arms and legs quivering like a marionette's, she closed her eyes, pushed it over the rim of her mind. Forgotten. Gone, if she could keep it gone. And if sometimes at night she was too frightened to sleep, she frantically lay herself flat on the clean linoleum floor of her room, silently sobbing, her cheeks rubbing wetly, hot, on that cool smooth surface, her arms outstretched as if she could with her body mimic and so exorcise the suffering she felt in spirit, whose cause she had systematically forgotten—if in the night this happened, she would remind herself that this bedroom had a door.

"Everything's fine up the road, Gene says," Aunt Lois might announce after one of what the Leavitts came to call his "borrowing visits."

"Well, good," Crelly would say pleasantly, with a little smile.

The land belonging to Uncle Elder and Aunt Lois rolled toward the south and down to the Edgar River in acres of sculpted green. On the north were stands of pine trees so large that two men touching hands couldn't span the girth of one of them. The barn was small but pleasant. Flowers edged the lawn, and below it was a vegetable garden that kept Crelly and Aunt Lois busy all summer.

Crelly especially loved summer evenings when the trees at the pasture edges made cool, dark shadows. The hills and pastures were arrayed in so many shades of green, in such a variety of shapes. There was a particular pasture fence of crossed, silvered boards, a gate there to swing on. Aunt Lois and Uncle Elder would herd their sheep toward the fold, and she would swing on the gate. The grass was smooth; all the heat of the day was gone; a chill came down like a blessing.

The sheep approached. Their eyes were dull, but their ears, small and black, stood upright at Aunt Lois's calling. Crelly would leap off to hold the gate open. As the animals passed, trotting docilely at the sound of their own hooves, she would despair of them. Their wool was thick after spring shearing but already dusty, ratted with grass and sticks. Whoever thought sheep were woolly-white was wrong.

In summer there might be sweet peas with lavender blossoms in a vase on a table in the kitchen. Or maybe the first tiny new carrots had just been set there by Uncle Elder, sending a skirl of garden dirt across the oilcloth.

"Sorry," he would say.

"Proves they're real," Aunt Lois would reply.

Golden, small and moist, those carrots melted on the tongue with a taste that was almost melancholy, both tart and sweet.

Examining the gate to make sure it was shut tight, Uncle Elder would shake his head. "Sheep, they're awful dumb critters."

"Can't help but like them, though," Aunt Lois always said.

The three of them would be helping with the gate, as if it took all three to do it. Aunt Lois might touch Crelly's hair. "Here's a very good girl, Elder."

In the barn there were a dozen cows. Each had her name painted on a board at the front of the stall. When she had first come to Uncle Elder's, Crelly had been afraid of cows. Their hooves planted themselves heavily, their dark sides blew in and out like great bellows, their tails snapped like whips, and their heads swung widely around. It was a long time before she had come to the barn, but as she grew older she learned to love to help hitch the milking machines, throw down the hay bales.

To one side of the barn was a tiny milkroom. Every day Uncle Elder brought fresh milk into the house, strong-tasting stuff so different from the milk in cartons at school that at first Crelly hadn't been able to drink it. The milkroom was a wonder of stainless steel sinks and scalded milk pails. There was a refrigerator and a separator, each in its own niche. In the morning Aunt Lois worked to skim cream for butter, store milk. She scrubbed and sterilized for an hour, running boiling spray for a rinse-down, over sinks and pails, even walls and floors, until all was glistening.

"There," she'd say, coming in from the milkroom with two small covered pails of cream, "guess that'll hold back the bugs." She would be steaming herself, wide wet loops of sweat under the arms of her blouse. She would shake her head, her glasses covered with tiny water drops. "Just point me to the tub, Crelly. I don't think I can find it on my own."

The bathroom had pink tiles and two soft lights in it, from pink light bulbs. "Can't see without my glasses anyway," Aunt Lois said. "Might's well be comfortable."

There was a pink rug on the floor and a pink plastic shower curtain suspended from a circular rod over an old-fashioned tub. The place smelled of Dutch cleanser and rose body powder.

Children from all over the town of Edgar went to school at Breaks Mills; Edgar was part of that school administrative district. Some years, Crelly rode the same bus with her brothers. They nodded at each other, separated by grades, friends; Gene and Jimmy attended for the bare minimum of school days and often didn't pass. It was all right; Crelly hardly knew them.

Aunt Lois and Uncle Elder went to every conference with Crelly's teachers and as she grew older began to realize that she must have more education. "May as well get used to it," Uncle Elder said. "Our Crelly's got to go places."

"When you go to college" was how some of Aunt Lois's favorite daydreams came to begin. "When you go to college," she would say, "I will have to lay my hands on enough tweed to make you at least one good suit."

This summer Aunt Lois sped Crelly, age thirteen, past the children's section at Sears and on to women's lingerie.

"I'm going to shop here?" Crelly said, pleased.

"Well," Aunt Lois said, "when you get to changing in those gym classes over at high school, you got to be able to hold your head up."

Standing in the gentle snowstorm of shining things hanging from little hangers she reached out, touched a half-slip edged with lace. "Course, the stuff has got to last you, it's got to be durable." Aunt Lois sighed. "I'm a sucker for lace."

Her plump hands examined the slip, felt along its seams. Head back, she turned the garment inside out, frowned farsightedly at the stitches.

She let go of it and, Crelly in tow, wandered up and down the aisles, pausing here and there to test elastics or hold material up to the light. They looked until Aunt Lois put her hands to her flushed face. "I don't know," she said. "For the money, it's all kind of dinky."

They were standing once again by the first half-slip they'd seen. Crelly touched its lace with one finger. "It's pretty, though," she said.

"Oh, hell," Aunt Lois said. "If it's pretty, we better have it."

Up and down the aisles they went again, selecting the best they could afford; they made an odd-shaped sloop. All the lightweight sails of underwear luffed as they headed for the cash register. Aunt Lois spoke words so risky she rarely dared to use them: "Charge it, please."

To make ends meet Uncle Elder and Aunt Lois sold mutton, wool, fresh vegetables. Uncle Elder was also a carpenter and ran his business from his home, going out every day after the chores were done to work on building projects.

In the late part of the summer, before she was to attend high school in Breaks Mills for the first time, Crelly went along with Uncle Elder into town; he sometimes had to make a trip into Pomfret to plan his buying at various hardware stores and lumberyards.

"Elder, how the hell—" With an eye to Crelly the men in the stores amended this. "How are you?"

"Can't complain."

The men greeted Elder Leavitt by name, called out to friends and employees that he had come. Uncle Elder only nodded. His style was to telescope speech into the fewest possible words. What he did say, people paid attention to. Crelly held his lists, as she had for years, with a certain pride. The letters of his handwriting were square, as if he'd tried to make a good straight box frame out of every one.

"One by eights," Uncle Elder said on this August afternoon. "Got to have a price. Clear, is it?"

"Best we have, Elder. For you, twelve cents a foot, running."

Uncle Elder and the lumberyard man faced each other, dressed in work pants of brown chino and much-laundered sport shirts, now a little smudged from the day's work. Uncle Elder's Red Sox cap was set on the back of his head. The other man's Red Sox cap hung to the side of the counter on a nail; when he had finished with customers for the day, he would put it on. The man had rolled up his sleeves. On his wrist was an expensive gold watch.

"Got some awful good pine over to Prince's, eight cents," said Uncle Elder.

"That so?"

Uncle Elder adjusted his hat, stood squarely by the counter.

"Doin' your homework, I see," the man said.

"Have to." Uncle Elder's face looked cool, rested.

The man cocked an eyebrow. "How much pine you goin' to need, Elder?"

"A hundred and seven twelve-footers."

The long counter was a single plank eighteen inches wide, three inches thick. It had seen a hundred years of trade and was covered with fine scratches from goods and tools being scraped over it, yet it was polished and solid. "Never saw the beat of it, how you know exactly," the man said. "It's a fair amount. Elder, would eight cents suit you?"

"Might." Uncle Elder's face revealed nothing.

The man shook his head. "I guess you haven't gone over to Sayley's yet."

"They're next."

"Oh, hell. We'll match it, Elder, whatever it is. Jesus." The man caught sight of Crelly again. "Sorry."

Uncle Elder nodded. "Good enough, then. I'll be phonin' orders on Wednesday, Roy."

"You know to the day? Course you do. And probably pass the discounts right along, too. They don't run carpentry business like this anymore, Elder."

"I do," Uncle Elder said.

The man reached across the counter and shook his hand. "Good to see you. Always is."

"Pretty quiet, young one," Uncle Elder said that evening at supper.

Crelly wanted to share with them the snarl of her thoughts. "If," she said, "Uncle Elder could go up and work on Aunt Alice's house and fix it up, wouldn't that—I don't know—help?"

Aunt Lois put down her fork. Uncle Elder hesitated. It was as close as Crelly had ever come, in the years she had stayed with them, to making any reference to her life at Aunt Alice's. In the beginning they had asked her often, then they left off asking since it seemed to make her unhappy.

Uncle Elder cleared his throat. "I once thought I could do some work up there."

Aunt Lois said, "I often wonder how Alice manages."

"The house is all broken," said Crelly in a low voice. "I used to think, if we could just fix up the house—" She stared across the kitchen table, over the remains of supper. Aunt Lois's kitchen smelled of meat loaf and baked potatoes and squash, all cooked in the oven at the same time to conserve electricity. The pleasant odors lingered. Aunt Lois and Uncle Elder were looking at her.

"A—a house that bad," Crelly said, "it would be quite a job to fix it."

Uncle Elder looked at Aunt Lois. "That's true," he said. "Some houses, better to raze them to the ground. I would far rather build new than tackle some rebuilding jobs."

"Crelly, what happened?" said Aunt Lois. Her eyes were soft, troubled. "You can tell us after all this time."

Crelly didn't know what to say, didn't remember anything worth saying. All she wanted was for life to remain like one of Uncle Elder's new construction projects, straight and plumb and good. She slipped away from the table to sit on the living room sofa.

Uncle Elder came in to sit beside her. "One thing I can see each person's got," he said. "It's the choice, Crelly, whether to speak or stay still."

Crelly said nothing.

He cleared his throat. "We wanted you here, we've always been glad to have you. If we could have had the boys, we'd have had them, too, but we were afraid we'd lose you if we asked. Alice and Bib have legal custody of you all. They need that money. She's my sister. We didn't want to rock the boat."

Crelly nodded, staring out through Aunt Lois's Priscilla curtains, lightweight cotton with big ruffles. In the distance she could see a circle of the river, shining like a coin. If I could pick that up and carry it, she thought. Something of my own.

"When you slide away from the table like that," Uncle Elder said with a trace of humor, "we think we've lost you, too. We don't want that."

He sat with one hand flat against the sofa, but his arm moved back and forth, as if it needed someone. After a moment Crelly moved sideways, crept beneath it.

2

One activity fascinated Crelly in high school, drama. She had little courage for auditions, but quite often she sat in the back of the gymnasium to watch the theater club during rehearsal. After a while she joined the club and worked backstage, painting flats, tracking down props, learning tricks of stage makeup, lighting.

As Crelly watched the plays from backstage, she muttered the lines right along with the characters. She could sometimes supply a phrase before the prompter, and by her sophomore year she was not too shy to sing words out when they were called for.

"Crelly, you ought to be up here," an actor would say.

"We have new auditions coming up," the drama coach, also her English teacher, would tell her. Crelly always shook her head. She was afraid to go onstage. She knew, however, that some part of her took to acting, as if she had been doing it all her life.

Parts to play. Script lines had special voices, were meant to sound in certain ways. High school actors often couldn't hear the lines, or so it seemed to Crelly. Seated in the back of the auditorium, she would want to cry out "No! That's not it! Listen!"

The auditorium was dark, the stage a small box of light. Crelly remembered a frantic child, feet aching from cold ground. Crossing to the Leavitts, she had walked on knives, the hollow dark around her like a great dark room. Going to the Leavitts, she had been reborn. The light and warmth had also hurt, but she had never wanted to leave them again. She would act anything that was required to stay. She had listened, got the lines right, got them by heart. Her life had depended on it.

Sitting in rehearsal, Crelly's lips moved. The way the lines felt onstage was either with or against her deepest yearnings. The stage, with its possibility of light, of spotlight and footlight, that blessed aperture, was a window in the dark. The actors should care utterly about what they were doing, know of its vital importance.

As for her, how could she climb onstage? She was not worthy. She was a small dirty thing, feet cut with knives. If she failed, she might have to slink away, discovered for what she never wished to be again.

So she sat, watching rehearsals. Sometimes she swallowed pain, as if the knives were at her heart. She tried to stay hidden at such times, head down, muttering, one finger across her lips. One day as she whispered the litany of the play along with the actors, however, she happened to look up. Standing not too far away was Myra Buckfield.

Crelly knew the woman slightly, once a teacher, now town librarian. She and Mrs. Buckfield exchanged a glance. In it was power, sheer understanding, like a reading of souls. Yes, Mrs. Buckfield seemed to say, when the lines fall badly, it hurts. Why are you waiting there in the dark? Before Crelly could say a word, the woman nodded, turned away, left the auditorium.

A few weeks later, the Leavitts had a visitor.

"Oh, Lord," Aunt Lois said, looking out the window. "It's Myra Buckfield. Here I am in all this mess." Balls of various colors of yarn were piled around Aunt Lois in little heaps, and to one side sat two empty apple boxes into which she was sorting them. As she looked about her, unsure what to do first, a knock came on the seldom-used front door at the far end of the hall.

"You talk to her." Uncle Elder, who had been sitting in his stocking feet, got up, ducked out through the kitchen.

"Coward," Aunt Lois said. "He's a big help." She opened the front door. "Well, Myra, you come right in, glad to see you. I've got yarn piled all over the living room, hope you don't mind."

"Lois, I don't care about that."

The voice was abrupt. Mrs. Buckfield's face was long and pale. She had on steel-framed glasses tied in the back with a piece of grocery string. Her hair was gray, skun neatly back, and she wore a flowered dress, its white collar closed precisely.

"There," she said to Crelly. "You're the girl I'm looking for."

She used a learned Maine accent; she was among the few college graduates in the town.

Aunt Lois's hands flapped. "Would you like a cup of tea, Myra?"

"Haven't got time, thank you, Lois." The woman's gaze swept the room, came back to Crelly. "What I want to do is give this girl a job. I called the school. I said, I have one job to give a high school student this summer. I want the brightest one you've got." Mrs. Buckfield looked at Crelly. "They sent me here, for this girl."

Sudden tears pricked behind Crelly's eyes. Aunt Lois only nodded. Of course her Crelly was the brightest one.

"Won't you sit down, Myra?"

"Can't, Lois, though I'd like to. No time these days." The woman remembered something. "Well, perhaps I will sit, thank you. A minute wouldn't hurt me." She took a seat, frowned.

"Lois," she said, "you know me from of old. If a thing is so, I say so, and if it's bad, I say that." She pressed her lips together, spoke again. "I'm not as well as I could be. I have a lump in my stomach the doctor says is cancerous. If it gets much bigger, he says, it'll break my hip. So. I have to have seven chemotherapy treatments before he will operate, the first one quite soon."

Aunt Lois made a shocked noise.

"Lois, I have never intended to be sick," the woman said severely.

"You never were sick." Aunt Lois's voice was disbelieving. "Not once."

Mrs. Buckfield laid her hands just so, fingers together in her lap. "I don't want to be sick, but if I am, this girl could help." She looked at Crelly. "The job is daily, nine to one, this summer. Cataloguing, care for the books."

Crelly met the woman's eyes. In them was knowledge and the determination to see clearly, in whatever direction.

"Well, Crelly is a good worker," said Aunt Lois. "Myra, I'm just so sorry you're not well."

"I intend to beat this thing." Mrs. Buckfield stood. "I intend to try. Crelly, what do you think?"

"Oh, I'll come," Crelly said, "if it's okay."

Aunt Lois nodded.

"Good," said Mrs. Buckfield. "I'll pick you up at the corner, take you to the center, eight-thirty every morning. Lois, you've got a bright girl here, you should be proud."

"We are proud. Please, Myra, let us know if we can help."

"Well, I will, thank you. And you tell Elder not to be so shy next time. I'm never going to scold him over his homework again, he's too old." Mrs. Buckfield smiled.

Aunt Lois shook her head. "I always thought you could look through walls."

"Crelly, Monday?" Crelly nodded. Mrs. Buckfield left the house, walked forthrightly through the grass.

Aunt Lois watched her drive away. "We were so afraid of her, as kids. Now all I remember is how we children played in the grass every day before school. We didn't know we were happy."

Uncle Elder stuck his head around a corner, grinning. "Has the old biddy gone?"

"Elder." Aunt Lois spoke sharply. "Mrs. Buckfield's got cancer. She has seven sessions of chemotherapy coming up, then the doctor will operate."

"No."

"She came to ask Crelly to help her this summer, at the library. Elder," Aunt Lois said, "our Crelly's almost grown. When did all this happen? When did she get to be my big girl, with a job in the summertime? Why, I remember I used to look out, see her running around, not much bigger than the tall grass, picking dandelions for me. Elder"—Aunt Lois's voice rose—"Mrs. Buckfield has cancer." Uncle Elder held out his arms, folded her close.

Crelly's loneliness was unbearable. She wanted to reach out to them, keep them as they were. "When I go to college," she offered from across the room, "you'll come and see me all the time so I can show you off." This was an old formula, the best she could do.

"Not in these hand-me-downs." Aunt Lois's head was still against Uncle Elder's shoulder.

To Crelly at that moment the room seemed very long, the space separating her from the Leavitts a ramp, a runway, a gangplank. Aunt Lois turned. "Can't hold back the world, I guess," she said.

Uncle Elder spoke softly. "Come on over here to us, kiddo," he said to Crelly. "We'll be all right if you do."

That summer Crelly set off each morning in warmth that had not yet turned to heat, to the sounds of bird songs, the slow movement of air in pine branches. Now and then would come a sudden crackle as some small creature rocketed through the leaves on the floor of the woods. She stood at the corner to wait. The countryside breathed sweetly, full of promise.

Mrs. Buckfield drove a big white car with white leather seats. In the back, on his own pillow, sat an orange and gray tabby cat who went wherever she went. His name was Oliver.

In contrast to the Leavitts' sometimes dusty pickup, Mrs. Buckfield's car was sparkling clean. On the seat between them lay her glasses case. In the glove compartment were maps and tissues and cough drops that gave off a peculiar smell. "Horehound," Mrs. Buckfield explained. "Settle my stomach."

The Grange Hall rose steeply for its length against a backdrop of pasture and bushes. At the far end of this building was the town library. An artist in wood had created its two rooms, which emptied into each other through a wide doorway. To the far end was a fireplace covered at top and sides with shining wood, the mantel carved with wonderful maple curlicues and curves. On each side were eight long sets of wooden shelves, as smooth as the pews in a church, where the books were placed; some of them were never moved, except for a dusting, from one year to the next. The floor shone. The large doorway was encased in several kinds of woodwork, as were the windows. An oak desk stood near the door.

Crelly "read" the shelves to keep the book titles in alphabetical order. She climbed on stools to dust the upper shelves and moved chairs to get the last remnant of gravel from daily traffic. She had a dust mop with an old nylon stocking over its head which she used on the floor. Finally wax paper was laid down and rubbed in every direction, to pick up dirt too fine for the mop.

Crelly tried to be as fussy as she could, and she felt she passed muster. As the summer progressed, Mrs. Buckfield went in for her treatments, each one a series of four IVs over a twenty-four-hour period, during which she must lie still, tubes running in and out. She began to remonstrate with Crelly's fussiness. "I've just decided there are more important things."

But the corners of the room shone and it pleased Crelly to keep them that way. She was young and death seemed far away; life could be wasted on details.

A few people visited the library in the course of the week. "Too few," said Mrs. Buckfield. "The others don't know any better."

No matter how ailing she was, Mrs. Buckfield came to the library in her flowery dresses and, sometimes, a dark sweater. On bad days she would say, "I feel a little down," and spend much of her time seated behind the big desk, changing the library books to a new cataloguing system. It was half a century overdue, she said, but she was glad to get this far at least. She sat forward in her chair, which was large, and behind her curled Oliver. Now and then she would lean toward the cat and say, "Ollie is my baby, aren't you, Ollie?" The cat would arch his back and purr and rub lovingly against her arms.

"Conceive a love for dumb animals, Crelly," Mrs. Buckfield said. "They don't talk back."

Fragrant with summer smells, drying grasses in the hayfields outside, the sweet odor of oiled wood and cared-for volumes, the library was a pleasant place. Many of the books were old, religious tomes, histories of small Maine towns, music books, volumes of poetry, sets of Shakespeare, books about agriculture and home economy and travel to distant continents, cookbooks and gardening books. To one side were more recent novels, thrillers, some detective stories. The library's budget was small for more recent items. Mrs. Buckfield read the new book catalogues with great care, memorizing their offerings, choosing the best she could. Her knowledge of books, writers and reviewers was extensive.

Books! When they were in exquisite order, Crelly could take her lunch to a table in the back and sit and eat and read. She took armfuls of books home with her to share with Aunt Lois. When she returned them, Mrs. Buckfield rarely said more than, "Did you enjoy these?"

Crelly nodded. There existed between her and the librarian an understanding. In the borrowing, devouring and estimation of these books was high adventure. Without a word, she and Mrs. Buckfield shared an excitement that amounted to a private, blazing triumph.

In and out of books, Crelly met interesting personalities at the library. It was new to her to greet people she hardly knew, to talk to them on a daily basis, but it was as important to her as learning one's lines, to try to understand the people she met. Fascinated by people's actions, speech, gestures, she was rewarded by a growing reassurance. There were fine people everywhere, there was nothing to be afraid of.

Sometimes, hidden in a corner by herself, Crelly imitated the people she met. She was a natural mimic. As someone else might collect flowers or seashells, she collected these imitations, having a special facility. It was not a sign of disrespect to imitate, Crelly thought, but an avenue to confidence, a form of admiration, of light. And sometimes of gentle amusement.

Mr. Wheelock was an old man whose head quivered as he walked. He blinked bleary eyes rapidly and pursed thick lips before he spoke. Crelly sometimes went to her hidden corner of the library and took a few steps, allowing her head to bob on its stem. She blinked, pursed her lips, whispered judiciously to herself. She liked Mr. Wheelock.

Mrs. Dumfreys was a fat woman whose chin nestled in folds of flesh. She smiled by drawing her head back, raising her eyebrows, and pulling her lips in without showing any teeth. "Hmm, hmm, hmm," she would laugh. Crelly, in her corner, practiced laughing: "Hmm, hmm, hmm."

Mary Shay was a busy young housewife, her three children under the age of five. She came in with a baby on her back and a child at each hand. The two walkers were really runners who pulled their mother along like a kite behind them, her hair flying, glasses awry. In her corner Crelly seesawed along in the same way. "Diapers!" Crelly whispered to herself. "I buy Pampers, it's my one little luxury."

One day Mrs. Buckfield took out a key, opened a closet, and dragged a cardboard box into the light. In it were stacks of old playbooks.

"Now, a girl like you might be interested in some of these." She looked at Crelly over her glasses. "You mimic people who come in. Is that true?"

"Yes, I'm sorry. It's a—a habit."

"Mr. Wheelock," said Mrs. Buckfield severely, "the other day? Best thing I ever saw. Uncanny. Reminded me of these playbooks. Ever act in plays?"

Crelly's jaw dropped.

"You take these home," said Mrs. Buckfield. "See what you think. No use wasting your talent."

Crelly did take a few home, sliding them along the kitchen counter to Aunt Lois, who took one look and exclaimed with a little laugh, "My land!"

In the days when the whole community of farmers got together at the Grange Hall and put on plays to raise money, Aunt Lois had been quite an actress, Uncle Elder told Crelly that evening.

Aunt Lois, her feet up on a footstool, her hands busy patching work pants, waved at the air. "One of the few who could learn lines, was all," she said.

"No, no, Crelly." Uncle Elder spoke seriously. "She was good. She'd get up on that stage and the hall would go dead quiet to hear her speak."

"Oh, phoof." This was Aunt Lois's special exclamation, somewhere between "poof" and "phooey." "You might as well know, Crelly, that your Uncle Elder and I got acquainted on that Grange Hall stage. Well, I was having some thought I might be an actress, and he—he was an awful old farmer. But at least he could learn his lines, unlike some. The night of the play he was so scared, his voice squeaked. He went right on with it anyway. I thought, You have to have respect for a man who keeps on like that."

"Damn right." Uncle Elder chuckled. "Course, that was the first and last time I'd ever get on a stage."

"I think it sounds nice," Crelly said wistfully.

"Nice?" Aunt Lois began to laugh. "Got me into all this! Getting up at four in the morning, sewing on work pants, and cooking and canning, and the garden! And don't forget the milkroom. Never forget the milk." She bent double, laughing. "And making butter." She gasped for air. "And the foolish sheep."

" 'Tain't as funny as that," said Uncle Elder.

By the end of the summer, Aunt Lois never saw Crelly without a playbook. Crelly read straight through everything in Mrs. Buckfield's box, then began on the plays in heavy volumes not lifted from the library shelves in years. There were church dramas of biblical stories, written in the fifties. *Peter Pan* was there, as were several collections by George Bernard Shaw. Crelly disliked Shaw, although she would have liked to play St. Joan.

There was a collection of plays by Goldsmith, including *She Stoops to Conquer*, and another collection, Marlowe's *Tamburlaine, Dr. Faustus, Edward II, The Jew of Malta*. These were heavy going, but someone had long ago underlined some good lines in pencil: "To entertain divine Zenocrate" and "Cut is the branch that might have grown full straight."

There were several volumes of Shakespeare, some of which had been published in the last century. Crelly labored through them page by page, sometimes hardly able to sustain her interest, sometimes borne along by lines that beat like the heart.

By the end of the summer, people had to speak to Crelly more than once before she answered. But she could often hear characters speaking. She tried to train herself to talk as they did. At home she practiced in the barn, in front of the cows. This tickled Uncle Elder, who more than once had to back out of his aromatic rehearsal hall so as not to disturb her.

Mrs. Buckfield was thinner by the end of the summer. Aging spots had appeared on her face and hands. Sometimes she stayed in her chair behind the big oak desk, did nothing at all. Oliver would climb onto her lap, and the two would sit as still as china figures.

When school started, Crelly got hold of a script for the first drama club production, went over it and over it again. Early September was lovely, with leaves crimson and yellow as fire, the sky a deep blue. Crelly saw none of it. She was, Aunt Lois said, higher than a kite.

On the day of the audition Crelly couldn't eat. She felt sick, unprepared. Her legs shook so that she could barely walk onto the stage, and when the call came—"Next!"—she would have run in the opposite direction, but someone standing nearby pushed her out. Her heels made loud, echoing noises on the boards of the stage, forcing her to lift them in an odd way.

"Good," said a voice without a face behind the footlights. There was a pause, a conference. "Now, Crelly," the voice spoke again, "to your left is a chair, there. Pretend that is the sofa, okay? To your right—see that board up on boxes? That's the desk, for now."

Crelly nodded. In her extreme fright it was easy to allow things to blur. She looked at the sparsely furnished stage and saw the colors of an imaginary sofa, the depth of its cushions. Here was her desk. It had three good drawers on one side—she could see them. The character in the play was expecting bad news. Crelly went to her sofa, sat. This once-familiar home was dark, threatening. Crelly began to speak her lines.

"Okay," came the voice when she had finished. "Good, Crelly."

The next day her name was posted with the others who had gotten parts. Why, she thought, I can do this!

Uncle Elder and Aunt Lois celebrated by taking her the several miles to a hamburger place. Home again, Crelly called Mrs. Buckfield.

"Hello?" The voice was that of a woman who did not expect to be phoned trivially.

"Mrs. Buckfield? It's Crelly. I just thought I'd tell you, I tried out for the play and I got a part."

"Well, Crelly! Of course you did!"

"Listen," Crelly said, "without the playbooks you gave me—I want to thank you for—"

"Oh, well. Thank me later." The woman hung up. Crelly stared at the receiver.

"Well, now," said Uncle Elder, "what'd she say?"

"To thank her later. You know, I don't think she likes telephones."

"Figures."

3

The play went well. Soon Crelly was in another, and another. Just before Christmas of 1980, Mrs. Buckfield was admitted to the hospital for her operation. Her arms and legs were thin. She had taken to wearing a curly wig that looked odd about her long face. She greeted anyone who visited her with a grimly cheerful "Happy holidays."

The surgery was successful, according to her doctors, despite the woman's subsequent long stay in the hospital. All Mrs. Buckfield said was: "If they don't get you in one end, they get you in the other."

Aunt Lois and Crelly went to visit her at home. It was amazing, Crelly thought, how many people the woman knew. Mrs. Buckfield kept beside her at all times a large wicker basket full of cards, which she answered as promptly as they came. "My lifeline," she would say. Once Crelly came upon her sitting in her chair, holding a handful of cards in a small stack. The hand that gripped those cards was fleshless against their sharp gray edges.

During that year there was off-and-on contact with Gene. Three hard knocks on the door in the morning, and there he was in their kitchen, asking for this, for that, almost as if he already owned the objects himself. "You don't mind if I take one of your hammers," he would say. Or, "I could put that saw to use if you don't need it."

Whose tools were they? Whose hills? Whose fields? They were hard put sometimes, Aunt Lois said, to tell whose charity it was.

In late July of 1981, at raspberrying time, Crelly and Aunt Lois went up several afternoons, after the heat of the day, to pick their usual quarts of berries. They dressed in jeans and heavy shirts against the brambles, and they fought off the big mosquitoes that came out with the fall of evening by borrowing two of Uncle Elder's old hats, dosing the brims liberally with Woodsman's Fly Dope, an evil-smelling brown concoction that seemed to do the trick.

"I'll never be able to wear those again," said Uncle Elder.

"Fuss, fuss," said Aunt Lois.

In the late evening after supper, the three of them would sit with bowls on their laps and pails of the berries beside them on the doorstep, their hands stained red, the sweet smell as heavy as an intoxicant in the air. Long lines of jars of raspberry jam marched down Aunt Lois's counter to the storage cupboard that summer, and when the sun shone through them, red lights glowed like rubies on the counter. There was raspberry pie for breakfast, its exquisite sweetness and tang forgotten from one summer to the next. They greeted each new bite with an exclamation. "I forgive you the hats," Uncle Elder murmured. "You are both forgiven."

"Big deal." Aunt Lois smiled.

Still-soft red berries hung in the shade, growing larger and riper, begging to be picked.

"One more time," Aunt Lois said in early August. Crelly nodded.

Through bracken and bushes, underbrush and tall grass, they moved like treasure-hunters farther and farther into the farm's wild acreage. Sometimes they separated to cover more ground, each with an old plastic cup in one hand, a pail in the other. The pail you set down carefully at a distance and you picked into the cup. The raspberry bushes grew taller than your head; they were treacherous and brambly. A sleeve might catch, a foot trip, berries could spill. Better a cupful than a pailful.

That evening while Crelly picked she "played people."

First, here was Edmund Cooper, come to the library to borrow a book. He said to Mrs. Buckfield, "Guns and huntin's what I want."

His shoulders hung a little forward in their plaid shirt—Crelly's shoulders hung forward. His hands, down at his sides, were cupped as if to hold a rifle. Crelly made her fingers curl in the same way. Edmund's head and neck moved slowly, all of a piece, as though he were stalking game. Standing there in the raspberry bushes, Crelly looked at an imaginary Mrs. Buckfield, then down at an imaginary library floor, pretending to stalk her book across it.

Here was Mrs. Buckfield, smaller and thinner this summer, her glance as piercing as ever. Her shoulders were straight in their dark blue sweater. Her chin thrust out and up. Mrs. Buckfield took Edmund Cooper's measure. "Got just one recent one," she said.

Crelly said this, turned on her heel. Her shoulders bent forward, her hands curled. She put Edmund Cooper's I'm-no-fool look on her face. "Don't care about that," she said in his voice. "Sometimes old's as good as new."

"Sometimes old's as good as new," said Crelly again; it was Edmund Cooper. Or as close as she could come.

Then, realizing that her cup was only half full of berries, she fell to work, picking rapidly and ignoring the stinging cuts that appeared on her hands.

One bush cleared, she whirled to another, reached up, gasped. In front of her hands, a face had appeared.

Crelly blinked. The sun was just setting, and she couldn't see well. "Who—what—"

Is it Jimmy? Here is my brother, she thought. She didn't want to get anywhere near him.

"You know me, do you?" Jimmy came toward her through the bushes.

Crelly moved away. "How—how are you, Jimmy?"

"All right, I guess. Hear you're in some plays."

Crelly nodded. He was so thin, she thought. "Yes. I was—just practicing."

"Is that what it was?" Jimmy's lip curled.

"Yes." Before school had been dismissed that spring they'd taken their play to a local high school contest, and it had won. Crelly had won a prize for best actress. This had been in the town newspaper. She spoke again. "Yes, it was." His eyes were odd, she was thinking. She cast around for another subject. "Well, how is Uncle Bib?"

He stepped back, swallowed. "Fine. Ayeh. Not that you care."

"Jimmy, I—"

"Busy being comfortable, that's you, Crelly, right?"

"Is that what you think?"

"Uncle Bib's been gone for some time," Jimmy said. "And not likely to be back, far as I can see."

"Look, Jimmy," Crelly said, upset, "why don't you come home with us, have a piece of pie? Aunt Lois makes the best raspberry pie."

"Too late for that." The boy looked away. His neck was thin, delicate. His Adam's apple worked like a hammer.

"Please," Crelly said. "You're right. We don't even know each other anymore. My own brother."

He shook his head to refuse with the bitterness of an old man.

"Crelly?" Aunt Lois called. "Are you there?"

"Oh, yes," Crelly called back. "And Jimmy's here, too."

"Well, hell, yes, I am." Jimmy addressed a spot behind Crelly's head. "And wonderin' who was strippin' all these bushes."

Aunt Lois had come up. She pulled back the brim of her cap. Uncle Elder had never had the money to go to a Red Sox game, but the radio played in the barn as he cleaned it, over the fields as he hayed. Aunt Lois expressed this as she touched her cap, pushed it back. What they had was worked for, her gesture said. These fields they owned were part of it, and the raspberries in them. "I know it's all right with Elder if you pick here, too, Jimmy," she said by way of reproof.

Crelly stood beside Aunt Lois. "I—I asked him to come and have a piece of pie."

"And a good idea, too. I got jam, Jimmy. You could take some—Oh, in this light, I can't see! Jimmy? Whyn't you come along with us right now?"

"Oh, I guess not. Guess you'd be happier without me eating your berries."

"Why, that isn't true! Don't you want to take some things home?"

"Jam?" he said. "Raspberry jam?" He turned, disappeared into the bushes.

Aunt Lois called out to him; they waited. He didn't come back. They started toward the farm. Midway there Aunt Lois stopped, laid a hand on Crelly's sleeve. "What did we do, Crelly, to make him hate us so?"

4

*I*n March of her senior year in high school, Crelly was given the part of Juliet. The drama coach, their English teacher, left her largely alone. He might say to one of the other actors, "Don't lift your hand so high, pick up your feet now." To Crelly he said, "Do you think, a touch more lightness?"

The gown she wore for Juliet was pieced together, like all the other costumes, from whatever the school could find. She practiced wearing it, practiced Juliet's walk onstage, worked hard at the speeches from the makeshift balcony. With the lights on, the gown was beautiful, the balcony real.

There existed a spot where the castles of Verona were as substantial as this old stage, where Romeo and Juliet did love and die.

"I can't remember this, how does it go?" "Listen, tell me what you think." "My lines, I can't remember my lines." On the night of the play, the actors clung together backstage, whispering to themselves, to each other, and all the time their minds were somewhere else. Their whispers were like messages to Crelly of her own hope, as was the clasp of their cold hands.

The gymnasium that evening was crowded with parents and relatives. Crelly looked out through a peephole someone held for her: women in colored dresses, men in homemade sweaters, children rustling uncomfortably in metal chairs. The auditorium was filling up; perhaps as many as two hundred people talked, laughed, greeted each other, found their seats. There were florid faces, pale ones, children who bounced up to run in the aisles. An adamant, pregnant young mother stood up and hollered, "Get over here! You get over here. Now!" A little boy slunk to her. People nearby smiled behind their hands.

Frail old women in their Sunday best, their hair carefully dressed and their complexions powdery, clasped each other's tight, gloved hands; old men whose suits hung from their thin shoulders as from wooden hangers in a closet nodded at each other and rumbled greetings. To one side sat one old man, all alone. Two more approached. As all three walked away, their arms intertwined briefly. They touched each other's backs in a gesture of long-standing regard. There sat Aunt Lois and Uncle Elder, looking pleased. In front was Mrs. Buckfield. Her glance glowed under the houselights.

Beside Mrs. Buckfield sat someone Crelly didn't recognize, a woman wearing a stylish red dress. There were large red stones at her ears, and on her lips was red lipstick. Her hair was pulled back so smoothly it seemed oiled. The woman spoke earnestly with Mrs. Buckfield, who reached out and touched her arm as one might an old friend's.

Crelly closed the peephole. Her knees had begun a quiver she now knew was normal.

"Places!" Actors moved, lights came up, the houselights went down. Behind the fusty curtains the footlights cranked upward, throwing odd, scalloped shadows of curtain onto the boards of the stage. The stage manager tugged, then swung on his curtain ropes, and the huge folds of material pulled back with iron slowness. The play was about to begin.

First, a couple of boys in tights. There was some giggling from the metal seats in front as the boys were identified. The chatting in the audience seemed endless. But when the swordplay began, mothers gasped. And well they might, thought Crelly. These boys had practiced hard for this.

The prince entered, a child cried and was hushed, some latecomers found seats. There was some whispering as a fond relative identified the prince, tried to wave at him. He kept his dignity.

Minutes old, the play was in trouble. In the wings, the waiting actors suffered. This audience was wrong, they thought. The lines were falling badly.

When it was time for Juliet's entrance, Crelly's heart pounded so hard that she seemed to step outside her body to watch.

" 'What, Juliet?' " cried the nurse.

" 'How now?' " Crelly asked faintly. " 'Who calls?' "

Later Crelly decided it was the nurse who started it, and said so.

The girl was a senior, already engaged to be married. She was well liked in the school, had tackled this part on a dare. Determination lay in the girl's eyes as she stayed sturdily within her part. She began her long speech slowly, with enjoyment; the attention of the audience shifted, centered. People began to listen, to laugh in the right places. Their energy poured over the footlights, all the well-wishing of the crowd. The nurse and Juliet looked at each other, found, suddenly, what they should be doing.

Romeo, a tall, fair basketball player, managed his entrance well and spoke his lines straightforwardly, his youth softening his manner. Mercutio, a small-boned little junior and an excellent speaker, got a round of applause.

They were rolling! Shakespeare goes anywhere, their teacher had insisted, despite his students' dubious looks in audition. He had been right. This audience was as good as any Crelly would ever have.

They had worked on the balcony scene over and over. Now it was new. Who was this fair-haired young man? The sudden connection between him and Juliet shimmered. She loved him, she knew it; the bond was thin as a thread, strong as a cable. Crelly's voice deepened in a way it hadn't before. She was in love. It bordered on religion: " 'And all my fortunes at thy foot I'll lay/And follow thee my lord throughout the world.' "

"Listen," whispered Romeo when they were backstage. "The chairs are quiet."

Very little sound was coming from the metal chairs.

Onstage, all the actors worked, and behind the scenes, touched each other for reassurance. The play was going well; they tried not to be afraid that it was going well.

Desperately Romeo cried out, " 'Tell me/In what vile part of this anatomy/Doth my name lodge?' "

Juliet, awakening in the tomb, asked the friar, " 'Where is my lord?' " and then again, " 'Where is my Romeo?' "

The play neared its end. The relatives of both of the dead hurried onstage too late, began to put together the patchwork of what had happened. " 'The sun for sorrow will not show his head,' " the prince said. His dignity lay upon him like a mantle. The curtain closed.

There was a crackle of applause. Actors gathered, clinging to each other, some in tears. The curtain parted. Crelly saw Mrs. Buckfield rise to her feet, applaud. There were Uncle Elder and Aunt

Lois, standing and clapping. Crelly and Romeo took separate bows. We are your sons and daughters, Crelly wanted to tell them as she leaned toward the crowd. Do you see who we are?

From the back of the hall the high school principal called out the traditional cry, "Brava! Bravo!" At his words, all the chairs could be cleared away for a dance. Juliet or Crelly wiped her eyes, went backstage with the others. Juliet or Crelly waited her turn at the mirror, swabbing on cold cream and wiping it off with tissues. Then she went to wash.

"Crelly? Crelly Kemp?"

Drying her face on a towel, Crelly looked up. Before her was the woman who had been sitting with Mrs. Buckfield.

She held out a hand. "Crelly, I am Marta Davis. I coach drama at the University of Southern Maine at the Gorham campus, and I'm director of the Russell Square Players. Myra Buckfield asked me to come tonight. I want to tell you what a wonderful performance you gave this evening. Very good indeed. Listen, I've seen your college application forms. You have no money?"

"No."

The woman sighed. "No. Well, we shall have to see. Myra gave me a message for you. She can't manage the stairs, I'm afraid, so she's waiting for me in the car, but she wanted you to know she loved the play. Well, good luck. Perhaps I'll see you again." The woman nodded, walked off.

"Did you hear that?" The whisper went around the dressing room. Crelly was too dazed to say anything.

She went into the cubicle for changing, shut the door, took off Juliet's clothes carefully, hung them up. Then she put on Crelly's clothes and sat for a moment, her head in her hands. They had had before them such a wonderful illusion. Now it was gone. She felt desolate. She was left here, with herself. After a moment she picked up the wisps of this self and put them back on again, as she had her clothing.

"I knew it! I knew it!" Aunt Lois danced around her kitchen, spun to the door. "Elder! Look what's happened! Elder! 'It gives me great pleasure to inform you that you have been awarded a scholarship in drama in the amount of thirty-five hundred dollars a year.' " She was reading from a letter Crelly had just received. "There!" she cried. "There."

"Well, all right!" Uncle Elder knocked off his boots, did a little soft-shoe in his stocking feet. "Tippity-tip tee tip!" he sang. "Oh, tippity-tip tee tip! Way to go! Now, Crelly, I want you to go down to that university, and I want you to show them what a farm kid from up here to nowhere can—can—" Words failing, he tossed his baseball cap in the air, catching it behind his back.

"I know," said Crelly, grinning and weeping all at once. "I'll try."

"You bet you will!"

Mrs. Buckfield had been taken to the hospital a few days before. She was on IVs for nourishment. The doctors had decided to operate again as soon as she was strong enough. They wanted to install a pump that would bypass the functionless parts of her intestines. It was an experiment, but Mrs. Buckfield told them to go ahead. "Let them. If it doesn't help me, it might help somebody someday."

A few days after Crelly's letter came from the university, Mrs. Buckfield did go into surgery. Crelly was there to hold the woman's hand as far as the elevator, but the hand was pitifully thin, the face a skeleton with skin stretched over it: humanity reduced to the essentials, oddly beautiful. As they moved down the hall, the woman's eyelids fluttered. "Just like going to sleep, Crelly," she murmured. She didn't survive the operation.

Two days later there was a funeral at the church that Mrs. Buckfield had attended faithfully for years. Up front was her casket of dark, polished wood, closed. The church was empty of flowers, at her request. "Let them put the money to some better use," she had said. The minister read some passages from the Bible, spoke a few words about her career, children she had educated, people she had helped. Above the pulpit a small stained-glass window cast shadows of red and green and gold onto the casket.

All the flowers you need, Crelly thought, here in those lights. Free.

Crelly remembered that during Fourth of July week the summer before Mrs. Buckfield had served Liberty Bell cookies to library visitors on paper napkins of various patriotic designs. "Leftovers from all my Fourths," she had said. "Been saving them for years, time to use them up."

Day by day the hand with that uncompromising grasp on life had opened a little more, let go. How much suffering it had taken to teach her! Around Crelly, people wept. Her own eyes were blurred with tears. She thought, I should have known her better.

"She was a woman of distinction, she demanded our best, and she commanded our respect," the minister was saying. "She was a faithful churchgoer and in her quiet way helped many of us. In our hearts we all approve mightily of her life, and we aspire to that same approbation that we hear in the words we use when speaking of her: 'Well done, thou good and faithful servant.'"

The choir in the little church sang music of Mrs. Buckfield's choosing: "'All in the April evening/April airs were abroad./The sheep with their little lambs/passed me by on the road.'" Crelly could not stop crying during the singing. At home she stole away from the house to be by herself.

For a long time she had attended church with Aunt Lois and Uncle Elder. She wanted to believe its teachings, to align herself with them as closely, as safely, as she could. But now some of her tears were angry at what was hard in life and without explanation—hard living, hard dying, hard taking hold, hard letting go. The hardness of God, Crelly thought in her tears, was having to be lost in the dark before one could be found.

"I wish I'd known Myra Buckfield better," one person after another said in the days that followed. "I'll tell you this, she was good to me."

"She was a fine teacher and a good woman," Uncle Elder agreed. "And you know, our Crelly wasn't a bit afraid of her from the start."

5

Crelly adapted to dormitory life, along with a knot of other theater majors, in a large frame house close to the theater's back door. The others laughed ruefully about the narrow halls, inadequate bathrooms, small closets. To Crelly it seemed like home. It didn't matter that the tile floor was old and cracked or that the toilet was an old-fashioned water closet. The bathroom lighting was also Victorian, but Crelly didn't care. She stood in the bathroom and looked at herself.

She was not bad-looking, of medium height with a narrow face, angular cheekbones, dark blue eyes. Her hair was brown with reddish lights. She wore it shoulder length so that she could dress it up on top of her head or let it fall, depending on the part she might play.

Aunt Lois had been collecting things and had run up the good tweed suit she had always promised. She had put money aside by going without herself so that Crelly could have new shoes, winter gloves. In great excitement they had packed all her things in Uncle Elder's old green metal footlocker, laying them in, taking them out again, putting them in still more carefully.

Crelly's spending money was tight, but it was fun to walk down the street to the drugstore and wander up and down the aisles, looking at the many different kinds of soap, the perfumes, shampoos.

She loved the city of Portland. In the small shops in the center of town were dried flowers, fine clothing, furniture, woodworking items, pottery, paintings. Up and down the streets she went, shivering a little in the sharp sea air, looking at the store mannequins whose life, it seemed to her, could be as real as that of women on the street. Those mannequins met people at airports, they had silver place settings, they lay between satin sheets or played grand pianos, lace next to them, lace for a covering.

Wherever she went she was hungry. She wanted to taste every kind of food, write back to make Aunt Lois's eyes shine. From restaurants she walked by wonderful smells wafted. She watched people hurrying down the streets, women shopping, secretaries in their good coats and high heels, the occasional limousine, its interior faces shadowed behind darkened windows. She saw the cold and hungry asleep on benches and could only turn helplessly away. At heart, she was one of them.

The dormitory was homelike. The women in it became close friends. Sometimes they were able to drag Crelly away from her studying. She told them she didn't see how anyone could dislike studying, it was so easy. This was greeted by good-natured groans.

And if sometimes the old black figure hovered, shaking its marionette limbs, she managed to keep going, bury herself in studying or the theater. All was well here; she was safe. Life would be pleasant if she could continue to act.

She worked hard for Marta Davis, mending costumes, clearing out backstage. She learned every part of a production that she could; she was as happy to work up in the light booth as on the general manager's stool. But when it came time for auditions she was too afraid to go to the theater, afraid to fail.

Marta sent for her. Marta was only an inch or two taller than Crelly, slim, with narrow shoulders, but when Crelly came into the auditorium the woman had grown much larger. She spotted Crelly. Her eyebrows drew together, a lowering smudge. "You get up there and read," she said.

Crelly stumbled onto the stage. Bare black wings, tape-marked floor. Someone brought her a low stool, and as she sat on it she saw a grave, a tomb. " 'I have a faint cold fear thrills through my veins,' " she began; this was Juliet's hardest speech, in the scene where she takes the potion that puts her to sleep. She is afraid sleep is death. " 'As in a vault, an ancient receptacle/Where for this many hundred years the bones/Of all my buried ancestors are packed . . . Romeo, I come!' " she says finally. " 'This do I drink to thee.' "

Marta gave Crelly the part. "But we have some work to do," she said. "Work of the body. You take everything so hard. Somehow, somewhere along the line, your body has become closed, Crelly. It doesn't respond as well as it might."

Crelly couldn't look at her for shame.

"Heavens!" said Marta. "You don't look bad onstage, you look fine! But you need to know how to relax, and when, and how to conserve energy. Otherwise performances will make you far too tired, and your health will eventually break."

This became Crelly's work: to teach her body how to move, to use only the muscles she needed, let the rest relax. With every movement she had to stop and think: What muscles am I using?

"Crelly, you are walking with one shoulder up! Crelly, your neck is tense! Crelly, do relax your right arm, yes, there. You only need your left. Shift your feet, a little apart. Now. Move toward him! Yes! That's better!" Sometimes Marta would sigh. "Getting Crelly to relax is the hardest work I do."

Gradually the training began to make sense. Daily exercising put muscles within her control, helped her use them more efficiently.

Uncle Elder and Aunt Lois came to Portland for opening night. "Hard to believe it was our little girl up there," said Aunt Lois after the play. "Not so little anymore. It was good, Crelly. The best I've seen. Are you getting too tired, lambie? Are you hungry? Are you eating enough?"

This brought a guffaw from Crelly's friends, who watched her put away twice as much food at the cafeteria as any of them.

"Don't listen," Crelly said, hugging her. "Oh, I've missed you!"

"No waterworks, now," said Uncle Elder.

"Elder," said Aunt Lois, "we're taking these girls out to eat."

"Can you?" Crelly was already dragging them to the street. She knew Uncle Elder's taste in restaurants. It would be what he called a with-or-without place, the food served with or without ketchup.

When they got back it was late. "Oh, gosh," said Crelly. "You're never going to get any sleep. It's almost midnight, and the cows are up at four."

"I guess I can lose a night's sleep and still manage," Uncle Elder said. "Even at my advanced age."

"Oh, he's too excited to sleep," Aunt Lois confided. "He won't go to bed when we do get home. He'll be out there plucking the cows' eyelashes up to see if they're awake yet."

The play ran for several more performances, got excellent reviews. One evening, Marta went backstage and brought Crelly out to introduce her to a group of people, a professor and his wife and a tall, quiet young man whose hair shone like honey under the lights.

No one thing happened to charm John Werner or make him suddenly aware that here was a good actress. The acting seemed natural to the period, yet young and free. From the beginning he felt oddly attached to this Juliet.

Up on the stage was a young woman, delicate and substantial, slyly humorous, desirable. He felt her thrill of first love in himself and, as the play neared its end, her confusion and dread; at last, his own pity. What parents would set such deadly strictures on their children? At the final curtain he was on his feet as around him came the noise of other people rising to clap, for the whole cast, for Juliet most of all. She came out alone, stretched her hands to them and bowed, went away. The crowd clapped. She didn't return.

John, staring up onto the empty stage, felt admiration and a personal connection to the woman who had been there, whose face beneath the makeup had seemed to him full of wonder, the eyes huge and glowing. He wished to climb onstage and find her, but he wouldn't have dared.

Here was Emil Brunholtz wiping a tear away, hugging his wife. Other people picked up their ordinary lives with a kind of wistfulness.

Here was Marta Davis, bubbling. "We must go downstairs, Gretta," she said to Emil's wife. "It will be mobbed, but you must meet her."

They waited for a long time in the lobby. One by one the actors came out, got a round of applause, were greeted by friends. "I'll go and get her," said Marta. "She's inclined to skip this part."

At last Crelly Kemp allowed herself to be drawn into the lobby. There was much applause. She came forward, nodded, smiled. John saw delicate narrow wrists, a thin face. It was only when she turned toward him, looked at him with dark blue eyes, that he recognized her for the actress on the stage. Uncertain, challenged, he stood in the row as she was introduced. She held out her hand to him, a chilly, strong little hand. He held it for a moment, finding with surprise that he wasn't afraid of her.

Around them people made plans to go back to the Brunholtzes' hotel for a meal, but John hardly listened, looking down at this person. He thought she might blow away from him, he wished it wouldn't seem odd if he offered her his overcoat.

"Pleased to meet you," he said.

She gave a nod, the flicker of a smile. Her hand rested in his.

Marta was laughing with the Brunholtzes. "Oh, Crelly will come if there's food," she was saying.

"Don't you listen to them," Gretta told the actress. "Such energy demands fuel. You will come with us? It will be our pleasure."

"All right, yes." She spoke in a low voice. "Thank you."

At the hotel, John opened the door for her. She climbed steps, floated more than climbed. Where had she learned that?

John wanted to dance, wished he knew how. He did a few steps when no one was looking, but she saw. The tilt of her head told him she was amused.

Emil's and Gretta's suite was nice enough, furnished comfortably. Crelly looked about as if a hotel room were a new experience. She examined every furnishing. Trays of sandwiches, relishes, fruit, were brought. "So this is room service," she murmured.

John sat beside her on the sofa. A kind of warmth circulated between them. She didn't know what to say; he didn't either. More acquaintances stopped to chat with Emil and Gretta. Crelly didn't move.

"Aren't you going to eat?" John said.

"I'd like to. First I want to remember how it looks. I don't usually go to parties."

"I don't either. Could I get you something?"

"Everything."

He gaped. "Really?"

"Just don't tell them who it's for."

The room was quite crowded. "They'll never know."

John began to fill two plates with mathematical precision, jealously eyeing the seat beside her. Several people spoke to her. In an agony lest he lose his place, he heaped the plates and went back, sliding in underneath a woman who held Crelly's hand, congratulating her on her performance.

The woman glanced down at John, moved away. He sat with a heaping plate balanced on each knee.

"This is just like home," Crelly said.

"Oh?"

"Well, like a potluck supper, then. You know?"

"No, I guess I don't."

"Well, people put the food on the sideboard."

"Sideboard?"

"A kind of buffet, you see, beside the tables, where they put everything on display, all the different kinds of food. And you take a plate and serve yourself. You put the scalloped potatoes here, here the macaroni, the cold cuts, rolls, sandwiches, pickles. You pile up your plate. Sometimes the men even get dessert at the same time and put a cupcake or a piece of pie on top of everything else. You go up with an empty plate, come back with a little mountain—stuff yourself silly, as Aunt Lois would say, with everybody else's cooking."

In a little while, talking all the time, she presented him with her empty plate.

"I'll go back if you'll save me a seat here."

"Could I have an apple, too?"

Amused, he filled her plate again, setting an apple artistically on top of a heap of pickles.

"Just like home?" he asked.

She nodded.

"Now, who is Aunt Lois?" he said when she had had time to eat.

Crelly picked up the apple, rubbed it to a higher shine on the knee of her skirt. But it got away from her, rolled onto the floor. Before John could move she had picked it up, breathed on it, rubbed it on her sleeve. "Good as new," she said as she took a bite.

Then an extraordinary thing happened. John saw it only in profile, a handsome blush that played up her face to the roots of her hair. Her lips trembled a little. His soul bottomed out on nothing; he felt vastly humble.

"I come from up in Edgar," she said, "where I live with Aunt Lois and Uncle Elder Leavitt. They are like parents to me. They have a little farm, some cows, some sheep."

"And you love it there?"

"Yes. I miss it. I miss them. Now, how about you?"

"Well, I've been staying with the Brunholtzes out on their island. I don't think I ever really saw the ocean before. You would like it."

"They own an island?"

"A small one. They come in here for some events, take a hotel room for a night or a weekend, a special treat."

Marta Davis hugged the Brunholtzes. "I should be going." She put on her wrap, spotted Crelly at a distance.

"It's all right," Gretta Brunholtz said. "John has his car. He'll take Crelly home."

Marta nodded. Emil Brunholtz hummed a little tune in three-four time as he showed her to the door.

Much later Crelly became aware that people were leaving the hotel. "Oh, I'm so sorry. Where is Marta?"

"She went a little while ago," said Emil Brunholtz. "But perhaps—John, you have your car?"

"Oh, yes," said John. "I'll be happy to drive you home, Crelly, if you don't mind?"

She nodded. "Thanks."

"It's quite a walk to the car," John said when they were outside. "Look, your coat isn't too warm."

"It's fine," she said. "Aunt Lois made me this coat."

Here was something he hadn't expected, a little vein of iron. He stood still. Crelly walked on a few paces, came back to him.

"What is it?" she said.

"Sorry if I offended you."

"It's okay."

She slipped into the car, quelled a shiver. His mother had put a lap robe in the back. He thought of bringing it out, then discarded the idea. Nothing he did should make her take offense.

"Do your parents live around here?"

"At Prouts Neck. I have a place in town, a condominium, but I spend most of my time at the Brunholtzes'."

John wanted to talk. He told her a little more about the Brunholtzes' island, about his work. When she asked questions, he added a bit about his childhood. She told him about acting, about her dormitory room close to the back door of the theater. They were parked outside of this little room for quite a while.

"I should go," Crelly said at last.

"Wait," John said. "Could I see you sometime?"

She studied his face. "Well, maybe," she said. "Maybe you could call me. Thanks for the ride home." A smile, and she was gone.

When John awoke the next day, Crelly was the first thing he thought of. In a way, it was hardly fair. He was used to squinting at the light and planning the day of work to come. Instead, there she was. He thought he should call her. Then he thought he'd better wait, so as not to seem too anxious. He should probably wait at least a week for good measure. Nothing much lasted. He would see how he felt in a week.

At the university Emil Brunholtz twinkled. "Have a nice evening?"

John became even more organized than usual. "Very nice, thank you. Now, about these quantities, Emil . . ."

In the ensuing days he was engrossed in his work. Now and then Emil would throw him a puzzled look. "Well, John, what is new?"

John wouldn't tell Emil that Crelly was constantly in his thoughts; she had become a kind of obsession, subtly altering everything he did.

A week passed. "When I think of all the time I wasted when I was a young man," Emil said one evening at the island, more to his wife than to John. "I was too proud. Too busy. You know."

Gretta smiled at him over her knitting. "You never did tell me, Emil, what took you so long? Just to come and see Papa? To ask if we might go for a walk?"

"Your family so well-to-do," Emil replied. "And you, knowing so many people. I—what did I know? Mathematics, nothing else."

"Finally," Gretta told John, "I had to arrange to bump into him on the street."

"It puzzles me, Gretta," said Emil. "What if you had done nothing and I had continued to be frightened?"

John rose abruptly. "Time for bed."

"Call her," said Emil. "Call her! A blind man could see you want to. Tell her you want to see her. Tell her she should come out to the island and visit."

"The phone book is upstairs," said Gretta softly. "But don't listen to an old man and an old woman. Listen here!" She rose, tapped him on the chest, which was as far up as she could reach, then groped for his shoulders, pulled his head down, gave him a kiss on the cheek.

"Thanks," John mumbled.

In the upstairs hall was the phone, connected to the largest island, Peaks, by underwater cable and from there to the mainland. John sat down, took the phone book in his hands. He didn't know the name of the dormitory, so he called the theater.

"Crelly Kemp is not here right now. May I take a message?"

"Will you tell her I'll meet her outside the theater on Monday evening at seven? This is John Werner."

"Yes, I'll leave a message."

John went off to bed so bemused he didn't see, below on the newel post, a hand pause or hear, under the breath but perfectly timed, Emil's little whistle.

Emil Brunholtz was, John had discovered on their first meeting in the fall of 1982, a short, round man with a white circlet of hair about the back of his head, thick spectacles across the bridge of his nose, and a sonorous German accent. John and a few others were admitted by special permission to his classroom at the university. Uneasy in their own prestige, all took their seats without speaking. It was a large room, a different kind of schoolroom from what John was used to, the desks made of tubular metal and light wood, the walls of Sheetrock with big modern windows. There were generous unframed blackboards on the front and sides of the room, and over the door was a plain round clock.

On the blackboard in front were some notations. John arranged paper and pencil in front of him and stared at the equations, began to scribble them down. The last class here must have been advanced, because these equations were deceptively difficult.

There were six other students in the quiet classroom. When he glanced up all were scribbling away, reading from the board. Later John thought to look up again, and there, behind the table in front, sat an old man working on a piece of paper.

Half an hour passed. Some people finished. They stared out the window or moved restlessly in their chairs. The old man continued to work. John shrugged, got busy again. On the hour he looked up. Brunholtz—if this was he—hadn't taken attendance, hadn't announced what the class would be doing, when the exams would be. One by one, bewildered, the students got up to leave. At last there were only two people left.

John sat back for a moment, rubbed his neck muscles, slumped forward, and went at the equations again. He thought he might have another class this period, but it didn't matter. Here was the first real companionship he'd had since he'd stopped working with Mr. Reed. He kept on.

At the next half hour Emil Brunholtz cleared his throat. John looked up and saw he was the only student left.

"Name?"

"John Werner."

"I am Emil Brunholtz."

Giving John a glance both shrewd and merry, as if this were the world's greatest joke, the round little man left the room.

At home John waded into the equations again, saw that of course no class had preceded theirs. Brunholtz himself must have put the equations on the board. John became snarled up in his computations. He checked, rechecked, sat up most of the night.

The next day he walked into the classroom, saw that all six of the other students were back. They sat at ease, probably much better mathematicians than he.

The blackboard was clear; John's head was full of jumbled numbers and coefficients. Brunholtz entered, looked over each face, turned to the board, began to lecture. His voice was deep, the accent thick; at first he was hard to understand. Now and then he paused, tapped an equation. His intonation a question, he waited for someone to supply the portion he looked for. At first a number of people called out the answers. He nodded merrily.

"Ah, yes, good."

John didn't say anything. Any moment now, the equations would pull ahead of him. All the bright people, who knew the answers, would leave him behind. Stiffly, he followed along. The hour drew to its close, the prescribed time for the class was up, but Brunholtz showed no sign of winding down his lecture. John was surprised to see a couple of his classmates leave, but Brunholtz didn't comment.

There was about the little old man a kind of merry watching, a zest and bounce in everything he did, and a keenness as well. He paused. The voices answering dwindled. In a few minutes, when the intonation went up, there was no answer at all.

"Ah," said Brunholtz, "allow me to repeat." Slowly he went over this segment of the work again. The intonation went up. He paused. Three people were left in the classroom. They sat stiff and embarrassed. John cleared his throat. "Ab squared over x," he said, but it came out in a mumble.

Brunholtz inclined his head. John repeated himself.

"Ah, good." The man continued to write. When he paused, John mumbled out the answers. The second hour passed. Others got up to leave. "I don't get it," one muttered. "I don't get it at all."

Brunholtz seemed not to hear. He continued to write. John saw that the man approached the center of the muddle. He leaned forward in his chair.

"And now," said Brunholtz, "we see that the correct avenue is not this, as we had thought." He made notations that John recognized as his own faulty figuring. "For," said Brunholtz, "we have computed this and we see it leads nowhere and we must have faith in that. Intelligence tells us, therefore, that we have not fully examined all the options. If all these points are true, we must step back from the computation and see—"

"That the basic logarithm is faulty," John said slowly, aloud. "Of course."

"Of course." Emil Brunholtz smiled, satisfied. "Name!"

"John Werner."

"Ah." The man made a little note in his book.

"But—what about the others?" John said.

"Oh, don't worry, they'll speak up for themselves. The complaints will come down. But"—the little man sighed—"if they want me here, they must have my methods. And they want me. Mr. Werner, I am pleased to meet a fellow mathematician. I can see that your friend Mr. Reed is right. I have at my home some examples of your work. It is very fine."

"Thank you." John stood up.

"What I would like," said Brunholtz, "is to run quickly down the history of mathematics, then concentrate on spatial relationships. I don't have time to teach basics. Let them go to the other good teachers for that. Do you know computers, Mr. Werner?"

"Some."

"Have you seen the computers here?"

"Yes, they're good."

"I have a better one. This is Thursday. Go to your classroom tomorrow, Mr. Werner, and plan to come home this weekend with me. We will begin our work."

"But—"

"The others? Will we not show up for every class period?" Emil Brunholtz shrugged. "Will we not take every intelligence as far as it is inclined to go? What is the greatest problem in mathematics today, Mr. Werner?"

"In physics, spatial measurement of the infinite."

"Ah, good. Meet me here at four in the afternoon tomorrow. Plan to spend the weekend with me and my wife."

"Thank you. Thanks very much—"

But by that time Emil Brunholtz had begun to hum a little tune. He waltzed out of the classroom and disappeared.

In Casco Bay, off Portland Harbor, islands are set to either side of the ferry run like green-upholstered arms on some great blue rocking chair. A study of maps might lead one to assume that life on these islands is more isolated than in reality it is; most of the larger ones are inhabited by colonies of people who live there year round, the populations swelling in the summer.

For the full-time residents, however, the Portland Ferry is taxi, school bus, sometimes ambulance. Perhaps it is also a solace, its steadily pulsing mutter predictable, even welcoming, and tickets, clutched in mittened fists for many months of the year, are tickets to reverie, blue distance, a rocking in the waters of Hussey Sound, the measuring of weather in sky and sea.

The ferry makes several runs a day. It was for the four o'clock trip that John parked his car near Custom House Wharf and walked the long drafty boardwalk to the Casco Bay Lines ferry office, where he met Emil Brunholtz.

"By midwinter," Brunholtz said, "we may be sorry we decided to live on an island. So chilly, and only September."

As they climbed on board, the horn blew a blast that made them both jump. The ferry backed, turned to leave the wharf. To one side John could see a fishing trawler, men in sweatshirts on its deck. They had stretched long pieces of netting over a boom and their hands wove shuttles in and out. Their heads bent toward each other as they worked, then all tipped back to laugh.

John was suddenly lighthearted along with them, as if he'd shed a mainland of duties and worries.

"It's this sailors must feel," said Emil Brunholtz, the collar of his dark wool coat up, a knit cap pulled about his ears. "Bound for adventure, free as the gulls. Look." Off the tankers on the southern shore, off the bright blue dry dock of Bath Iron Works, shipbuilders for the nation, gulls sailed against the sky, riding upward on air currents, wheeling. They were scavengers of the coast.

The ferry pulled past two century-old forts, neither of which had ever seen battle, on the way to Peaks Island, the largest in the bay. John drew his light jacket up protectively about his neck.

"Gretta will have to find you some warm clothing," said Emil over the noise of the motor. "Look, she made this for me." He pulled out of his black topcoat a scarf of red, orange, blue and green. It lay like a rainbow at his throat. "Warm," said Emil Brunholtz, smiling. "You never felt such warm." The ferry slowed, pulled in at the landing.

"We're here?"

"No, no. From this place we take a smaller launch. Look, there's Owen."

A man in a dark blue work jacket and work pants waited for them at the landing. His hat was fur all over and hung in flaps about his ears, making his long face look even longer. His complexion was florid, beaten red by hours of facing into the wind. Deep grooves at the eyes and the man's habit of frowning made it seem as if he measured not only weather and ocean but character.

Owen's bare hand, when John shook it, felt like steel gloved in leather. The man nodded at Emil and without a word started his motor, which thumped and rumbled; they were off. Their craft was a lobster boat, the cabin buttoned tight against the chill. John and Emil stood to one side, gripping stainless steel handles set in the woodwork. Owen stared out across the water, one hand negligently upon the wheel, his body alert. They passed between two islands. The ocean opened out, lay before them in gulfs of green, dark blue. To the left appeared three more islands, emeralds on silk.

"Mile away, five knots," Owen hollered at Emil.

"Ten minutes," Emil hollered back. They nodded at each other.

The boat chugged through heavy water, rose, sagged into troughs. "End of the sound, a little rough," said Emil Brunholtz in John's ear. The boat lifted, sank, moved into still water at the lee approaching the foremost island.

John stared at the island formations. There were two larger ones, each several acres across, and in between a smaller. The island at the far left seemed to float. On two sides of it were beaches, the sand rolling down to sea level. The inner island was separated on both sides by channels, to the left a small matching beach, to the right a formation of cliffs, duplicated on that side by the cliffs of the third, larger island. From a distance the chasm that separated these two seemed narrow, the striations of rocks like two faces.

"Day after day those islands frown," said Emil, following John's glance. "Gretta and I wonder what they see."

The cliffs were some forty feet high, John saw as the boat approached. Blackened bands of rock rose gradually. The channel of water separating the two islands was thirty feet wide. The water licked upward, spinning suds over barnacled boulders. Above the cliffs on the inner island was a stand of evergreens that extended all the way from its high edge to the opposite end of the island, its beach. The island to the far right seemed to be pastureland, fenced along the cliffs with barbed wire. Farther to the right were a small red farmhouse and a boat landing where a dinghy was moored.

Owen putted toward the island at the far left, cut the motor, unbuttoned the cabin. Without a change of expression or inordinate exertion, he unlatched his boat hook, grasped a piling with it. Over the piling he tossed a looped rope easily, like a cowboy, his lasso two inches thick.

"That is style, Owen," said Emil.

"Ought to be." The man pulled the boat close so that they could get out. "Done it enough."

"Well, thanks," said Emil. "As always. See you first thing Monday?"

"No, be over tomorrow. Storm windows."

"I had forgotten." Emil's words were lost in the gunning of the boat's motor. With one squinted glance Owen continued on his way.

"See there, not the first one close to us but the next island over?" said Emil. "That's where he lives. He has a farm there—cows, everything—and makes ends meet fishing, some of the year. Owen is self-sufficient."

"He lives alone?" said John.

"Oh, yes."

"Somehow I thought so."

Emil chuckled. "Come on now, I can see you are chilly. We'll go up to the house."

The curve of the path led upward then down, and in a small valley lay an old house with an addition to one side. The house had been set with an eye to the curved line of the valley, as Maine ancestors knew so well how to do. To the south and west, windows flared gold and blue in the setting sun.

It was warm inside, cluttered, comfortable. A little old woman bustled toward them down the hallway. "Well, Emil," she said, and gave him a kiss. "And this must be John Werner. Welcome! I'm Gretta. Why, Emil, he's frozen, his hands are frozen! It must be fought! It must be guarded against! I have a fire going, we will have some nice tea. Come on now, come on."

She bustled John down the hallway, came back for her husband. "We must warm him up! Oh, Emil!"

John found himself in a cheerful room with many windows and a warm blaze in the fireplace. Gretta Brunholtz pushed him closer to it. "Now don't you go out of the house until I find you some warmer things to wear. The air is wonderful here, but this is only the fall, and it is cold. No, no, sit here. Here is a shawl, put it about your shoulders. Oh, the tea!" She hurried out.

She was small, with a plump pink face. Her eyes were dark and keen. She had a wealth of white hair, which she pulled into a bun on the top of her head. Her bustling warmed John, made him feel at home. He looked about. He had an impression of many kinds of things, balls of wool of interesting types, some bits and pieces of wildflowers drying on a shelf, a shell collection, herb wreaths of bay and sea lavender.

The furniture was dark, but fabrics lay upon it—soft plaids, warm colors—so that the effect was one of comfort. When he spotted the sunset, reflected in shimmering paths on the water, John rose from his chair and went to stand and watch, startled.

"Now you see," said Emil's wife. "The beautiful light. At every time of day, the beauty here. This light cannot be equaled."

Emil stood beside her. Together they watched the sky change and darken.

"Now," said Gretta, bustling again, "a little supper. Cheese, bread and butter, apples—Owen brought them from his trees, Emil! So fresh they make me cry and I thank God I have all my teeth. Tea? Yes?" She looked at John.

"Yes," he said. "That will be fine."

Nodding, she left for the kitchen. Her voice sailed back. "Emil! Yoo-hoo! Will you make the tea?"

"Yes, dear!" Emil called. "Excuse me, John. You stay." The old man went to the kitchen in his stocking feet.

They ate from trays placed near the fire. John couldn't keep his eyes from the windows. "I have never seen that color in the sky before."

"Not gray, not rose, not even color, more like light," said Emil. "As if one looked through a semitransparent filter, a foil."

"A dye to duplicate that light. If one could reproduce, even come close, with yarn." Gretta sighed.

The bread pulled from the crust in buttered tufts. The tea was hot and sharp. John selected an apple from the dish, peeled it neatly as he had been taught, with knife and fork, sliced it, and ate, expecting the usual pale purchased taste. But this apple shouted in his mouth, raucous, sour, wildly sweet. He swallowed, not at all sure he liked it, then found he did, eating all the last slices as Emil and Gretta did, with a small slab of white cheddar on each bite. After a while he stared at his empty plate. Had he really been thinking about food? He didn't usually.

"John," said Gretta, "perhaps you will tell us about your home?"

"Well, we live on Prouts Neck. The house is large and in the historical register. My dad calls it the hysterical register."

"Ah." Gretta smiled. "And have you brothers and sisters?"

"No." He paused. What should he tell her? John wondered. What did he remember about his life? What could he share? Suddenly words stumbled from him. He found himself saying more than he'd meant to.

Paths were what he remembered. Prisms of light, another John Werner, age seven, who stood on a mossy spot, looked up through the branches of trees, a little boy who had escaped from the house while his nanny napped.

The branches were like arms, with fistfuls of leaves. A mosaic of shapes fell together as he turned. There were prisms of space between the leaves.

Light fell on rainbow particles. He closed his eyes, saw but not perfectly, opened them and looked, closed them again. If he could draw those prisms on his heart he would have them to hold on to.

"Get him out in the real world," Jack Werner had said the summer John was ten. "Don't bring him up in a hothouse!" John's parents had argued. The result was his attendance at the nearby public school. Every day John's mother had sent her son off with a dissatisfied look, his school year a growing blight on his appearance, his character. He was one of the smaller boys in his class, didn't get particularly good grades, didn't play sports. The kids in public school were polite to him. Everyone knew he was different. He came to school in a limo. He was rich.

Most recesses, kids left him alone. John jogged round and round the playing field by himself. Running was one thing he could do; the daytime pills helped.

One day in school, in the spring of 1972, the pills seemed to work even better than usual. John wiggled in his chair. Miss Everett, a woman in her late thirties with a pale ugly face and a sweet expression, went so far as to frown at him. Miss Everett didn't know about the asthma pills.

If there was anything John wished he could do, it was to play ball. Right now, he guessed, he knew more about the game than any kid in this school. He had been sick, but he hadn't been asleep. He had studied the statistics, listened on his radio. He knew the strategies of games as early as 1871, when Boston, John's team, finished third, having won twenty-two and lost ten.

John kept what he knew to himself. At recess he exploded out the door with the others. There was warm spring in the air. Everyone seemed to move faster than usual.

The girls played softball in one area, the boys baseball in another. Miss Everett alternated as umpire. John hung around the baseball field, jogging away when the boys chose up sides, coming back to watch. He wouldn't stand there waiting to be the last man chosen.

The field was not regulation size, he had studied the distances.

Wiry-armed boys threw baseballs hard into their buddies' gloves. These kids weren't professional. They did their share of striking out, missing catches, bungling throws. They pretended they were good, arching their necks, scratching the ground like bantams. When something went wrong, they all hollered. The kid at fault twisted his hat, threw his glove on the ground, spat with a high, wild carelessness.

There was one kid in particular John liked to watch, Marty Blackstone. Handsome, popular, athletic, Marty could snag a catch by hovering in the air until the ball smacked into his glove. He would land on both feet, throw the ball just where it needed to go.

Sitting on the bench, John watched a high drive from a bat. Marty sprang into the air, shagged it, winged the ball to first for an out. John hollered, "Hey, Marty, all right!" Marty looked over, seemed to see him sitting there on the bench to one side for the first time. John's ears reddened.

Between innings Marty came over. "You got a bat?"

John shook his head.

"Ball? Glove?"

John shook his head again.

In disbelief Marty looked away, spat like a bullet into the dust. "I been watching you run. You look like you could run bases. Go on up behind the school. They got all kinds of stuff there. Get a glove. Get a good one, if you can find it. Go on, now."

It never occurred to John to disobey. He jogged to the back of the school and found gloves, a box of them. He picked one out, tried it on, thunked its flattened fingers. They were bent out of shape and didn't make a pocket, but he didn't want Marty to forget him. He jogged back down to the diamond.

"God, Marty," said one of the other kids. "You gonna let him play?"

"He can run," said Marty. "And he can catch. You can catch, can't you, John?"

John had never caught a ball in his life. He nodded.

"Sure," said Marty. "Watch this." He let one go.

The ball hurtled; John flung his glove up as one might wave a hanky. There came a thudding, pain, bursts of light. John found himself sitting on the ground, his glove to his eye.

"Oh, God," said Marty. He pried John's glove away. "Oh, God." A crowd began to gather. "Go get a teacher!" Marty cried. "Go get somebody! His eyeball is all bloody!"

Two or three kids set off. There were many others ringed around John and Marty.

"Does it hurt?" "Are you all right?" "Oh, ugh, look." "Hey, let me see, does it hurt?"

John's eye throbbed. He thought he might throw up. "Heck," he said. "Heck, no. Doesn't hurt. Look, I'll show you."

On rubber legs he stood, wove about a bit, moved the glove to give somebody a glimpse. He was hanging on to his thin breakfast by a thread. The ring of kids crowded closer. "Do you see it?" somebody said. "Hey, John, lemme see." Their voices were awed.

Miss Everett came swiftly down the field. "John, let's look at you."

He lowered the glove. Miss Everett's mouth pursed. "Who did this?" she said. "John, how did it happen?"

"It was an accident." Everybody relaxed, especially Marty.

Miss Everett shook her head. "Well, you've got an awful shiner, I'm afraid. Can you walk up to the school?"

"Oh, sure," said John.

Rubber-legged, aching, he wobbled up to the school. All the children followed.

"You people stay right here, he doesn't need any help," said Miss Everett. "Thank you for your concern."

"Can Marty come?" John asked.

"All right. The rest of you stay outside."

Marty was allowed to hold the ice pack in place. John's eye throbbed.

His mother came to get him. "I was in a meeting," she said to Miss Everett.

"It's okay," John told her at once. "Just a little black eye, Mother."

Helen Werner turned to John's teacher. "I would like to know what happened," she said.

"Marty," said Miss Everett, "thank you for your help. You have my permission to return to the classroom now."

"Yes, Miss Everett," said Marty. "Hold the ice like this, John, that's it. Hope you feel better." The boy left.

"I'm so sorry, Mrs. Werner." Miss Everett sighed. "He's been very brave."

"The problem," said Helen Werner, "is just how one ever achieves healthy interchild contact in this sort of environment."

Miss Everett didn't let that faze her. "It's hard anywhere," she said. "John should be better by tomorrow, though. I know it hurts, but I've seen worse."

"If there are lasting ill effects, Miss Everett, I'll hold the school responsible."

"That's what we have insurance for. Look, I don't blame you for being upset, Mrs. Werner. I feel a little upset myself."

"It was an accident," John began weakly.

"I'll handle this, John," said his mother, frowning.

Miss Everett didn't give her time. "Just keep ice on it, John," she said. "And be sure to stop by the office to let them know you're taking him home, Mrs. Werner. I must get back to the classroom." She nodded at John. "Hope you'll be better soon."

Helen Werner's eyebrows went up. She led John out of the school.

Once home, his mother settled him among cushions in the living room, disappeared to write some letters.

Now and then that afternoon John tiptoed to the front hall powder room to see how he looked. The initial hurt had subsided to a dull, slow pain. It pleased him to stand in that little room and glare at himself in the mirror.

The powder room off the receiving room in the downstairs hall was a wonder of delicacy, done in faintest shell pink and green and white. The white linen towels hanging near the sink were immaculate and pressed, monogrammed in pink stitching. The room had been redone by his mother just recently. Everything was new.

John stood in the center of the floor, careful not to touch or dirty anything. To one side a full-length mirror had been set into white tiles. He stood before it, scared to see himself. The one eye was violet and plum, yellowish at the edges. His eyebrow, cheek and eyelid were swollen, and he had to squint because of the swelling. When he managed to open the bad eye at all, the eyeball loomed out, flooded with scarlet.

It made John tremble to look, but as the afternoon wore on he gulped horror down, held it quaking in his gut, and managed, time and time again, to stare coolly at the mess on his face.

That evening at six, as usual, John's father came home from work.

"Jack? Is that you?" John could hear his mother come down the stairs. "Do look in at your son, will you? We really must do something about that school!"

The lid on the bottom of John's world jiggled open. He reached down, fastened it. Surely they wouldn't make him change schools over a little thing like this?

"I feel I can't take much more," said Helen Werner.

"Now, dear." Jack Werner turned abruptly into the living room, caught sight of John, came closer. He squatted by the sofa to get a good look, a squat well clothed in precision-cut gray flannel. He smelled of the office, John thought, a combination books-carpet-cigarette smell. John felt the wish to please him, find himself in his dad's embrace.

"A shiner, eh?" the man said. "Good big one, too. Get into a fight, did you?" He seemed pleased.

"He did not!" Helen Werner adjusted the gold chains at her neck.

"Now, John, what happened?" Jack Werner said.

"I got hit in the eye with a baseball."

Jack Werner had long before given up on baseball for his sickly son. He gaped. "Line drive or something?"

"Somebody drilled one right at me," John said as picturesquely as possible.

"And you missed?"

"But he doesn't play baseball!" Helen Werner interrupted. "Those teachers should know that!"

John and his father ignored her. They were deciding the success or failure of this event.

"Yeah," said John. He tried to grin. "Hole in my glove."

Jack Werner looked down at the floor, up. He smiled at his son, a skinny sickly kid whose grades weren't too good, who had never learned to play baseball, and who just might be the evidence of his father's success or failure in life. "All the colors of the rainbow. Attaboy." He patted his son's knee.

"Yeah," said John.

"Jack, we have some negotiating to do." Helen Werner twisted an opal ring around on her finger. The light in it was muddled, a rainbow drowning in white paint.

"All right." Jack Werner straightened. "But not now, okay? I just got home."

Much later, alone in his room in the dark, John began to feel really bad. Slow tears gathered, worked their way beneath his eyelashes. He hated himself for being a baby, turned in his bed, muffled his face painfully in the pillow. Half suffocated, he lifted his head, sobbed out loud. "I hurt my eye. I hurt it bad."

He was really crying, unable to stop, unsure just where all these tears were coming from or what this deep grief was for. Unable to control his sobs, he got off his bed, moved blindly into the sitting area beside his bedroom, but no one waited there to comfort him.

Nothing there but books. John laid his hands flat along them, but it was a while before he could make out any titles. *New Mathematics* by E. W. Driscoll. He took it down. Gripping the book hard he went back to bed, opened it, began to read the first page, forcing himself to concentrate, afraid of crying anymore.

The sobs became a hitch in his breathing. He picked up one tissue after another, wiped his face. His lips moved as he tried, before his night pill took effect, to get everything on the first page by heart.

The next morning he found the book still in his hand.

"Jack," said Helen Werner the next day, "I would like to invite you to a working lunch."

"Oh?"

"Yes. I have a list of things to work on, goals for the coming year. John may accompany us if he wishes."

John's father sighed.

At the restaurant, John had polenta with minced chicken and a curried bechamel sauce, his mother had salmon mousse with capers, and his father an omelette aux fines herbes. They sat at a very small table. When they'd been served, John's mother got out her list.

"I'd like to begin right away, since my agenda is lengthy."

Something in her voice reminded John at this moment of his

grandmother Ashley, his mother's mother, an old woman propped up on pillows. "We never knew what to do for Helen," his grandmother had said once. "Always on the brink of unhappiness. Your grandfather brought her presents to chase the clouds away. He had to!" The frail old woman had pounded one tiny fist on the embroidered sheet. "Otherwise, we lived with a storm!"

At the top were a number of items John paid little attention to: trading cars, hiring a new gardener, a trip to New York to shop. "But they have beautiful furs here," John heard his father say. His dad was losing the argument.

Polenta was like cornmeal mush. The chicken minced on top, sawdust. John's interior eye was on a little interior baseball diamond. Rice came to the bat.

John's mother and father spoke on and on, impersonal voices of business associates driving for compromise. The count on Rice was two and two, three and two. The final pitch rocketed. John heard his father say, "Helen, we've been through this before."

"It's important to me!" said John's mother, a sharp whisper.

"How it looks!" said John's father. He frowned. "You brought us to this restaurant so I wouldn't yell, didn't you?"

"Nonsense."

All was quiet. Both adults looked at John.

Jack Werner tapped the table. "Your mother wants to send you to Gresham Latin next year, John."

"What? But I like the school I'm in!"

"Gresham Latin is a fine school," said Helen Werner. "If you go there, you can walk. We won't need to have Harold drive out early in the morning. Gresham Latin is the best school in the country—well, one of the best, anyway."

"But I don't want to go to Gresham." John's throat was full of cornmeal mush.

"You don't get a vote, kid," said his father in a poisoned aside. "All you get is a price."

John couldn't tell if his father was joking or not. "I don't want to go to Gresham Latin. I like it where I am. I've got some friends there now."

"A boy of ten, all upset." Helen Werner looked at her husband. "I hope you're satisfied."

"Let him alone, Helen."

"I don't want—" John stopped. There was a click in his chest, a whine, mush in his bronchial tubes. He wheezed. "May I be excused?"

"John, did you take your pill?" His mother shot him a sharp glance. He nodded. "Go, then."

It was too late. By the time he got to the door, he couldn't catch a breath. He clung to the jamb, wheezing.

"Come on, son." His father took him to the car, found the inhaler in the glove compartment. "You'll be all right."

They took him home, put him to bed. The whine subsided. They left him to rest, but he could hear them talking in the hall.

"We must do our best," his mother was saying, "not to be manipulated by his infirmity."

John went to sleep. It was easy to sleep. Being awake was what hurt.

No excuse to feel sorry for himself. After all, he had money. Of course, at Gresham Latin there were plenty of kids with more. Gresham Latin was not a place for coddling. If his mother hadn't been so determined, giving enormous grants for school facilities, John knew, he would have been dropped, skinny and unfledged as an ugly duckling. But he was not dropped. Instead, he stumbled around for several years, was held back twice, passed on.

Once an attitude had been struck at Gresham, it often became the rule. If you were bright, you were bright all the time. If you were suave you conversed with instructors in the halls and drank among friends late in the evening. If you were a loser, half drugged with asthma pills, too weak to play sports, wondering where your next breath might be coming from, you slid along the halls dimly, grateful for any nod or glance.

He remembered a day in the spring of 1980, when he shuffled into Gresham's science room, sat down. He realized that, in his medicinal vagary, he'd put on his jacket instead of his suit coat. At Gresham Latin, where the sons of legislators and diplomats were educated, suits were the required dress.

"Feeling casual, Mr. Werner?" Old Toothy, his science teacher, came close. John could see how spittle spun a tiny thread between the man's upper and lower teeth.

"I'm sorry, Mr. Tuttle," he mumbled. "I'll go home and get my coat."

"No, no, Mr. Werner. You might get lost on the way." Young

men in ties and jackets snickered. Old Toothy returned to the front of the class. "In a fog, Mr. Werner? Again?"

John's eyes slid to the windows along one side of the paneled room. He had often counted the panes, mentally making multiples of twelve in binomial numbers, with exponential increases.

"Mr. Werner, you will write us an essay, complete with a family tree, classifying all the animals we have studied. We will put it up here." Old Toothy touched the wall behind his desk. "You will like it up here, Mr. Werner, since you seem to spend so much time studying our walls and windows."

A snicker in the classroom. Boys liked it when John kept old Toothy off their backs.

After science came math.

John should have done well in his math courses, but he never did. He'd never learned discipline. Homework was tiring, often unnecessary. Still, this particular teacher, Mr. Reed, was excellent.

John opened his math book. Mr. Reed, a tall square man, came into the room. His suit was wrinkled into accordion pleats at the knees and lower back. His tie flapped. His hair was in an unfashionable cut. He was a well-known, often-published young mathematician. The school just tolerated his appearance.

No one dared to move. Old Toothy was a gothic leftover beside Mr. Reed.

He started right in. "Well, now, Mr. Anderson, what's going on in the world of factoring today?"

Mr. Anderson, a slim, dark-haired boy, rose to his feet.

As if his chair were too quiet, his desk too stationary, Mr. Reed, too, stood up. He threw the numbers of an equation onto the board. John fastened his eyes on those numbers. The lettering fell away; he couldn't help himself, he drowsed. Mr. Reed laughed. John looked up. Mr. Anderson was standing at the front of the class; his ears were red.

"—object is not to embarrass you!" Mr. Reed was saying. "Not at all, Mr. Anderson. The object is to teach you. You can't learn if you already think you know. Sit down, Mr. Anderson. Those of you laughing, can you do any better?" He moved with rapid steps from one end of the platform to the other, making lively motions with his hands.

John steeled himself to be called on. Usually he could put something together that caught Mr. Reed's interest, even if it wasn't, precisely, the assignment.

Mr. Reed went on to someone else. "Mr. Davis was mightily amused. Well, Mr. Davis, do you know the answer to this problem?" Mr. Reed sprang to the blackboard, gesturing at Mr. Davis, who was now standing. "Because you do, perhaps we should add this and this."

A complicated construction was added. The chalk sounded like a tuning violin. It broke in several pieces. "There, Mr. Davis."

Mr. Davis appeared to think. Mr. Reed clapped the erasers. Chalk dust lay in the air, a puff of yellow smoke. He threw down the erasers, beat his arms through the dust, confronted the class. "Are these our minds?" he inquired.

No one answered.

"Mr. Davis, sit down. We'll take out our homework."

John took out his. He hadn't finished it. He waited to be called on.

Mr. Reed's chair crashed. "Mr. Mayer! What did you think of problem number one?"

Mayer, a thin, bespectacled boy in the back, stood up, cleared his throat. "I took the equation ab squared plus—" he began.

Mr. Reed shot into the air, alighted at some distance from his desk. "No! I asked you what you thought of the problem, Mr. Mayer, not how you did it!"

Young men froze.

Mayer's Adam's apple bobbed. "I—I—didn't like it much, sir!" he blurted.

Somebody snickered. Mr. Reed shook his head, laughed. Quite a few of the students laughed, too. "I daresay!" He hauled out a handkerchief, mopped his forehead, went and sat in his chair, which exploded in a minor way at his sudden weight. He lifted first one foot, then the other, to the edge of his desk and leaned back. John wondered if the chair would hold. Somehow it did.

"You didn't like it much?" Mr. Reed's face was far back, his body horizontal. He stared at the ceiling.

"No, sir."

"That troubles you, Mr. Mayer."

"Yes, sir."

"You wish you had some other way of thinking about this problem?"

Mayer nodded. How Mr. Reed could have seen the nod was anybody's guess.

"Good. Sit down. But remember this day! Critical thinking!

This is a good basic equation!" He sat upright with a bang. His tie had come loose and flapped over one shoulder. "It is part of the structure upon which the larger equation is built. It demonstrates the efficacy and importance of the good basic equation! Mr. Graham! Proceed!"

Mr. Graham had done his homework. While he described the steps he had taken, Mr. Reed paced, nodding and rubbing his hands.

The bell rang. Students got up to leave.

"Mr. Werner!" said Mr. Reed. "Will you please wait to talk to me after class?"

John's head felt too heavy for his neck.

"Mr. Werner, are you feeling all right?"

John searched the man's face for irony, found watchfulness, concern.

"Yes," he muttered.

"Ah." Mr. Reed turned away. "Mr. Werner, do you have time to do the equation on the board?"

John nodded, went to the board. The equation was long and complicated. He picked up a piece of chalk.

Mr. Reed took a seat at a front desk.

John examined all the letters and numbers before him. Mr. Reed must have added to them while the other students were leaving, increasing the complications.

John twirled his chalk, stepped back, glanced at the board, small and black and framed in dark wood. He measured it, went to the far left-hand corner to begin with the simplest part.

"Good," said Mr. Reed.

John was lost to the world. He used the blackboard in columns, throwing figures onto it with Mr. Reed's own rapidity until two columns ran from top to bottom. Neatly he drew a line, began again at the top. This was a calculation in ideal numbers. It didn't occur to him that ideal numbers hadn't been introduced in class. He kept on, the reasoning theoretical. Mr. Reed stood beside him. "Good," he murmured. "That's enough. You could stop there, Mr. Werner."

John couldn't stop, had a sense of ease within difficulty. He began a fourth column of figures, moving slowly at first and then faster, checking and rechecking, circling his answer. "There. I think that's it. This is a beautiful proof."

Mr. Reed stood beside him. "It's better than I had done."

"Where did those final pieces come from?"

"Mine," said Mr. Reed. "I found them the other day, part of a big proof of Lobachevsky's. Where have you been studying?"

"I have some old books," said John. "My grandfather was a good mathematician, I guess, before he went into business. I've been sick a lot, so I've looked at them, played with them a little."

"Not only play, I think?"

"No," he admitted. "Once you get started, it's hard to stop."

"John, have you been sick?"

"No. Well, yes. I have to take asthma medication. Makes me sleepy."

"As today?"

"Yes."

"John, I've noticed that when the homework is just practice, you don't do it. That brings down your grade. Is this true in your other classes as well?"

"Maybe."

"You don't care for your homework?"

"I try. But something reminds me of mathematics, and pretty soon I'm busy thinking of that and not doing what I'm supposed to be doing."

"You must let me see what I can do for you. Look, if I brought you a problem from time to time, would you work on it?"

"I would be happy to. Honored to."

"All right. On the condition that you would also make some modicum of effort to satisfy your other teachers."

"Yes, sir."

"Good. I'll give you some advice. When you get home in the afternoon, do your other homework first. Don't neglect it. Clear?"

John nodded.

"That will leave the evenings free. I'll share a problem or two with you. We shall see. I will be watching you, John."

"Thank you," John said.

Mr. Reed dismissed him with a wave of the hand. "You should know by now, John, you have the makings in you of a distinguished mathematician."

John, halfway out the door, turned. The classroom was dim, but Mr. Reed, standing in the middle of it, was nodding, smiling.

The next days at school were no easier. John worked. It wasn't that easy, paying attention. Often he had to drag himself away from the contemplation of windows, force himself to listen to words as they came from his teachers' mouths. Sometimes he was mesmerized by the mechanics of speaking. They could be stated mathematically. Each sound made its own interior map of placements for tongue, lips, teeth. *Analysis situ,* examined by the mathematician Gauss, had to do with relationships, the geometry of position.

Even literature had its pitfalls. How fast might a ship be traveling, how quick the tide, when one read in the *Aeneid:* "The anchor drops, the rushing keel is stayed"?

A few afternoons later Mr. Reed stopped him again after class, handed him a sheaf of papers. "Take these home. See what you can do. Not before your other classwork. Agreed?"

"Yes."

After he had finished his other work, John took out the math problems Mr. Reed had given him.

"All distances measured from any fixed point along a given straight line 'correspond' to 'numbers' that 'measure' the distances. Now, let us examine classes of cuts, or points on this line." John was off.

"Here!" said Mr. Reed one day. "Often, in our society, the word 'mathematician' is preceded by the word 'mere.' Is that right? Old sticks, right? Stuck in cement cubicles at large universities? Let out into the sunshine twice a year, for air?"

Mr. Reed pounded his desk.

"Meanwhile, what are we really? All the physical universe is ours! Not some cubicle filled with a desk. Come with me. I think you need exercise. Ever do any running?"

"No. That is, not for years."

They strolled to the gymnasium, looked at the indoor track.

John wondered. He hadn't had an asthma attack in a long time, but he'd been so tired, weak. Could he be hooked on pills?

That evening, before he went to sleep, he didn't take his usual medication. The next day he was surprised to find that he had slept the night through and he wasn't wheezing.

On the shelf in his bathroom was the brown bottle of his daytime pills. He knew he should take one now while he could still breathe. He reached for the bottle, replaced it. This was an experiment. If he got sick, he'd go back to taking them.

He let himself out of the house. Air seared at his chest. He was afraid. At Gresham he sat at his desk. All around him were healthy young men. He was tired of worrying about being sick. He wanted to set one foot in front of the other, count his steps, make multiples of those steps, run. He wanted to be normal.

Funny, shuffling steps in highly polished school shoes. The muscles in his legs and arms shook. He jogged home that day. Every joint hurt. There was a grinding in his stomach, a withdrawal symptom.

He made it into the powder room, where he threw up at length, settled back against a wall, still sick to his stomach. All he would have to do to feel better would be to go upstairs, take a pill.

John looked around his mother's powder room. It was now lavender and blue and peach, redecorated in honor of twelve linen hand towels given to Helen Werner by a Morgan aunt who had married into the Saltonstall family. "For poor dear Helen, stuck up there at Prouts Neck all year round." His mother had not been at all put out by this. When anyone commented on the towels, she would say carelessly, "Oh, yes, they were a gift from the Saltonstalls."

John crept up the stairs, stumbled into his bedroom in an agony of aching joints, shut the door, locked it, lay on his bed. The pills were on the shelf in his bathroom. A lifetime refillable quantity, thanks to Dr. Brinkley.

The door rattled. "John. Didn't you see the light? Dinnertime." He looked up. The red light over the door was on, a signal from the dining room below. The doorknob turned, hesitated at the lock. "Be right out," he called. "Changing my clothes."

"Don't keep Cook waiting."

At dinner his parents' conversation flickered back and forth, candles in conflicting drafts. John's mind wandered. His father suddenly pushed back his chair, shoved it under the table, left the room. The front door slammed.

"Temperament." John's mother spoke in a shaky voice. "Very bad, Dr. Brinkley says."

John nodded, excused himself.

Too sore to study, he climbed onto his bed, turned out the lights. He was alone. The world, which might seem in daily life to have form and structure, was revealed. He was a bit of organic matter slanting into a slippy, insubstantial surface.

He opened his eyes, shut them. In his bowels a worm of fright wriggled, made him shiver. Panic moved into his abdomen, tapped with silver delicate fingers muscles under the skin.

One pill. All it would take. He stared into the dark, gripped the bedclothes, saw a geometrical figure, a triangle of equal sides and angles. He began to write an equation. Something needed to be rebuilt, straightened. Climbing inside the triangle he went to work.

Then he saw himself climbing into it, thought with relief, I'm dreaming. I'm asleep. I'm all right, then. I'm asleep.

The next morning he awoke, examined the early light. He could still breathe. He dressed.

That afternoon he went to the indoor track. Circles, he thought as he shuffled around it like an old man. The circumferences must add up to some crystalline amount.

There was never any need to go away for the summer, since their home was on the ocean. Anytime they wanted, Harold could pick them up and take them by car down to their beach. The approach had been made into a stone path, and stone steps led to the sand of a little cove with a cliff overhang. No one in John's household went. They could go anytime. John's mother was fond of telling visitors: "It's so hectic, you know. Everything in motion, all the time. Quite tiring."

John spent his summers working on proofs for Mr. Reed and jogging down to the ocean. His mother tended to fill the house with garden parties and tea parties and little cocktail hours. A tray of invitations of various sizes went with her everywhere, and she was continually checking off lists. John went down to the beach, weaving in and out of the background plantings so as not to be seen.

"John," said guests when he was spotted, "you've grown up."

He was at last filling out, into a height of more than six feet. "Such a handsome young man!" they said. He nodded, escaped. Jogged. Proving he could be somebody, himself.

One day in midsummer of his last year at Gresham John jogged to the little private beach, stood watching the rollers heave onto the rocks. In a moment he was out of his clothes, walking into the waves. Stars of light dazzled on the surface of the water. He looked down at his arms and hands and saw thinness but muscle, the tense ridge that went the length of his inner forearm. He waded out until the water was at his waist, and when the next wave rolled in he dived over it and came up with his hair soaked and a feeling of exultation within.

He swam strongly out against the tide, turned, shot inshore on a breaking crest. In a blaze of joy he put on his clothes, jogged back to the house. His mother was receiving guests, so he took the back stairs three at a time, thick sandwiches from Cook hidden in one big hand. Taking huge bites of the sandwiches, he sat at his books.

Mr. Reed was away that summer with his wife and family, but

he wrote to John. Sometimes John sent some work he'd finished. It was a lively correspondence as they worked from one equation to the next, tightly rigorous in their approach, creative, humorous as they reached for something new.

One problem John worked on all summer, polishing, changing, perfecting. At last he sent along a proof so brief its form was a haiku.

Mr. Reed wrote back: "This is so perfect I can't understand it, John. I can't see how you got to it, and it's taken me all this time to write to you and admit it. Please, from now on, share a little more, even if it isn't just right or a bit muddled. *Pauca sed matura* is one thing, but if Gauss had shown the roads he traveled to his proofs, as you and I know, and as his contemporaries begged him to do, mathematics would be half a century or more ahead of where it is today. You don't need to fall into his trap."

In September, when Mr. Reed returned to Portland, John went to meet him and take him the latest sheaf of papers.

"Great guns!" Mr. Reed jumped up, wrung John's hand. "Look at you! What did you eat, Vita-Grow?"

John grinned, handed the man the papers, stood in silence while he looked at them. Mr. Reed laid them down, banged a desk a few times. "Yes! That is more like it! You made it as obvious as you could, didn't you? And still, I can see, it's going to take weeks to catch up! Now, been exercising?"

John nodded.

"I can see it! We have to start thinking about college, don't we?"

John cleared his throat. "Look, I want to thank you for everything you've done."

"Don't thank me yet!" Mr. Reed swung one foot about the other, twisted himself in a circle. "Look what I've got. This young giant grinning at me."

"Brunholtz is the man," said Mr. Reed one day that October. "Emil Brunholtz."

"Who is he?"

"Mathematician, lecturer, man of letters, most well known for *The Science of Arithmetics*. He creates his own systems. High degree of spatial intuition, very rare. His systems have advanced the theory of measurements in theoretical physics."

"But where is he?"

"He's been traveling in Europe for several years. Now he's in this country, and he's moving up here to an island hideaway he and his wife bought some time ago. He wrote to me that he's accepted a small teaching position at the university to keep from feeling too isolated.

"In my opinion, Emil is the man you should see for, say, a year or so. After that, you will know what you want to do. Go to the university, John. Learn something new. There's a lot you haven't done."

"So," John finished, "that's about all. I don't want to give you the wrong impression. My parents do the best they can. I don't have any reason to feel sorry for myself. We all . . . suffer."

"Of course," Gretta murmured. She looked at Emil. There was a silence.

Once, John wanted to tell them, I saw my father look down a street as if he couldn't see to the end. Once I heard my mother cry so that only Dr. Brinkley could quiet her.

"My dear." Emil sat forward. "We thought we might go up and have a look at the computer this evening."

"Surely." Gretta frowned at her husband. "And I should see you next week. Emil! Tonight is a time for music! For playing cards, yes? Tomorrow, when you are fresh, won't that be soon enough for computers?"

"Oh, yes, music." Emil sat back. He tapped a waltz cadence on the arm of the chair, smiled. "I had forgotten."

To one side was a small German piano of intricately carved oak, its keys yellow with age. Gretta went to it, began to play. John, who had never really listened to a waltz in his life, found himself counting—one, two, three. Emil closed his eyes, his head back. His finger danced on the arm of his chair. "Such humor," he said when she had finished. Gretta looked pleased.

"Yes. Thank you, Mrs. Brunholtz," John murmured.

"You will call us Emil and Gretta, and we will call you John, would that be all right with you?"

"It would be fine." John found himself wondering: Could they use an extra man around here? He could do odd jobs. He wouldn't cause them any trouble.

"Good," said Gretta. "Now, do you play cards?"

"I used to. A nanny taught me."

A table was brought before the fire and there began a game of three-handed whist. Both mathematicians counted to themselves.

There was no sound but the slap of the cards. Gretta laid her hand down. "There."

The men groaned.

"Oh, no," said Emil. "Not again."

The next day he and John worked with the computer, beginning right after breakfast. About two o'clock in the afternoon, Gretta brought trays of food in to them. "Emil, I expect you to be finished by four. That will be enough for one day."

"Yes, dear." Emil Brunholtz looked at John, shrugged. "She knows I would work the clock around."

That afternoon John went outside to jog while Emil napped. There was something in the air here that made him want to caper a little as he ran. Later, comfortable enough not to have to do anything, he sat alone in his room and stared at the ocean, watching the light on it change.

The next day he and Emil worked hard, but there was more time than he would have expected simply to be, to feel the movement of light and breeze, to have small, undemanding conversations with these people, to watch Emil glance at his wife, or she at him, and see the understanding they enjoyed. On Monday, he hated to go back to his condominium.

The following week he attended classes and worked at home; then Emil invited him again to the island. It came to be accepted that John would come to visit on weekends. He and Emil became engrossed in a big project.

Many times as John jogged about Emil's island he found himself fascinated by its configuration and that of the other two. Separating Emil's from the inner island was a swirl of deep water, fifty yards across at low tide. Emil's boat landing faced the coast of Portland, but to its right the ground sloped down to a small natural beach. On the inner island the land also sloped into a beach. It seemed likely that the two had once been connected. Emil agreed. "A sandy spot, eroded. That water is exceptionally deep, the undertow quite murderous. We never allow anyone to swim on that side of the island, despite the sand. In past history, the lives of two boys were lost there; they were dashed against underwater rocks."

One Saturday John inquired if Owen might take him to the inner island to look around and if Emil might arrange this. It was necessary to catch the tide before its peak, to make it easy to row in one direction, and after its peak to row in the other. Owen wouldn't take a larger boat in; there were too many boulders.

Owen squinted off across the water. "Yup. Take him at three. That suit you?"

"Excellent. You are a good neighbor, Owen."

The man's expression didn't change. "Try to be."

"I don't think he likes the idea," said John to Emil later. "Maybe he doesn't like me."

"Nonsense," said Emil. "It's not you. He doesn't like anyone. That's why he lives on an island."

"You live on an island."

"That proves it." Emil walked away, whistling.

At three, feeling like a tenderfoot at the O-K Corral, John followed Owen down to Emil's little boathouse. Uselessly he stood by while Owen pulled a dinghy off its mooring and held it in the water so John could step in. Then Owen let the boat out, climbed into its exact center, and without a word pulled it over the top of the tide to the opposite shore, where he was out again and dragging it in toward the beach before John could offer to help.

"Stay put in there," Owen said. "You ain't got the boots." On Owen's feet were boots that fit him halfway up the calves.

When John was out at last, he pulled the dinghy far up the inner shore.

"No need to take it with us," Owen said mildly.

John set the boat down. "What I was wondering, Owen, is why you live on an island."

"Feel like it."

"Oh. None of my business, right?"

"Hell." Owen spat. "I had a wife. Died—leukemia. We built the house, I had the boat. I dunno, when she went, I didn't ask anybody else." The man turned away.

John followed.

They started out around the periphery of the inner island, through a forest that tangled in a dense undergrowth of scrub pine. The sticks of the lower branches were woven together in an impenetrable gray webbing. They skirted them, climbing a narrow path along the edge of the cliffs that swung up around the border of the island to the south and west.

At the height of the cliffs they paused. Below, waves fought, crashed against the rocks like thunder. It seemed as though a giant ax had fallen between the two islands, taking out chunks, then a final, wedge-shaped piece. The narrow cut was dark, treacherous.

"Make your hair stand up a little," said Owen over the noise.

John nodded. Rock jutted toward the bottom in rifts and switchbacks. Near the bottom it was ribbed sharply.

"When the tide goes out," Owen said, "it's no more than three feet deep down there."

"Ever walk across?"

"Thought of it. When that old tide comes ripping, though, it'd make a person look some. Me, I'm not much of a climber. When Indians lived here, they cut some niches in the cliff over there, little footholds. But those quit halfway down. You look real close, you'll see a little tree, about three feet up. That ledge, that kind of apron? Well, up beyond that the steps go. Good enough for Indians. Old Windigo." Owen snorted. "Good way to get killed."

On the far side John could make out the little ledge, the pine, the apron. He looked down. Cliff faces fell away, giving him a sense of vertigo.

The men turned, pushed on into ocean wind. Woods also rose on the ocean side of the island. The climbing was treacherous.

"Chapel's this way." Owen nodded up the slope of an interior clearing, enclosed by forest on three sides.

Painted white once, the clapboards of the little square building at the head of the clearing had peeled and weathered. "Needs upkeep," said Owen. "Built well enough. Once had its own wharf on the inland side, wooden stairs leading up. Gone now, course." A cleared path to the rear of the building led, no doubt, to the cliff view they'd left a while before. As he approached, John could see to one side a narrow graveyard whose ancient, thin gravestones seemed to be sliding into the ground at an angle.

Owen opened one of the two doors, neither of which had a lock, only an old-fashioned wrought-iron latch. One door led into the sanctuary, the other into the ell. Inside, the two were connected by an entryway. The floors of the tiny chapel creaked under them.

Owen said, "Emil owns this now. Grew out of use. Too far for the summer people to come. Here it sits."

"Songbooks in the pews?" John said. "Bible in the pulpit?"

Owen allowed himself the trace of a smirk. "Don't want to let that fool you."

John followed him into a tiny back kitchen. Owen had sat down at a table there. John joined him. "Listen, who is Windigo?"

Owen shifted in his seat, planted his boots far apart. John was reminded of some fishermen he'd seen once, three of them sitting at a dock, each with his feet planted just that way.

"Windigo," said Owen. "A bad old Indian spirit. I never knew him personally. Unholy cannibal."

Owen's voice became cadenced, gravelly. "Old Windigo, Weetigo, some tribes called him. The Indian god which is as close to ours as the devil. Roamed the earth, Indians said. Ate whoever he saw fit. Now, a long time ago on one of these islands, a man and his wife and their wolf dogs lived. As nice a couple as you'd ever want to meet. No one saw them all one winter. When they were found in the spring, the bones of humans and dogs were all thrown together near some rocks by the shore. Hard to tell, people said, who had eaten whom. But the Indians, they knew. Old Windigo. Who blows through when the going gets tough. Who points to this one, to that one, and says, 'I'm going to suck your insides first, 'til your skin is hanging on your bones and you can't even grow a hair. Then I'll chew the skin and pull on the bones.'

"Lots of stories around here. Spirits everywhere. You know Bailey Island, to the north?"

John nodded.

"Well, just go up there 'round Christmastime, wait 'til it begins to get dark. Look for a headless pirate astride a milk-white horse. And that horse has wings."

John snorted a laugh. "Oh, come on."

"Now, you don't want to be laughing. Out on Cliff Island, Captain Kieff swings his lantern these hundred years, luring ships to sail onto the rocks there. When the ships crash, the sailors are never heard of again."

"Owen . . ."

"Or go to Long Island. See the sea captain tramping around in his whirling cloak. There's a ghost of a girl who runs at night over all the islands, begging for help, gore coming from her nose and throat." Owen reached over, gripped John's arm. The two sat nose to nose. "Bring me a Bible," he said. "I'll swear on it."

John looked him in the eye, raised one eyebrow. "Aren't you ashamed to be telling such tales in a church?"

Owen's face cracked into an approving grin. "Had you going for a minute there, though."

"You never," said John.

"All right. Let's get out of here."

"You know, I could row back," said John, "if you told me how."

"Well, put her in, then. Let's see."

It was a slopping job, but John managed. He pulled at the oars as he had seen Owen do.

"Up a little," the man said. "You're shipping water."

"It's not that hard, rowing?"

"Not if you've got the current. Tide's everything in these channels."

"Look, thanks for the trip." John helped Owen secure the little dinghy in the boathouse.

"Yup. I'll go along." Owen boarded his lobster boat, nodded at John, chugged away slowly over the water.

6

One Sunday night, a week or so after meeting John Werner, Crelly went to the theater and found a message on the bulletin board. "Crelly Kemp, John Werner called, said to meet him outside the theater at seven on Monday."

Crelly didn't like to be summoned. She stood frowning at the bulletin board, took down the message, turned it over in her hands. She meant to practice for the next semester's auditions, do some studying. She stood debating. She could see John Werner's blond hair, serious eyes. For a week she had wondered if he would call.

Marta Davis came to her doorway.

"I ought to practice," said Crelly, flicking the note through her fingers. "I ought to study."

"Yes," said Marta with a deep laugh. "Constantly."

Crelly went into the theater, to one of the rehearsal rooms. She wanted to figure it out. What would Aunt Lois and Uncle Elder think about John Werner? Would they like him? Would they trust him?

All she knew about him was what he'd said the week before, polite conversation. All she had was this note on pink paper.

She flicked at it.

Crelly had gone out with groups of young people in high school, boys and girls together, but not often with just one boy. A group of happy young people could seem golden and invincible, but one boy was too often insubstantial, somehow too weak. Crelly started to throw the note away, hesitated.

She could see the serious, even hurt, quality of John Werner's eyes. Picturing his face, a reverie came to her, a warm ease. Instead of throwing the note away, she folded it into a tiny, neat package, slipped it into her pocket.

On Monday night when she opened the back door of the theater, she saw his low-slung silver car immediately. Crelly was aware that the car was expensive, something one might see in an advertisement on the back of a magazine, but she forgot it when John got out, came toward her. His eyes were clouded.

"Hello," she said, more gently than she expected.

"Hello." His voice was a little broken. "I'm sorry about the message, Crelly. I meant just to ask you, but I was too nervous."

"It's all right."

They went to the car. Crelly watched him fold his long legs under the steering wheel. The moon above the city lights made a ripple of silver across his knees. The night shimmered. They drove to a restaurant just over the bridge in South Portland. "Oh, it's beautiful," Crelly whispered. "Is this an expensive place?"

"Why, not very."

White linens, plants, thick carpet. Crelly stood still as a glass cart rolled by, a tall German chocolate cake in the center of it. John felt that if she continued to look about with those blue eyes, the crowd at the restaurant would fall at her feet. "This way," he said.

Crelly opened the menu, gasped. "Fourteen ninety-five. John, can you afford this?"

John Werner blinked. "I think so." He got out his wallet to check.

"I have eighty dollars." He smiled slowly. "How much are you going to eat?"

"Eighty?" said Crelly. "You could feed a farm family for—" She looked at him, forgetful. The grooves at his lips touched her, as if a finger had been laid sweetly on her breast.

"What would you like?" he said.

"Why—why everything, I guess."

"Lobster stew," John told the waitress. "The spinach salad, crabmeat fromage, filet of sole. Two glasses of Liebfraumilch, in honor of Emil, who loves it?"

"Yes," said Crelly. "Oh, this is going to be fancy."

She is radiant, John thought. He allowed himself to bask a little in her glow.

They ate, talked. "What I remember," said Crelly, "is that it's summertime, evening. We're bringing in the sheep. During the day they graze in the pasture, but at night they come down into the fold where it's safer. If you stand far away, they look like flowers in the grass. It's evening, cool. Damp, almost. Uncle Elder and Aunt Lois count the sheep. I swing the gate to. We all close it together." She smiled. "Now, tell me one thing you remember."

"Well," said John, "once I sneaked out of the house and walked —it seemed a long way at the time—to the edge of our property where there were some big trees. I stood there, looking up through the leaves, and I thought the spaces between them were like prisms. I knew I had to get back to the house, so I closed my eyes, opened them, until I had those spaces memorized. To this day I can see how they looked." He stopped. "I don't usually talk much about this."

"But it's wonderful, John."

"Dessert?" The waitress rolled up the glass cart. On it was the chocolate cake and, to the sides, a carrot cake and a cheesecake with fresh strawberries.

"The cake in the center?" suggested John.

Crelly shook her head. "Thanks, but I don't eat chocolate."

"The cheesecake, then?" She nodded.

When they were finished they drove to Back Cove in Portland, parked where they could see the ocean fill the bare inland harbor on the tide. A semicircle of city lights glittered like a bracelet around the flats.

"What I don't see," said John, "is how you can be here like this with me and then be up on the stage. It seems like you must be two people."

Crelly shrugged. "My work. Sometimes I am two people, sometimes more. There's an actress I work with who stays in character a lot even when she's out of the theater. She doesn't know who she is most of the time." Crelly laughed.

"Look," John said, "Emil said you might like to come and visit the island this weekend. Would you?"

"Well, it was nice of Emil to ask, thanks very much," Crelly said politely. All at once she felt a little afraid of the person beside her. Who was he? What did he want? "Do you want me to come?" she said.

"Yes." John was surprised at the question. "Of course."

"Well, then, I will." She smiled.

They sat, silently watching what was, now that the water had begun to come up in the bay, a double strand of lights.

"I suppose I should take you home," John said. His eyes were on her lips.

"But you'll pick me up when? Saturday morning, first thing?"

"Yes. Early. Seven." They drove back. He pulled the car to a stop, turned toward her, but Crelly's hand was already on the door handle.

"Wait," he said.

Crelly faced him. Suddenly their lips touched, light as feathers.

On Saturday, she was up early. It was wintry outside, dark. John wouldn't pick her up for an hour, but she couldn't sleep. Perhaps she would take a walk down to the all-night coffee shop.

Snow had fallen. It was fluffy and dry and sparkled under the streetlight. Between high banks the street looked as soft as the inside of a cocoon.

"John?" Cautiously, Crelly walked toward a low-slung silver car, peered in. The interior was littered with drawings and diagrams that seemed to be maps and pages of figures in careful, clear script.

John hunched over them. He lifted his head. Crelly saw what she had sometimes seen when wandering in the fields at home, the still startlement of an animal caught in the act of being itself. For a moment she was too surprised to move.

John recovered first, opened the door. "Hello, don't mind me. I'm just working."

"Oh. Sorry to interrupt."

"Not at all. I couldn't sleep. I thought I would come here and park and be near you, at least." He broke off, having revealed more than he'd meant to.

Crelly didn't seem to have heard.

Together they stacked the papers. She got into the car.

"Had breakfast?"

"No. But I need my bag, if we go on from there."

"Let's get it."

They stopped at a restaurant downtown, had coffee, eggs, home fries. Then they headed for the wharf, talking all the way. The sun in the harbor glittered like tinsel.

"It's warm below," John shouted over the sound of the ferry motor. Crelly went down the stairs, looked out every spray-stained window as the boat turned and left the dock. She examined the green walls, the benches. The ceiling was upholstered with strapped-up life jackets; it looked like an orange mattress.

John followed her about. "Too enclosed?" she asked. He nodded. Up on deck, they stayed out of the wind, watched the islands pass. This was the first time Crelly had ever been on the ocean, and she was entranced.

After a while, however, she did look up at John, who had turned toward her with his back to the sun. His face was in darkness. She could see only the outline of his head and body. His shadow fell across her. Involuntarily, Crelly grasped the deck railing. She was shivering.

She lifted a hand. He stepped back, and the sun fell on his face. Blue-gray eyes, blond hair: this was John, of course. Smiling at him, Crelly turned once again to look out over the water. Everything was all right: this was John.

A man named Owen met them at Peaks Island. He nodded at Crelly when John made introductions, helped her aboard, snapped the door to his cabin shut.

"Owen, Crelly comes from Edgar," John said.

"Does?"

Crelly felt too slender under Owen's weatherbeaten gaze, but she smiled. Owen nodded. The motor rumbled. Green-blue ocean swelled about them, evened into a kind of rhythmic lap. When she caught sight of the three islands, Crelly cried, "Oh! Look!"

Owen couldn't resist that voice. The man glanced up and away quickly, to hide his approval.

To John's surprise, when Owen had cut the motor, flung out the boathook, and pulled them in, he spoke.

"Out for the weekend, are you?" he said to Crelly.

She nodded. Owen took it further. "Up from Edgar?" It would have been "down" to anyone but a sailor, who knew the current and wind that came from the south and west.

"Yes, I am, thank you. Owen, I never rode on this kind of boat before. I really liked it."

Owen looked pleased. "I got some relatives out Breaks Mills way somewhere, I dunno but," Owen said. "I was out there myself some years ago. Pretty."

"Yes, it is. Well, thank you." Crelly held out her hand. Owen shook it.

The old pushover, John thought. "Owen, we'll be taking the rowboat this afternoon."

"Yup. Okay. Be sure to lash it good and tight."

"We will. Thanks."

"Yup." The man putted away.

Crelly looked about her, at the island, the landing, the water. "I love this," she said.

Her hair blew in long wisps against the sky, her cheeks were bright with fresh air. John would have kissed her. Instead he said gruffly, "Come on, let's meet Gretta and Emil."

Gretta bustled, drew Crelly down beside her on the living room sofa. They made quite a contrast, the white-haired Gretta, nodding as Crelly spoke, and Crelly, bright-faced and delighted.

"Well, John," said Emil, "time to go to work."

John nodded.

"Done by three!" Gretta called out.

"Done by three," Emil said over his shoulder.

Gretta asked many questions about Crelly's home and family. Crelly answered them as best she could. "My dear," said Gretta, "have you ever seen a loom before? No? Come with me."

Upon the large wooden frame of the loom was a length of crimson wool woven with a raised pattern of stars. "It must be calculated to the stitch." Gretta sighed. "So exacting. Sometimes I wonder if it's worth it."

"Oh." Crelly touched the intricate pattern. "I've never seen anything like it. I've never even seen weaving before. Will you show me how you do it?"

Gretta was pleased. "You must decide on the pattern first, of course." She sat at the loom, set her feet to the pedals. "Then you must be sure to have yarn enough. The shuttle is passed, so." The shuttle flew, the pedals were pressed, the loom adjusted.

"One row at a time is how it must be done," Gretta said. "No use to skip or ignore or misread. Each row is counted, or the pattern is muddled."

"So strong," Crelly murmured. "Warm. It will last a long time?"

"Oh, yes." Gretta moved close to the weave to examine it nearsightedly. "It should last."

That afternoon Crelly and John took the dinghy across to the next little island, pulled the boat up, walked along the shore as far as the woods, so that she could have a view of the harbor. As they walked, her hand swung near his. John caught it, held it tightly.

Crelly didn't pull away.

The wind had whipped the interior slope bare of snow. Before them was a plain building, once painted white, and to the side a little graveyard.

"Where are we?" she said. The building was so like inland places she had seen before.

Her voice was clear, musical as a bell. "This is the chapel," John said.

He was thinking of Owen's gruesome tales. He would keep them to himself, he decided.

Two pieces of granite, the stone steps of the chapel, sagged into the ground from years of the weight of snow. The doorsill was worn to bare wood, from the march of weather if not the feet of worshipers.

"Somebody walked away and left it," Crelly whispered. "Somebody said, 'We'll be back next Sunday.'"

They stepped into the small entryway, turned toward the sanctuary. There was a musty smell, somehow sweet. The windows were made of plain rippled glass that let in a dim light. The pews were of wood in a dark color. In the front was a wide, whitewashed center arch and platform.

"It reminds me of the church at home," Crelly said. "People came here, even got married, do you think?"

"Yes, maybe."

Crelly went to sit in a pew, staring toward the front. Her lips curved, slightly open.

John cleared his throat. "What are you thinking about?"

"A bride with a handful of flowers, standing just there." Crelly gestured to the front. "Her hair is in a knot at the back of her neck, and her eyelashes are very long."

"Oh?" said John, trying heavily for playfulness. "And what does the groom look like?"

"I don't see him so well. But John, the bride! The bride has on a white dress made of satin, gathered at the waist. There's lace at the neck. The groom," she wisecracked, "is more of a mystery."

"Just like a woman," John said. He meant to joke, too, but spoke more harshly than he'd expected. "That's the way it'll be for the rest of their married life." His voice grew sharp. "They won't really know each other, be enemies all their lives. Married enemies." He looked at Crelly as if she were to blame.

Crelly frowned. "I was just joking," she said softly.

John sat slumped in a pew, inside his clothes as inside careful layers of wrappings. "Sure. Look, maybe I should take you back."

This wasn't at all polite. Crelly stood, moved to the front of the sanctuary. He, too, stood. "Maybe we should get back," she said, puzzled.

John looked at her across rows of pews curved at the upper back like ocean waves. "It's cold out. Stay here until I drag the boat down."

"I could help you."

"No. Stay here." The door made a damp, muffled sound behind him.

I should never have come here, Crelly thought. I should know enough to stay onstage. You get applause for that.

Outside, John dragged at the boat. Its keel made a damp trough in the ice-crusted sand. How soon would the tide fill this trough, tear away its sides, smooth it out to nothing? What speed? What time? He tried to figure, couldn't.

He was in a moil. What was he doing talking weddings with this person he hardly knew? Damn her, anyway. He scowled. Tomorrow morning first thing he'd put Crelly on Owen's lobster boat. Let Owen take her to the ferry, he liked her so much.

He trod heavily on his way back to the chapel, made a lot of noise opening the door.

Crelly was huddled in a small bundle on the platform in the front. She looked frightened.

John would have given anything to reassure her, apologize, but he couldn't. Instead he motioned her toward the door, walked past her on the path, steadied the boat in silence. She climbed in, sat tense-shouldered, her eyes on the treacherous, quiet-looking water as he rowed.

At the landing John slid the skiff into the boathouse, fiddled with the rusty padlock. "You can understand why Owen is so fussy about keeping this boat locked up," he said, more friendly than he meant to be. She didn't answer. He decided this justified his own silence.

Without speaking, they walked back to the house. They'd returned early; Gretta and Emil were still napping. In the entry, they stood together taking off layers of outer clothing.

It was impossible not to speak. "You could tell me why you're so troubled," Crelly said.

"I'm not troubled." John would have liked to talk. He shook his head.

Crelly scowled. "Look, John, I see things, I have to, I'm an actress. Something's bothering you. You're denying it. That's not very honest."

John, who had opened his mouth to speak, shut it. He turned on his heel, walked away.

"That's right," Crelly said, surprising herself. "Run."

John's neck was warm. His ears were warm, too. He wanted to shake her. Instead, he walked through the living room and out to the computer room; if he could have locked the door, he would have.

"What?" said Emil, sticking his head around the door sometime later. "We haven't worked enough today?"

John, deeply engrossed, had managed to forget everything but work.

"Come, John," Emil said. "Gretta would be most upset if she saw you up here now."

"Women!" John muttered.

Emil had started out of the room. He turned. "Oh? Do you speak of Gretta that way?" A glint of steel was in the old man's eyes. He gestured around the room. "Without her there would be nothing. None of this. Come out of here, now, and learn."

Crelly didn't come down for dinner, saying she had a headache. Emil said he felt like reading in private after the meal and went to his room. Gretta played the piano softly, wound some spools of yarn. Her white hair gleamed in the lamplight.

"Well," said John, "I guess you're not mad at me."

Gretta glanced up. "There's something in the air tonight, John. What is it?"

"I don't know, really. Crelly and I went to the island today. We had an argument. Over nothing. How it started or what it was about, I'm not sure."

The old woman gave him a keen glance, collected her balls of red yarn. "I'm not the one you should talk to," she said. "John, will you excuse me? I'm going to do a little weaving tonight. And will you shut out the lights when you go up?"

"Of course."

Once the old woman had gone, John looked around the room. Colorful fabrics, interesting objects, comfort. Slowly he got up, turned off the lights, paused to watch the last embers of the fire. The coals were covered with ash. Inside they glowed like coral roses.

Later, the confusion of his dreams woke him repeatedly.

At last he gave up, padded down the hall, down the stairs, and up to the computer room, where he worked for a long time. In unsnarling some mistakes, however, he did fall asleep.

When it was almost morning he woke, went down for some milk. In the living room he stopped. Crelly had just come from the other direction.

"I didn't sleep very well," she said.

"Neither did I." They looked at each other, both rumpled, sleepy-eyed.

Crelly drew her robe about her. After many washings, its hem dimpled and the pockets were frayed. It wasn't a garment she liked to be seen in. "I was going after some milk," she said. "Could—could I get you some?"

John ached. It seemed to him that it was a great kindness on her part to offer. No one had ever gotten him a glass of milk, for free, before. "Thanks."

There was a cloudy misery in his eyes. Crelly felt sorry for everything that had happened. "Come on out to the kitchen, why don't you?" Crossing the room, she took him by the hand, led him out as one might a child.

"Now, just a minute." She poured milk, set it before him. With a grateful look, he drank.

Crelly spoke again. "An egg and some toast? That always goes good after an argument, Aunt Lois would say."

John looked rueful. "You don't mind?"

"No." She went from refrigerator to stove. Butter melted in the frying pan, eggs broke and began to sizzle.

"I never really watched anybody cook anything," John said.

"No? Well, don't mind this old bathrobe."

John stood up, nosed over the frying pan, inhaling the smell of the eggs. Crelly had put two dishes to warm in the oven. She lifted them out, squinting against the heat.

"My Aunt Lois made this robe," she said, setting a spatula under the eggs, lifting them onto warm plates. "Careful, it's hot."

"This is nice of you, Crelly."

She was touched. "Look, would you like some toast? Jam?"

"Yeah."

They made toast, began to eat, quiet at first. Afraid, Crelly thought, to break something more than silence.

"I'm sorry about yesterday," John said.

"Are you?"

"I don't even know what it was about. Do you?"

"No."

"But I am sorry."

"Can I—would you like a cup of tea?" She rose to get it.

"Let me help." He, too, stood.

"Oh, no. I just wish I looked better, that's all." She put a hand to her hair. She hadn't bothered to comb it, and it rose in a dark tangle about her head.

"I think you look beautiful."

For a second they stood still. Cautiously Crelly asked, "Are we friends, John?"

"Please. I'd like to be. Friends." He saw her narrow shoulders, her soft form under the robe. He held out his arms and she came into them, her hands creeping up around his neck. They kissed, lightly at first, then more firmly.

"I'll put the kettle on," Crelly murmured. She gestured to a side cupboard. "The cups are in there."

As John got them he thought, What looked better than a plain white cup, its ear rounded, its rim smooth to the fingers?

7

Cups of tea. Over the next weeks John and Crelly shared many, developing a connection as delicate as a sensitive plant, as full of action and reaction as the relationship between a touch on the palm and a clasp of fingers. They could walk down a sidewalk arm in arm, look at each other, and smile. They went to movies, to concerts and plays—more than either would have done alone. They shared cups of tea with Marta, with Emil and Gretta, seeing every friend from a new perspective, of two together.

This was belonging, Crelly thought: to find the jigsaw piece that was not at all like yours but fit around it.

There were less successful times, when they argued. Crelly might be afraid. John wouldn't admit to anger at all, walking away from disagreements as if, Crelly sometimes thought in the added rage of frustration, he had suddenly entered some remote garden of numbers, where all the flowers bloomed on schedule.

At those times she couldn't have said what held them together. There seemed to be nothing that could. But sooner or later one of them would turn to the other and say, "Friends?"

The reply would come: "Friends."

They ate tuna fish and potato chip sandwiches, crunching loudly in each other's ears. They got up to see the sunrise but were too chilly to wait it out and ended up at a doughnut shop instead. They developed their own private lockstep, which they practiced while waiting in line anywhere. They sat on a park bench behind a shared newspaper and spied for the federal government.

We're in love, Crelly thought. We must be. She pulled back from John's embrace one day in early spring. "Is this a good idea?" she said. She would have lifted her fingers to his cheekbones, only suddenly she couldn't.

"I know," he murmured. "I can't feel anything or do anything without its affecting you. Or you me."

They held each other, allowing between them a little pale afternoon distance.

"I had always planned—don't misunderstand me now—not to marry anyone," said John. "If you saw my parents, you'd know why. But even when you're not with me, Crelly, I don't do anything without you. If that makes sense."

She nodded. They moved off down the sidewalk, gripping hands tightly.

In the spring the islands began to thaw. The green ice of gnarled cliffs ran with chilled water. Rutted earth turned glistening and soft and blades of grass of a new sharp green pushed among last year's leaves. In the April woods dogtooth violets grew, with their small yellow bells and spotted leaves. Tiny stars of blue dotted the grass. At the back of the little chapel, lilac bushes began to leaf out. Tight buds showed on a runaway clematis.

Inside, Crelly moved away from John, to the platform in front, to the big old open Bible on the pulpit, turning the pages until she came to the heading "Praise of a Good Wife." " 'She is not afraid of snow for her household,' " Crelly read aloud. " 'For all her household are clothed with scarlet.' " She looked up at John. "Is this me, do you think? Could it ever be?"

On her face John saw the adventure they were contemplating. Did he dare? Would she make him a home? Would he make one for her? "If you want it to be," he said. They turned, walked back to the pews.

Crelly sat close to John, her face on fire at her own daring. She took his hand, opened it, stared at the palm, told herself she would not be afraid. She had thought of this so often. Slowly she laid his hand against her breast. John's face grew severe. She held his hand against her.

He leaned down to kiss, feeling the breasts change shape against his lips. Then he pulled away. "I don't want to hurt you," he whispered.

Crelly put his fingers on the hem of her sweater, helped him pull. In a moment she was out of her clothes. For the first time John saw the frailty of her shoulders. Her breasts were small and round. His pulses hammered. He saw dark veins, those pinkish tips. As he watched, they hardened into two round berries.

Crelly went to him. He fit her beneath his coat, held the heft of one breast in his palm. "Look how it lies in my hand," he whispered, and once again leaned forward.

His hairline was wet, his neck dark red. His lips at her breast were both comfortable and uncomfortable. "Easy," Crelly said. "Gently."

"Sorry," he whispered. "Sorry, sorry. Lie back. Oh, please, lie back." He spread out his coat for her, lowered her against it. "Please. I just want to see."

Crelly covered herself compulsively with her hands, hesitating. John pulled away. "Whatever—whatever you want," he said.

At the sound of his voice her hands let go the edges of the jacket. The rounded flesh of her breasts spilled sideways, tilting. Nothing in John's life had prepared him for this, the sight of a woman lying on darkness, bare to the waist.

Crelly watched his face as he came to lie against her. The weeks before, of speculation and planning, of unanswered wanting, came upon her with new urgency. Her fingers fit themselves into the space between his belt and his belly. She moved in her own clothing, making room for his hand.

"So strong," she whispered.

"I don't know what to do, Crelly."

"Touch there, touch there."

"Yes?" he whispered.

She nodded, sighed, murmured his name, tightened against his fingers, relaxed.

"Let me touch you," she whispered. "Show me how, I don't know how."

His body responded at once, wildly. He became still; then stiff and still, then wet. He made one small groan.

"Oh," she whispered, close to tears.

"Crelly." The pupils of his eyes were large, dark with feeling. "I love you. Marry me. We're married already."

Wedding

1

Out Route 26, up the old Grey road into Edgar they went, off into the west-central part of the state. The land grew hilly. Lakes shone in the sun over every horizon of highway. There were farms with the first flat carpeting of green on their pastures, little cattle ponds, acres of earth just rolled over. Mud, manure and flowers, all the smells mingled together. Fence and shrubs and plants in windows, daffodils blowing crazily at foundations and doorsteps, tall old trees with branches fine as hair.

"I didn't realize," John said.

By the time they were out of the car, Uncle Elder and Aunt Lois were hurrying from their house. Aunt Lois's heavy arms lifted up to hug Crelly. Uncle Elder waited for his turn, holding his hand out to John meanwhile. "Elder Leavitt, pleased to meet you." He gave John a glance both cordial and careful. "Well, Crelly," said Aunt Lois. "Crelly." Elder spoke up. "Give over, Mother. My turn."

Aunt Lois went to John. "And you are John. Now, I think anyone just home from college should have a kiss!" She kissed his cheek. He gave her a smile that looked, she told Elder later, almost grateful.

"Bring your things right in," she said. "We'll get you settled."

Uncle Elder reached into the back to pick up Crelly's suitcase.

"I could get that," John said.

"I guess I can manage," said Uncle Elder. "One or two more times."

Crelly and Aunt Lois did most of the talking.

"You like baseball at all?" Uncle Elder said to John at the end of the noon meal.

"Some. Statistics, especially."

"Hmm. Been listening in lately? How about those Red Sox?"

John grinned. "You see Rice, that last game? The Sox have to get the lead out of their pants if they want the pennant this year."

"John," said Crelly, "I didn't know you liked baseball."

Uncle Elder waved a hand at Crelly, as at a pesky mosquito, and turned to John with interest. "Know what I'd like to see? Some hustle. Now, in the old days, you had some base stealing. I'd like to see that again."

"So would I," said John. "Nothing like it. Boston hasn't had a good base stealer since—who? Jethro, maybe. Thirty-five bases, back in 1950. Thirty-five in 1951."

"Now, DiMaggio did steal some."

"Yes, he did. Eighteen in 1950, '51? But then, you know, we had to have Willie Mays. Mays, Aparicio, Mays. Chicago. New York." John made a disgusted sound in his teeth.

Uncle Elder looked pleased. "You know, the game's on this afternoon," he said. "Red Sox and Yankees. Owners of the Sox spend their summers up here, so we get a good clear broadcast. I'm going down and build a dam, take the radio with me. You want to come?"

"Sure," John said. "Crelly?"

"Not me." Her eyes were large. "You go ahead, though." Aunt Lois snickered.

"He never talks baseball to me," Crelly said after the men left. "Never once. Not that I ask."

"Well, some people hide it," said Aunt Lois. "And some people can't help talking about it. Either way, it's a sickness in the blood."

John followed Uncle Elder down over the fields to a small stream. About a yard wide with a graveled bottom and many large stones at its edges, it rippled gently downhill toward the river.

"Going to take a few of those stones," said Elder, "set them across here, make a little dam, so's to have a pool for the cows when I let them onto this grass. You ever built into a stream?"

"No."

"Well, we'll start with that big one over there." Elder pointed out a small boulder. "It'll roll downhill, we just put our backs to it. First we'll tune in, though."

In a little while the two men were straining shoulder to shoulder, their feet digging into the stream gravel, pant legs wet to the knees. The boulder didn't give.

John was enjoying himself. He might dig out a fulcrum of pebbles in the gravel bed, but this was a great day for brute force. "Hold on." Digging his feet in, he shoved. His face turned bright red, his lips drew down in a ferocious mask of effort.

Uncle Elder dug in, too. Nose to nose the two men glared at each other, snarling. Then both expressions eased. The stone began to roll, gathered momentum.

"Yahoo!" John yelled.

"Hold her now! Hold on!" Uncle Elder bellowed. They grappled, tearing the skin of their fingers against the slippery bottom of the rock, rolling it along.

"Hell," said Uncle Elder. "Just like a hoop."

They shifted, jimmied until the boulder lay wedged into place in the middle of the stream. It glistened with water. Both men sat on the bank breathing hard, watching the shine of it dry.

"Going to build up the sides," Uncle Elder grunted.

"Yes," said John. He held up a hand. "Was that Rice, flying out?"

They listened. "Sounds like it." Uncle Elder sighed. "And here comes Jackson. That jackrabbit."

All afternoon the men worked, pushing stones into the stream, listening.

Up at the house, Aunt Lois glanced out her sink window. "They could have used the tractor shovel, but they're having a whale of a good time."

Crelly went to look. "They're soaked," she said. "The radio is so loud I can hear it from here."

"Of course. Or it wouldn't be any fun."

"I'll say this for him," Uncle Elder told Crelly later, when John had gone up to change. "He's a good worker. That dam looks pretty, and it'll last. And we did it without chewing up the ground with a tractor, either."

Aunt Lois was wise to him. "How'd the Red Sox do?" she asked.

"They lost." With two hands Uncle Elder set his baseball cap so the brim fell over his eyes. He went to the barn.

They ate around the kitchen table, bringing from the stove dishes of thick pottery, one for mashed potatoes, one for carrots. The pot roast came in on an old-fashioned cream-colored platter webbed with hairline cracks. Any other plate, Crelly told John, and the roast wouldn't have tasted so good.

"See," explained Elder, "that plate is seasoned. All those cracks hold the gravy from one time to the next. Extra flavor."

"Oh, don't tell him, Elder," said Aunt Lois. "What will he think? John, maybe this isn't quite what you're used to."

The round table, the windows, the warm room, dishes on the stove and counter, the smells of food. "It's fine," he said. "I eat alone when I'm not with Crelly. At my parents' house—" He stopped.

"Doesn't your mother like to cook?" Aunt Lois said sympathetically. "I get sick of it, myself."

"John's mother has a cook," said Crelly.

"Has a cook?" Aunt Lois blinked. "Why, the answer to a prayer!"

"I never had a meal as good as this," said John. "Thank you, Mrs. Leavitt."

"Lois. Call us Lois and Elder. Everyone does."

Never had John wished so much to be liked. As for Crelly, it seemed to her that Aunt Lois and Uncle Elder, who had always been in the foreground of her vision, had faded to the sides now, and instead she saw only John, his broad shoulders, blond hair. She was, she decided, just so proud of him.

There is a certain kind of glue that sticks people together when they're made for each other, Aunt Lois told Uncle Elder. You couldn't see it, but when it was there, you knew it. Watching Crelly walk down the lawn beside John Werner, her hair shifting to the side in a tangle so that she could look up at him, her face bright as she hesitated, or seeing John's hand reach for Crelly's in odd moments when they were almost alone and obviously couldn't wait to be alone, Aunt Lois saw that what she called the glue was there. It seemed, she said, that one was always calling and the other answering.

"It's not so much what they say," she told Elder. "It's what they do. Have you watched?"

"Try not to."

"But this is another sign," she told her husband as he reached for her. "What they have makes us new. Do you know?"

On the second evening of John's visit, Aunt Lois sat in the living room with her knitting and Uncle Elder snoozed in his easy chair, *Time* magazine spread out on his knees. Now and then he turned a page, snored. Crelly and John came downstairs slowly, their intertwined fingers chilly, damp from nerves. So far Uncle Elder had not replied to Crelly's "What do you think? Isn't he something? Do you like him?"

They hesitated at the door, John in the lead, Crelly peeking around his arm. John was aware of Elder's reserved judgment. He turned to leave, but Crelly, to be helpful, gave him a little shove. Propelled backward into the room, he laughed too loudly.

Aunt Lois looked up, smiled, went back to counting stitches. Uncle Elder snorted, turned several pages, blinked, rubbed his eyes.

John and Crelly sat on the sofa. They waited.

Aunt Lois looked at them over her glasses. "Was there something you wanted?"

"Yes," Crelly blurted. "We want to get married."

"What?" Aunt Lois put down her knitting.

Uncle Elder's magazine slipped off his knees. "Damn," he said. "Crelly, you're too young."

"I am not. I am of age." Crelly frowned at her uncle. He glowered back. It was one of the few times they had ever done such a thing except in play. Carefully she watched his face for some sign that he wished, as she did, for an eyebrow to waggle or lips to turn up. Neither face moved a muscle.

"Lois, is she of age?" said Uncle Elder.

"You know she is," Aunt Lois said. "Eighteen."

"Oh, for God's sake." Uncle Elder swung his big feet and long legs off the hassock. He scowled at Crelly and John. "I suppose you think you're serious about this," he said to John.

"We love each other, Elder." John spoke warily. Nothing so far had gone as rehearsed. "We've worked it all out. With my allowance and Crelly's scholarships, we should be fine. We can stay in my rooms." He refused to call them his condominium, especially here, where the word would seem outlandish and false. "Until we've finished school. Then, I don't know, depending on where Crelly needs to go for theater and me to study, and depending on what Emil says about what's next for me—it might be Boston, or one of the larger cities for a while."

"Cities?" Elder heaved himself to his feet. Cities for Uncle Elder, Crelly knew, were places to go when there was no other choice. John gripped her hand tightly, his fingers dead cold.

"Elder," said Aunt Lois, "we knew that would come. Married or not, Crelly has to have her try."

Uncle Elder bowed over the empty fireplace. "Guess I thought you'd just come home, Crelly," he said. "After all this schooling fuss. We'd go on as we were before. Even when I knew you wouldn't."

Crelly went to stand by her uncle. "You gave me everything," she said quietly.

Uncle Elder touched the black andirons with his toe. "I don't care about that, Crelly. Whatever we gave we wanted to, and we never had a minute's regret. Not a minute." He cleared his throat. "But, will you be safe?" His voice squeezed through his throat in little words. "Will you be warm? Who will watch out if you get sick? All's I care about."

John stood up. "Look, Elder, I'll take care of her."

"You seem to think so." From underneath lowered brows Uncle Elder gave John a glance. "And Crelly seems to think so. But I don't know you."

Aunt Lois lifted a hand. "Elder, please."

"Now, Lo." Elder straightened, looking hard at the tall blond fellow who had stolen Crelly's heart. "What I'm thinking is, I never knew anyone living on an allowance from his parents who amounted to a thing."

"Elder!"

"Uncle Elder, you don't understand—"

"I understand, Crelly. We each have to support ourselves in this life." The older man held up his hands, creased, bent, scarred.

Somewhere in the back of his mind John could hear his mother speaking. "It's a good investment. We'll make it all back." He was, always had been, part of her investment scheme. She fully expected that eventually he would be in business with her. To lose Crelly because of the grind of those wheels was more than he could stand.

"My parents have money," he said. "That's not my fault. They give it to me, so much a year—that, or pay the federal government. I'm a convenience, a savings for them. The dividends come to me through accounts they've set up. This is also not my fault or any of my doing, but it would seem a damn fool thing to turn it down."

"A man stands on his own two feet," Elder Leavitt said.

"A man doesn't turn down what's already his, Elder."

They eyed each other.

Aunt Lois sighed.

"Now, Crelly, this fellow here is polite and well intentioned," Uncle Elder said, "and he may be pretty smart."

"Only brilliant," said Crelly.

"Brilliant, maybe," said Elder. "He's well-off, and except for this one reservation I have, I like him. I do."

The room was still. Crelly blinked. "You do?"

"Yes," said Uncle Elder. "And if you have to marry anybody, it might as well be him. Just"—he shook his head—"I don't know."

"Oh, phoof!" Aunt Lois threw her knitting down. "Phoof, Elder! Why do you do this to us? Why, when you can see that Crelly has her heart set, just set on him?"

Crelly, radiant, turned to John.

"It's just, it makes me feel so goddamned old," Elder said.

"You are old," said Aunt Lois. "I am, too. So?"

In Maine there are woods roads in every trace of forest. The woods extend, sometimes over hundreds of acres, and these roads connect and intertwine, one leading to another, so that it's possible, even for those who know the area, to lose themselves. Sometimes a road opens out into a brittle, orange-needled slum of slash left years ago by loggers, where the smell of balsam and sun-oxidized pine rises high into the air, drifting like smoke. Sometimes the road is a single track of moss and wild oats that leads into hovering, dappled shade. You may find yourself on a damp bank where you must cast an eagle eye out over tender knee-high grasses for poison ivy. The air is heavy with moisture and wet earth. Then, suddenly, you are in some dry unnamed meadow, where yellow stems break underfoot and your throat stings, parched.

"If you look around," Crelly told John as they walked, "you might find a cellar hole. Up by those big old maples, maybe. Once I found a growth of rosebushes higher than a house. But that was on the other side, close to the river."

They strolled along, finding among some pine trees a wide expanse of pure white sand. John dug with his foot. "There are clamshells in it! Was this ocean once?"

"I don't know," said Crelly. "But there are lots of places like this around here." She smiled at him, flirting. "When the ocean comes back in, sir, will you take care of me?"

He grinned. "Are you worth it?"

"You!"

"Kiss me."

They wandered until at last Crelly felt it was time to turn around. She looked about speculatively. All John could see was trees. "Are we lost?"

"No. We've been moving west, facing the sun, away from the road. Now we turn and move east, toward it. Keep the sun at our backs."

It was some time before they fought their way clear, at the brow of a hill. Below was a cleared space, high bushes and saplings, and far below a ramshackle house, its small foundation green with mold, its windows covered with tattered plastic. Beyond were two collapsed piles of boards and masonry, a barn once, a shed.

"Where are we?" John asked, surprised by the look of horror on Crelly's face.

"Let's go," she said. "Now."

"What is it?"

Crelly fled down off the ridge to a clearing where two mounds of earth were overgrown with weeds; her foot caught in the loose dirt.

In her desperation she thought she saw a head, a body. A black marionette danced. She slipped, cried out, a bleat from the buried past.

John, crashing down the hill after her, tore through a line of saplings. "Crelly? Where are you?"

"Over here! Oh, John!"

He, too, saw the mounds of earth, but they were of no shape he could identify. He found her at the edge of a little clearing. "Are you all right?"

"Yes. I slipped." She would admit only that, not the face she had seen or the black quivering body.

This was a Crelly John didn't recognize, her shoulders trembling, her eyes wide with fright. "Please," she whispered. "I want to go home."

In one smooth motion John picked her up, settled her firmly in his arms. "We'll just walk along like this," he said.

Through the field and down to the road Crelly clung to him, her face buried in his shirt. John looked back only once. The house behind them seemed to sink into the ground. Although the day was warm, a little ribbon of smoke lay eerily straight up in the air above its chimney.

Gradually Crelly relaxed. "I could walk now."

"On that ankle? No, you couldn't."

It was two miles back to the Leavitts'.

John took her into the house, deposited her on the living room sofa. Aunt Lois scolded. Uncle Elder brought ice for the ankle.

"We got lost," Crelly said.

Later, Elder took John aside. "You carried her all the way home?"

"Yes."

"For a sprain?"

"Can't take any chances." John flexed his shoulders. "She did get a little heavy."

"You'll be lame tomorrow." Uncle Elder shook John's hand. "I guess she's going to be all right with you."

There were No Trespassing signs at intervals all the way to John's parents' home on Prouts Neck.

"We must be almost there?" Crelly asked.

"Almost."

"Are you sad? Are you worried?"

"No, no. I'm fine."

John stopped the car, pulled a plastic card out of his pocket. Fed into a machine, it opened a gate across a road. "Winslow Homer lived on this road," he explained. "There were so many tourists that no one felt safe."

They traveled along the ocean for quite a distance, turned, turned again into an area that seemed mostly trees. At last they came to a high stone wall. John got out, pressed a concealed button.

"Where are we?" Crelly asked.

"Almost home." A large steel gate opened, closed after them.

They rounded a curve. There was a long sweep of lawn and at the top of a rise a mansion made of stone.

"Where's your house?" Crelly said.

John sighed. "That's it."

"Oh, no." She saw the picturesque jumble of stone façades, with two wide wings.

John slowed the car.

"Sorry," she managed to say. "Just got a little scared."

Circular driveway, bricked pavilions, unusual flowers. John opened the door to the house. "Mother, we're here."

To the left was the living room, beyond that a conservatory. Crelly could see the brilliant red and white of a summery sofa cover and a lampshade of pearl beige. Straight ahead was a dark staircase, underneath it a small receiving room with glassed doors that led to a flower garden. To the right was a dining room, high and dark, buff-colored with Chinese tapestries. Crelly found herself staring at an ornately carved hall chair. Sitting in it would be agony.

A tall golden-haired woman appeared at the door of the living room. She wore a dress in an oblong shape, with extra material at the sleeves. Her jawline was as square as John's; her eyes were neither gray nor blue.

"So this is Carol. John wrote us about you. Very nice. Hello, dear." John leaned from the waist to peck at his mother's cheek. Crelly reached to take the proffered hand, but it was in and out of hers in a moment, as a letter might slide from an envelope. "Come in," said Helen Werner. "Do come and sit for a moment."

For all her height she seemed vulnerable, shaken. She was thin, the sort of woman one wanted instinctively to protect.

They went into the large, elegantly decorated living room.

"Oh, how beautiful," Crelly exclaimed.

"Yes," said John's mother. "The red-and-white-striped slipcovers, don't you think? A touch of excitement."

"Oh," Crelly said, "very exciting."

John sat on an arm of the plush sofa. He didn't look straight at his mother but to the side, or away.

"John, please don't sit there." Crelly patted a seat beside her on the sofa. John, frowning slightly, took it.

"Yes," said Helen Werner. "You are the first girl John has brought home to meet us. Certainly not the last, John, I'm sure? John is a late bloomer, but we expect he will have many years of dating."

"Any girl is lucky to know John."

John's mother asked a few questions about the university. John answered them politely. They went on to discuss some mutual acquaintances. Crelly studied the room. Two sofas faced each other. Chairs were set at intervals, each with its own shining table and elegant lamp. What must it be like to live in such surroundings?

"Come upstairs," said Helen Werner. "I'll show you your room, Carol."

"Crelly," said John.

"Crelly," said his mother. "An unusual name. Unfortunately, Crelly, I'm in the process of redoing some of the guest rooms, so we will give you one of the smaller bedrooms. I hope it will be adequate. You'll be with us such a short time." The woman's expression was politely solicitous.

"I'm sure it will be fine," Crelly said.

The wide stairs, a little room comfortably furnished. Spread, pillow sham, curtains and rug repeated the same flowered pattern in shades of blue. "Oh," said Crelly. "It's really very nice."

"Matches your eyes," said John.

"Quite a few servants have lived in here," said Helen Werner. "Now, John, we'll let Crelly unpack. Come with me. Your room has been completely redone. You don't mind, do you, dear?" Nodding at Crelly, Helen Werner led her son away.

It was a theory of acting that if one assumed an attitude, a position of the face and the body, some of the feelings of that position would reveal themselves. When she'd finished hanging up her things, Crelly stood as John's mother had, hands at her sides, straight neck, shoulders back. She re-created the tightened cords at the neck, the sadness in the eyes, and when she looked in the mirror, she saw a woman of fearful insecurities and, also, fearful strengths.

John didn't recognize his old room. The bookshelves were gone, the walls painted dark green with gray woodwork. Here and there were tall vases with pink and peach-colored china lilies in them.

"What do you think?"

"It's quite something," he said. "I'll be very comfortable, Mother."

"Good. Freshen up and come back downstairs. I suppose she'll know that we eat at eight?"

"Crelly? I'll tell her."

"No, I'll tell her myself."

As if that will keep me from Crelly's room, John thought when his mother had left.

A little while later, he took Crelly on a tour of the house. There were many empty bedrooms, several with private baths. Along the hallways was a dark, hand-painted wallpaper depicting scenes of Portland Harbor a hundred years before.

"Oh, my," said Crelly.

John waggled a hand. "Great for museums."

They completed their tour of the house by entering the green-painted kitchen, where a short plump woman, her hair in a tiny ruffle on the top of her head, felt her way about blindly.

"I hear you, who is it?" the woman said, peering down at the pages of a cookbook, which she held two inches from her bespectacled nose.

"John Werner and a friend."

"The little boy?"

"Yes. Well. Katie-Four-Eyes, may I present Crelly Kemp?"

The old woman didn't appear to have heard. "Is there some message from upstairs?"

"No."

"Then why are you in my kitchen?" She turned to a pot on the stove.

"Sorry." John and Crelly left. John sighed. "Getting cranky. She used to make me sandwiches."

"John, why does she have that name?"

"Four-Eyes? Once two Katies worked here; she had glasses, the other one didn't. Her real last name is—I don't know now. I don't know if I ever did know it."

Back in the living room Crelly held out her arms and they embraced.

"What is going on here?" Helen Werner's shaken voice came from the doorway.

"Sorry, Mother," said John formally. "Didn't know you were here."

"Even so, John," Helen Werner said. "Now we'll play Peggoty until dinner."

Crelly and John followed her into the conservatory. "The board is of teak, inlaid, Crelly," Helen Werner said, setting the game on a small table. "You must be careful how you touch it." The board, eight inches across, was set up on legs, with a tiny drawer beneath. Inside were the pegs, of carved ivory, each two inches long.

"Scrimshaw," said Helen Werner. "On my side of the family, we trace our line back to the first ship captains in this area, the owners of sailing ships."

Alabaster eggs, Crelly thought, looking into the woman's eyes. Laced with red cracks.

The game was easy to learn, but not to win. John beat Crelly several times. "Now," he said, "try it again. This time put your pieces here and here." He began to lay the game out, to play both sides. "Put your piece over there, yes, that's right. Careful. If you do that, I'll do this."

She continued to lose.

"In our family, we tend to be very good at this game," Helen Werner said.

John was intent on something he called "triangularity." He didn't really see his mother, nor did he see Crelly until her pale, slightly tired face appeared some time later across the shining length of the dining room table.

Above it, an astounding chandelier shot daggers of light everywhere.

"We know a family of Leavitts out in Falmouth, connections in Boston," said John's mother as dinner was being served. "Are they related to you?"

"No." Poor Mrs. Werner seemed more rattled every time Crelly could not produce a relative with a family name she knew. This was like a code, a self-protection. To have the proper relation, Crelly decided, was to own the plastic ticket that fit the slot. "I have only one set of relatives," she said. "My brother Gene is the wage earner in that family. He drives a truck."

"Truck?" said Helen Werner.

"A manure truck."

John's father, at the far end of the table, chuckled, muttered something no one quite heard. No one quite saw Jack Werner, either. He was a form filling out a three-piece lawyer's suit. His eyes, canny and childlike in their bid for approval, he averted. Crelly thought him a cipher until she realized the undercurrent between him and his wife.

Dinner did not go well, despite Crelly's attempts to please. It seemed to her that the harder she tried, the more disappointed John's mother became. The next morning, at breakfast, she tried again.

"More cream, my dear?"

A heavy little silver pitcher, to match the heavy silver napkin ring at her place. Crelly stared at it. "No, thank you. I wonder where John is?"

"Out for a morning run." His mother sighed. "He likes to be alone, you know. Tell me, what are your plans for education, my dear?"

"Well, right now I'm studying theater at the university. I might sometime look for acting work in one of the bigger cities."

"The theater." Helen Werner lifted her hand, let it flutter to the table. "How terribly interesting. No one in our family has ever been on the stage. We all have such terrible memories for the lines, you know."

"Well, I do like it," said Crelly.

At that moment John came into the dining room.

"Have you taken your pill?" said his mother.

"Yes." John's eyes fell to his napkin.

Ever afterward Crelly would remember that picture of him, eyelashes sweeping his cheeks as he fibbed. "What pill?"

"John is on medication," said Helen Werner. "Every day of his life."

John's eyes stayed down. He was the picture of health. "I thought you and I might go for a walk, Crelly," he said. "To the ocean?"

"We might all like to do that," said Helen Werner, "and then lunch with a dear old friend of mine, Laura Stearns. Tonight, John, Clydy McPherson is coming for dinner. She said she's missed you over these last few months."

John nodded.

"I'll go upstairs for a sweater." Crelly escaped. She didn't know any of these people.

John followed her up into her room, took her in his arms.

"John, what pills do you take?"

"No pills. Haven't for several years."

"She doesn't know that?"

He shrugged. "It seemed simpler not to mention it."

Crelly leaned against him, her fingers under his shirt, on the cool muscles beneath. She looked up. In the doorway stood John's mother.

"Are we ready?" she said.

John nodded, let Crelly go. In a few moments all three of them set off down the path.

Laurie Stearns was a woman of Helen Werner's age, a quiet, thin little soul with a wreath of gray hair. "Crelly," she said. "How quaint. Darling, just darling." She used a cultured, widemouthed accent, a bit nasal, as if the openings in the back of the throat were partially occluded. Crelly throttled an impulse to imitate. "I understand," the woman went on, "you are interested in the theater?"

"Laurie is very creative," Helen Werner said. "She makes puppets."

"Thank you, Popsie," said Laurie. "That's my name for Helen. We gave each other names at Smith. Popsie and Laurie."

Crelly nodded, stole a look at John, across the table. He was staring at the window frames. He might have been a thousand miles away.

"Yes," she said. "I think someday I'd like to become an actress."

"An actress," said Laurie, on a somewhat horrified intake of breath. "Oh, Popsie."

Chastened, Crelly stared at her napkin ring.

John had abandoned them, in spirit at least. He spoke when spoken to, otherwise kept the door of his interior computer room closed. He examined the crosspieces around panes of glass in the windows.

"Don't you find, Popsie," Laurie Stearns said, "that the youth of today are unrealistic in their expectations?"

"I know, dear." Helen Werner sighed. "But how to tell them so? They rush quickly into doubtful liaisons that are no good for either party."

"Quite." Laurie Stearns also sighed.

Crelly pushed food around on her plate. She felt she hadn't had a good solid meal since she arrived.

When Helen Werner walked her friend to the door, Crelly turned to John. "Well, that was nice, wasn't it?"

"What was?" His eyes were a hazy sky.

"If you'll excuse me, I'm going to my room. I have some reading to do. Tell that to your mother, John. If you speak to her at all." Crelly marched up the stairs.

Helen Werner came into the hall. "Thanks for the lunch, Mother," John said. "Crelly has some reading to do. She will be down for dinner."

A storm brewed on his mother's face. "Really, John. Tell Crelly we must make plans together. I need to speak to Cook, and then Crelly must come downstairs. Please."

"In an hour or so?" John said uneasily.

"No. At once." At least his mother had gotten Crelly's name right. John took the message upstairs.

"No," said Crelly, "I'm tired. I want to read. Tell her that."

"Crelly, are you mad at me?"

Crelly gritted her teeth. "No," she said. "Why should I be mad at anyone?"

"Then would you come down, please, just for a little while?"

Crelly tried to think. Aunt Lois would have said, "Oh, the poor woman. Be kind, Crelly, to John's mother."

"All right," she said after a moment. "I don't know what's gotten into me today."

A little before eight there was a knock on the door. John came in, touched the light switch. Crelly, who had been napping, awoke and stared, not sure where she was.

"Crelly? Look, it's almost dinnertime. I thought you might want to dress." He had on a dinner jacket with black velvet lapels.

"John, I can't. I have no evening clothes." She buried her face in the covers.

John wanted to pick her up and carry her off, as he had in Edgar. "It's all right. Just that Mother has invited all these people."

"What will I wear?"

"Doesn't matter. You're always beautiful to me."

She looked out, looked him over.

"Let's just get through this, okay?" In his eyes was supplication.

"Okay," Crelly said. "Okay."

No matter how she arranged her belt of gold chains or how nice the modest gold loops of her earrings looked below her piled hair, it was still obvious that her dress was homemade and her low-heeled shoes were not proper for evening. At the last moment she uttered a prayer for survival and, like a prisoner on a long march, without thought of distance or destination, she opened the door, went down.

There were grand arrangements of flowers. There were gowned women and men in dinner jackets. A woman named Clydy attached herself to John, wouldn't let go. None of it mattered beside the performance Crelly felt forced to give. She was gracious and friendly but made of steel. Nothing could touch, nothing hurt. John's eyes swung toward her again and again.

At last the two of them sneaked into the dining room. Each person's place at the table had been marked with a hand-printed card. John was seated by Clydy, Crelly down at the far end of the table. John switched the cards. He and Crelly sat down, holding hands.

When Helen Werner came in with her guests, she saw them, said nothing. Her face was wary. Several times during the meal she glanced at Crelly, sizing her up. The woman's eyes had become quite red, cracked-looking, Crelly saw. Someone commented on this, asking if she were suffering from allergies, and John's mother nodded.

After dinner, guests moved in and out of all the beautiful rooms, talking. Clydy McPherson came, laid a hand on Crelly's arm.

"Good luck." She breathed alcoholically, weaving as she spoke. "You'll manage it all better than I have, I expect."

"Clydy, I've called a cab." Helen Werner took the woman's arm.

"Crelly will be a lovely wife for John, Helen," Clydy said. "John is in love with her. That's plain enough."

"Oh, Clydy," said Helen. "You are so refreshing."

Helen Werner glanced at Crelly repeatedly during the remainder of the evening. Crelly thought it was like a series of snapshots: Crelly with a wineglass, Crelly beside John or speaking to the elusive Jack Werner.

When the last guest had left, Helen Werner came back into the living room, sat. She looked sad, weary.

"Let's go for a walk," John said to Crelly.

"Capital idea," said Jack Werner. "I'm almost tempted to join you two." He glanced at his wife. "I'd better not."

"Well," John muttered as the door closed behind them, "you did that very well."

"Did what?"

"All those people."

"I enjoyed the party."

"Hmm."

Crelly walked a little ahead of him. When he reached out, she extricated herself from his grasp. "I think you'd better take me home, John," she said. "Back to Edgar. I've had enough of this."

"What?"

"Maybe you'd rather have Clydy. Clydy would fit right in."

"You fit right in. At least, you did tonight," John said grimly. "Don't you want to be married?"

"Your mother thinks I'm an adventuress."

He guffawed. "Crelly. She doesn't think that at all."

"Are you calling me a liar? I know people. I've been watching." Too quick for him, she turned, fled inside, up the stairs.

John followed her. "Crelly? May I come in?"

"No. Go away."

"Let me in or I'll pick the lock. They'll think you've driven me mad."

"Oh, for heaven's sake."

The door opened. Her long hair was tousled on her shoulders. He wanted to touch it. He wanted to hide his face in that hair.

She frowned at him. "All right, come in."

"Crelly, I want you to marry me."

"I know that! I just don't know if it's such a good idea!"

As if she'd hit him, he sat.

Crelly thought she should have hit him. Or walked out of the house on the spot. But then she saw his profile and felt more like weeping. Beneath his stillness was, she thought, a well of tears so profound there might never be a bottom.

"What are we fighting for?" She went to him, held him. "It's all right. We'll be all right."

"I know this is hard. I'm sorry. Look, friends?"

"Friends."

"I want to tell them tonight. Now. What we said, third week in August."

"John, what will you do if they forbid it?"

"Marry you anyway. We're of age."

"You're willing to do that?"

"That's what it's all about."

"All right then." Her hand in his, they headed back down the stairs. His parents were still in the living room, John's mother staring off into space, his father reading.

John cleared his throat. "Crelly and I wanted to tell you, we plan to be married. We've set a date. We hope you approve."

John's mother said nothing. His father looked up at them. "When is the date?"

"August twenty-second," said John.

John's father got up, poured himself a drink.

"You'll live at the Towers?" Helen Werner said. "We'll continue on as before, John? Same place? Same arrangements?"

The sunken, reddened eyes had a cash register gleam, Crelly thought, but the voice was not sharp. It was shaken, as if this were the least they could do.

John and Crelly looked at each other. Their agreement was fast, simple: nothing mattered if they could be together. They nodded.

"Better to run away and elope," Jack Werner said to the cut-glass Scotch decanter.

"We will be happy to welcome Crelly into the family." Pointedly ignoring her husband, Helen Werner rose, smiled, touched her cheek to Crelly's.

Crelly blinked. It was so sudden, so graciously done, with such obvious courage. "Thank you," she managed. "I know I'm not the sort of person you would have chosen for John."

"Nonsense!" said Helen Werner. "Whatever gave you that idea?"

"I don't know," Crelly said. "But I'll do my best to fit right in."

Helen Werner's laugh splashed into the room, water covering stones. "Don't worry," she said. "I have chosen you, my dear." Her hands touched a necklace of black opals, orange lights glittering within. Later, Crelly would remember the woman's deep-cuticled fingers, their nails shiny and hard from being manicured, gripping those stones.

At least, Aunt Lois told Crelly when she and Uncle Elder joined John and Crelly at the Werners' a few days later for a get-acquainted dinner, Elder had not worn his baseball cap.

"No," said Elder glumly as they all stood together for a moment on the gravel driveway. He fingered his tight dress shirt collar, ran a hand over his shining bald head. "Instead, I get to look like an egg in a cup."

Aunt Lois nudged him gently with her elbow. "Behave."

Elder's Sunday suit was shiny across the shoulders, though Aunt Lois had tried pressing it with a spritz of vinegar, to take off the shine. He would have a new one, she said, for the wedding. She herself wore a dress of flowered crepe with a detachable lace collar. The dress looked as nice inside as out, every notch matching, the seams overcast.

"Let's go in," Crelly said.

Helen Werner wore silk, an oblong shape. Jack Werner had on a brown three-piece suit. There was a drink already half finished in his hand.

"Mrs. Leavitt, I am so glad you're here," said Helen Werner, leading everyone into the living room. "With the wedding date so soon, we haven't a moment to lose."

"Please call me Lois. I know what you mean. Young people don't like to wait. I didn't, myself." Lois Leavitt smiled and glanced at Elder. "Long ago, now. Sometimes seems like yesterday."

The two women sat together on the sofa.

"Mm. Yes. Listen." Helen Werner sipped her drink. "What do you think of the larger sanctuary, at St. Luke's?"

Aunt Lois glanced at Crelly. She was too polite to contradict John's mother on such short acquaintance. "I believe we shall have to consult with the bride," she murmured.

"Crelly, such a dear girl," said Helen Werner. "Lois, do you know Les Pains?"

"In Portland?"

"Oh, yes. Excellent caterers, really excellent."

Aunt Lois stiffened. "Are we discussing Crelly's wedding?" she asked.

Dinner was announced. The women relaxed, took each other's arms. Everyone filtered into the dining room.

"Oh, my," said Aunt Lois. "That is one of the finest chandeliers I have ever seen. Look, Elder, isn't it beautiful?"

"Waterford," Helen Werner said.

"My Lord," said Aunt Lois.

Uncle Elder stepped back to the threshold, looked up. "It's a wonder, all right. How's your wiring?"

The question tickled John's father. "You know, I expect to throw the switch on that damn light someday," Jack Werner said, "and have the whole house short out."

Uncle Elder nodded.

"Jack!" said his wife. "Please. Now, John, you sit there, Crelly over here."

"Elder will sit by me," said Jack Werner. "Don't fuss so, Helen."

"I wasn't aware that I was fussing."

"It's really all right," said Aunt Lois. "We women can discuss Winslow Homer while the men put their heads together." Crelly knew how Aunt Lois hated it when men and women split up into separate areas at functions at home. "What are people so scared of?" she would ask.

Touching Aunt Lois's arm, John's mother sat down. The meal began. Among the many dishes served were tiny new beets in little glass saucers.

"Garden's growing well?" said Uncle Elder.

"These," said Helen Werner, "are hydroponic, water-nourished. They come from our greenhouse."

"Delicious." Aunt Lois cast a warning glance in Uncle Elder's direction.

Either he didn't see it or he chose to ignore it. "You know, as a young man I had to go into the hospital once, have my appendix out."

"Oh?" said Jack Werner.

"Elder, no," Aunt Lois breathed.

"It all went well enough," said Uncle Elder, "and I was getting ready to go home. Then, the night before I was to be discharged, what do they bring me? New beets. That's what it says on the menu, 'new beets.' "

"They are nourishing," said Helen Werner.

Aunt Lois shook her head. "Don't encourage him," she whispered.

"So next day," Uncle Elder went on, "I'm all ready to go home, and a nurse comes in. 'Mr. Leavitt, you can't go, you got to stay one more day. You got blood in your stool.' "

Aunt Lois groaned. Helen Werner meticulously wiped her lips with a corner of her napkin. From the other end of the table came a sound like wind in a canyon. Uncle Elder breathed like a bellows, in and out quickly, laughing.

John's shoulders shook, but he kept his face straight. Crelly looked away for fear she, too, might laugh.

Jack Werner said, "Hell, it was the beets, right?"

With complete understanding, the two men nodded at each other.

"That was one nurse who didn't know her business, nor mine," Elder said. "I had to stay right there in the hospital for twenty-four more hours. Damn tab running the whole time."

"Sue the bastards," said Jack Werner. "I had a man in just yesterday with a similar case."

John and Crelly caught each other's eye, a mistake. From then on throughout the meal, whenever they looked at each other they began to laugh, trying to hold it in mightily but unsuccessfully.

Aunt Lois sighed. "I won't even apologize for him," she said. "I won't even bother."

Jack Werner, enjoying his wife's discomfiture and the undercurrent of laughter around the table, told one amusing story after another about his work, each punctuated by Uncle Elder's appreciative "Is that so?"

"Well," said Helen Werner, "since we're all having such a happy time, perhaps we could take our coffee in the living room?"

"Certainly." Aunt Lois turned to her, eyeing Crelly for support. Crelly and John, staring at the walls, were trying to look serious. They all moved into the hallway.

"You get much mildew in a place like this?" Elder asked innocently.

"Some," said Jack Werner. "The stone, you know."

Crelly moved stiffly away, her lips clamped shut. She didn't glance at John, not wanting to see his trembling face.

Unexpectedly Jack Werner began to bounce on the floor. "Feel that?" he said to Elder.

"Beams." Elder nodded. "Better check for rot."

Without a glance at their wives, the two men left the room.

Helen Werner looked perplexed.

"Headed for the cellar," Aunt Lois said. "Or the attic. His only good suit, too."

Crelly began, helplessly, to laugh out loud. John joined her. Gales of their laughter rang out. They leaned against a paneled wall, and each time they caught sight of each other, even to a hand against wood, they dissolved in more paroxysms.

"Go ahead. Get it over with," said Aunt Lois. She turned to Helen Werner. "Nerves," she said.

"When you two have recovered," Helen Werner said, "feel free to join us in the living room."

"Yes," said Aunt Lois. "I can't take much more of this." Arm in arm, the two women left.

To be invited to laugh took some of the shine off it. Snickering, John and Crelly followed them.

"Now," said Aunt Lois, "let's put this wedding together." She leaned toward John's mother conspiratorially.

"Indeed," said Helen Werner. "We really must hurry if we are to have the invitations properly engraved."

"My dear," said Aunt Lois, "there's no problem. Our church will hold two hundred people, one hundred for you, if you like, and one hundred for us. Our own little church out in Edgar will do just fine for the wedding. Crelly would never be married anywhere else, isn't that right?"

"Yes," Crelly agreed.

"But—the caterers," said Helen Werner.

"Oh, well, our Women's Association is all set to do the food," said Aunt Lois. "It's all taken care of." She and Helen Werner had been leaning together like two old friends. Now each pulled back a little stiffly.

"It will be beautiful, Mrs. Werner," said Crelly softly. "All the August flowers, a long summer day." She looked up at John. Neither of them cared much about the wedding beyond getting it over with.

"Well." Helen Werner frowned at her hands, which lay empty

in her lap. "I have a wedding dress that has been in our family for years. All the brides in our family have worn it."

"We've already chosen a pattern," said Aunt Lois. "A Butterick Classic. I've cut into the cloth."

The two women were sitting quite far apart on the sofa. "Well, it seems," said John's mother, "that this is to be a homemade wedding."

Aunt Lois looked at the woman, looked again.

"Some of these guys, you never know." Jack Werner and Uncle Elder headed back into the room.

"True," said Uncle Elder.

"One of them I went out to see," said Jack Werner, "suing over his septic system. They were digging. The septic tank"—he laid a hand on Elder's shoulder—"was the body of a 1945 Ford truck."

The two men sniggered. "He'd rolled up the windows, hadn't he?" said Uncle Elder.

"Sure had," said John's father. "It was the sewer pipes that were the problem."

"Stovepipe?"

"Yes."

Helen Werner's voice sounded sharp against Crelly's and John's mirth. "Most of Jack's work is with my corporations," she told Aunt Lois. "Jack is usually too busy to deal with small, local cases." At "small" and "local," Helen Werner looked down her nose at Aunt Lois.

Aunt Lois sat straight. She spoke softly. "He seems to enjoy them, though."

"Sherry?" said Jack Werner.

"Don't mind if I do," said Uncle Elder.

"We'll send along the invitations when they come," said Aunt Lois. "Or address them ourselves, whichever you like."

Helen Werner eyed Crelly. "Either way. We'll be so glad to have Carol in our family."

"Crelly, Mother," said John. "Her name is Crelly."

"Of course. How stupid of me." Helen Werner smiled at Aunt Lois. The two moved a little toward each other on the sofa. "Do tell me," said Helen Werner, "a little about your family."

There were two hums in the room, the men a lower sound, the women, higher. John and Crelly listened in. At the end of the evening, Aunt Lois and Helen Werner rose, walked arm in arm to the door. "Well, thank you," said Aunt Lois, "for a lovely evening."

The women's heads bent together. "You're entirely welcome," John's mother said. "We were so glad that you could come."

Uncle Elder and John's father shook hands. The two couples smiled, waved at each other as Uncle Elder and Aunt Lois got into their pickup truck, drove down the long driveway.

"That was a good dinner," said Jack Werner to his wife when their guests had left. "Good conversation, for a change."

"Yes," said Helen Werner dryly. "Wasn't it?"

In their pickup truck the Leavitts rumbled down the road. "He's okay," Uncle Elder said. "But her I don't trust as far as I can throw her."

Aunt Lois stared out over the black reaches of ocean at night, hung on as the truck turned a bend and headed inland. "My feeling to a T," she said.

2

Gene hid in the woods and watched while Lois Leavitt made the long trip to the head of the driveway. Into the mailbox she set a letter, then lifted the red metal flag on the side of the box upright so that the mailman would know to stop. Gene waited until she was back inside her house, crept up, snaked the letter out, melted into the woods. He opened the letter, but there was no money.

His eye ran down the words.

Aunt Lois's round handwriting filled two pages easily with a few thoughts. At the end of the letter she had written, "Elder and I are delighted to see how well-off you and John are now. Just stay the same self in marriage, Crelly, as you were before the wedding, and know that we always love you."

The woods were still; cool fall air separated each tree from the next. The letter crumpled in Gene's hand. Crelly, he thought. Married, she had everything. She had always been able to make or break him.

He and Alice were dying. Slowly. No matter how he worked, they were going behind. Alice's savings had been used up. There was less food in the house, less hope. The cupboard was bare of that.

If Crelly was on his side, fine. If not and he was going to go down, he would take her with him. He would see to that. He would see to it.

He opened the crumpled paper, tore it into a million tiny pieces, which he scattered. They made the only movement there was in all the spaces of cold.

In the early weeks of their marriage, Crelly began to plan how she wanted their home at the Towers to look, wandering from bedroom to living room, dining room to kitchen, changing each to fit her own tastes.

She and John should have their own things, cups and saucers, blankets. Perhaps they could put some of the furniture in storage so as not to have to tiptoe around it.

I'd like a good wooden breadboard, she thought, instead of that heavy marble affair in the kitchen. White cups like Gretta's, a platter like Aunt Lois's for roasts, some crockery mixing bowls. I'd like to have some dishes with scalloped edges.

The living room needed a comfortable chair for John, a footstool, more bookshelves. The monochromatic covers someone had put on John's books would have to come off at once.

She would like softer lighting in the bedroom. On the bed was an ugly orange spread with silver threads running through it—that would have to go. Perhaps Gretta might weave them a new spread?

But while Crelly was making plans, Helen Werner paid them one of her visits.

"You won't give towels another thought. I've bought you yours already, all those lovely orange ones. And the place has been decorated within the year, so of course you won't change any of that."

"As a matter of fact," said Crelly, "I thought I might."

"My dear, if you did change something, we would have to call in a decorator to protect our investment. That would be an extra expense. You wouldn't want that. Now, the bedding is all fine. The kitchen is equipped. Cook will do everything."

"I can cook," said Crelly. "I'd like to."

"Nonsense. Cook is a nutritionist, dear. I go over the menus with her myself, all planned ahead of time. Now, do be careful about the water and electricity. All those bills come to us, you know. My dear, if you must operate the garbage disposer, be extremely careful. It is a special system. Let Cook do it. About the laundry—"

The woman opened John's closet. "Here are the bags for the laundry, good. Have you sewn labels inside all of your things? The laundry is an expense, so we must be careful."

"Yes." Crelly sighed. "I'll make a note of it." She was beginning to understand the look of John's father. She was beginning to feel like him, herself.

"Everything will be fine," she muttered to the well-ordered rooms when Helen Werner had left. "As long as I remember my lines."

Before the wedding, she and John had been so busy being The Couple, celebrated, partied, photographed. They had been rehearsed, rearranged, rushed. The vision she had had in the chapel on the island the year before must be true of brides, Crelly decided. Familiar with everything but the face of the groom.

What was this tight, fearful reservation she felt, so that it was necessary to act, to pretend that all was well? She loved John, didn't she?

"Friends?" she had said to him too often lately.

"Friends," John always replied, puzzled by her insistence.

On the silver sofa Crelly huddled against him, but after a visit from his mother she was unable to relax. Everything had been given to her on loan if she cooperated, she felt. What was it Helen Werner really wanted?

Crelly didn't want to think what she did think, that Helen Werner wanted her son for herself. Crelly didn't want to feel that Helen Werner was creating in her, Crelly, a personal representative, a carbon copy of the contract of ownership.

Marta was still in her office when Crelly left the theater one evening in October.

"Crelly?" Marta's voice rang out in the cement corridor.

"How did you know?"

"Your footsteps." Marta rubbed her eyes. "The story of my life, footsteps in these corridors. What are you doing here so late?"

"Working."

"Go home, Crelly. You're getting too tired. Take some time off, why don't you?"

"I should. Don't worry about me. Go home yourself, Marta."

"I will. Let the cat out. If I had a cat."

"I'll go home," said Crelly. "Put dinner in the oven."

"Late to begin dinner."

"It's all made."

John was wondering if something was wrong between him and Crelly in bed.

All the mechanics worked, but sometimes as he hovered over

her, Crelly's glance moved restlessly across his shoulder to his neck. It was a frightened look. She loved him, didn't she?

As the sexual rush ran over him, left him limp, Crelly often cried out his name in a lost voice, as if she had forgotten who he was.

How could you, John wondered, have a person naked under you, here her tipping breasts, there all the corridors of a woman, your wife, and still be afraid that you aren't what she wanted?

He guessed that his mother came over quite often to oversee Crelly, who didn't know much about running a household. Or so his mother said. But the book Helen Werner left one day was by Dr. Brinkley, their family doctor and his mother's counselor. The book was entitled *Love and Marriage* and dealt with the sexual experience.

John and Crelly read it together. This was the modern age. They were an enlightened couple. It turned out to be quite interesting and even improved his technique, John thought. Much as he had always disliked Dr. Brinkley, the setup of the chapters was appealingly mathematical. There were graphs charting male and female arousal times, orgasmic heights and frequency, tapering-off levels. There were average numbers of sexual encounters at various stages of married life. There was measurement of penises.

John had begun to see if he and Crelly matched the numbers in the book. It was a mental checklist. The weeks when they made love three times were above the national average. If he could perform the act just right, with the proper frequency, Crelly would have to be satisfied.

"You know," he had said earlier in the month, "we started out pretty well after the wedding, but I've been wondering. Is something wrong? Do I do something to worry you?"

"No, of course not." She had put her fingertips on the high soft skin at the insides of his thighs. He had lain back on the sofa that glittered like a silver tray, his body served in measured portions.

The only time he and Crelly were really happy was when they spent weekends on Emil's island. In that atmosphere they were comfortable. He could skip the pressures of making love by Dr. Brinkley's trendy book, touch Crelly when he wanted to because he loved her.

Crelly's key clicked in the lock. She should not find him worrying. John turned his gaze to his papers.

Crelly let herself in, kissed his forehead. "Sorry I'm late. Are you hungry?"

On Emil's island, John thought, they all wore old clothes. Crelly always had on new, here. She wore them to be nice to his mother. Oblong silk blouses. Nightgowns almost too familiar, his mother's brand. John reminded himself that clothes had nothing to do with love.

"That's all right," he said aloud. "I had plenty to do here. Sure, I can always eat."

"John," Crelly said, "did your mother visit your place so often before I came here?"

"I don't know. Maybe. I didn't notice."

"Sometimes I think she's not checking up on the condominium but on me. She lets herself in with her own key—that bothers me. She asks me things. How late you work."

"Mother's just careful."

"Yes." Crelly bowed her head, turned away.

John saw the head go down. An irritated thought came to him: Why was Crelly so dissatisfied? Was this, as his father had often said, the general condition of women?

Later that night he woke to find she had gotten up. He stood in the kitchen doorway while she poured herself a glass of milk, drank, set the empty glass on a drainboard and started out of the room. Then she turned back, rinsed the glass carefully, put it in the dishwasher.

That night he couldn't sleep at all. He turned to his books, computer sheets.

The concept he and Emil were dealing with had to do with measurement, the attempt to establish a general mathematical law for the spatial relationships of particles in beams of light. "Something that isn't there," Emil said. "That's what we need. Otherwise, what are we going to do?"

"Go over and over the same ground," John had replied. "Rats on a track."

The next morning Crelly answered the buzzer. "Yes?"

"Crelly, it's Gene. Let me up."

"Yes." My brother, Crelly told herself, but she could hear Cook in the kitchen and was for once glad of the woman's presence. Gene's knock on the door was unmistakable, accompanied by the metallic clamor of the door in the frame.

He brushed past her.

"Well, how are you?" Crelly said as Aunt Lois always had. "Can I get you something to eat?"

Gene turned. An odor came from him, of wood ash and damp must. His hair touched his collar in black strings. "Come on, I don't look that hungry."

Crelly shut the door.

"Nice and warm in here." Gene looked about. "Yes, I've always said it's just as easy to love a rich person as a poor one."

Crelly stood behind a straight chair, waiting. "Can I help you in some way, Gene?"

Crelly's outline behind the chair trembled slightly. She laid a hand on the back of the chair for support.

"Out in the country, Crelly," Gene began, "we're havin' an awful hard time. You folks here, all nice and warm, don't know what it's like out there. We're going to be cold this winter, Crelly. We're going to be hungry. The worst of it is, we don't have a thing to look forward to. We just got so damn little."

Crelly gripped the chair. "What is it you want, Gene?"

"Money," he said. "Crelly, there's a little store in town that's for sale. I want to buy it, fix it up. Alice and I have made a lot of plans about paint and carpeting and such."

"How—how much do you think you need?" she managed to say.

"Quite a lot. Five thousand dollars, down payment. Then maybe monthly payments." Gene's voice dropped. He sounded fond of her, as if they had some special attachment. "It's awful hard to get a loan if you haven't got anything. Hell, Crelly, you probably spent that much on furniture for this room. You can do this for me. Maybe, someday, you'll come for a visit. See what we're up to." His voice was strange, wooing.

Crelly shuddered. If she could only keep it simple. Take from the rich. Give to the poor. "Well, I don't know. It's a lot of money. I —I'll have to speak to John. I don't have any money, myself."

She could see he didn't believe her.

"Well, good. You ask." He stood, surveying her place as if he already owned it. "It's really up to you, Crelly. All depends on what you want. I'll stop by again in a few days." Crelly didn't move. He walked past her, let himself out. The door slammed.

Crelly lifted a shaking hand to hush it. Cook came out of the kitchen. "Mrs. Werner, I'm off to do the shopping. I'll be back at two to set up dinner."

Crelly nodded. A moment later came the sound of a key in the door. She backed away as the door opened.

"My dear," said Helen Werner, stepping inside, "you aren't ready to go? Remember I said I'd take you to the theater today? Here, let me get your coat."

Obediently Crelly put on the coat.

"You seem quiet today," said Helen Werner as they left. "You know, when I see a young bride looking pale, I think of pregnancy."

"There isn't the slightest danger of that, Mother Werner."

"Fortunate," said John's mother. "Dr. Brinkley says that it's so important to give people a chance to make their marriage work before there are children."

Crelly paused in the hallway. "Yes," she said, "I know."

She knew everything, thanks to Helen Werner and Dr. Brinkley. She had no doubt that if she and John ever had children there would be more volumes by Dr. Brinkley, to add to the one already prominently displayed on their bedside table, all about exactly how children should be raised.

That evening, at dinner in Prouts Neck with John's parents, Jack Werner spoke less than usual. John, abstracted, was present in flesh only. Helen Werner ran everything. Here was the fire in the fireplace, and here the thin demitasse cups, and here Cook, to take them away.

When dinner was over Helen Werner said, "Saturday at four, for cocktails, dear?"

Crelly accepted for herself and John. John hardly heard.

Later, when they went to the car, Crelly found she had forgotten her purse and went back inside to the hall table to get it.

"You ignored him altogether," Jack Werner was saying. "Why don't you leave Crelly and John alone?"

The back of his figure was turned to her. He poked at the fireplace, was speaking to an empty room.

Crelly tiptoed out of the house, got into the car. Silently she rode to the Towers, got undressed, went out to the living room. John was deep in calculations. She went to stand in front of him, stood there a long time before he looked up.

"John," she said, "why are you angry with me?"

"What? Me? I'm not angry. Of course not." John looked not at her face but at her nightgown. His glance shied away. He went back to work.

"John," Crelly said, "do you love me?"

"Of course." His eyes were on his work. "Crelly, it's just all these papers, this problem we can't seem to work out. Now that you're at the theater so much, I've just got very involved in this thing."

"You're involved in your work because I'm at the theater?"

"Nothing else to do," John mumbled. "But it's okay, really."

"You mean, it's my being at the theater that's at fault?" Crelly's voice rose. "John, what else do I have? When I do come home, you're working. Right now, while I'm talking to you, you're only half listening!"

John looked at her over the top of his figures. "I can hear every word you say."

"Then pay attention! Even when I'm here you don't pay attention to me!"

John didn't want to argue with the woman he saw before him. He searched for something to scatter the force of what might be brewing, remembered Dr. Brinkley's book.

"Crelly," he said, "do you realize that women are more likely to be upset at the same intervals each month?"

Kill this bastard, Crelly thought, horrified. "I'm surprised, John, that you even stop to count!"

"Oh, I count everything. You know that."

"Fine!" Crelly cried. "Count the trips I make!" She stalked to the bedroom, then back with pillow and blanket. "One," she said. "One trip!" She slammed the bedroom door behind her. The lock slid into place.

"Good!" John said. "A little peace around here!"

He sat with his papers, waiting for the door to open again, but it didn't. This, he told himself, was Crelly's problem. Locking him out of the bedroom, now what kind of woman's hysterics was that?

All night long Crelly dreamed there was someone outside her bedroom and there was no door. She was in danger—where was the window?—she had to escape. The person outside the room was wringing her heart. Could it be John, pretending to love her, taking everything she had?

At first light she was awake. She wouldn't get up. She didn't want to see John this morning; she couldn't get the word "friends" out once more. John left without his breakfast. She heard him go. She knew she would have to get up, carry back the pillows and blanket, and remake the bed before his mother came in and checked up on all her belongings.

Crelly frowned. On all whose belongings?

She got up.

That evening when John came home, no one apologized. "Friends?" he said halfheartedly.

"Friends," she said, loathing the word.

"Emil's asked us out to the island this weekend." It was a peace offering, almost an apology.

"We'll have to talk it over with your mother. She has plans," Crelly said quietly, viciously.

"Then just tell her we can't come."

"For once, you tell her."

"All right. I will."

They slept on opposite edges of the bed that night, packed for the island in silence the next day. Owen's eyes went from one of them to the other as they stood on opposite sides of his little cabin. He said little.

They were glad to see Gretta and Emil, and that made it easier for them to be friendly to each other. When the two old people sat near their fire and said, "Tell us, what has happened in Portland?" both Crelly and John began to tell pleasant little stories, surprised to find themselves smiling, once again listening to each other.

"In a week's time," said Emil that evening, "we have been called to New York."

Gretta shot him a surprised glance.

"No, it's true, Gretta," the old man said. "I haven't had a chance to tell you yet. I was thinking, if John and Crelly would like to come out here to the island and house-sit while we are gone, they would be welcome."

"Of course," said Gretta. "The very thing. What a good idea, Emil. Since we are going anyway."

With gratitude John and Crelly agreed to come. In bed that night, they made love.

The following Monday, Gene turned down Pearl Street toward the Towers. He hid his ears in his collar, his hands in his pockets, and reached toward the door of the place with his whole body, as a runner might lean toward a finish line. Today was the day he would know for sure. Inside he pressed the buzzer.

A ringing noise upstairs made Crelly jump. Gene's voice came, an old warning. "Crelly, let me up."

She pressed the button, opened the door a crack. The beginnings of jowls hung below Gene's jawline, she saw. His thin lips parted loosely, the lower protruding from the upper, the lips of a child waiting to be fed.

"Well?" He stood in the doorway.

Crelly clung to the knob. "I haven't talked to John." She didn't hold the door open; she didn't want him inside.

"That's no way to treat your brother."

"A little more time, Gene," she said. "We've been so—busy."

His eyes were murky. "Okay, two more days. That's all I've got. Let's be doing it."

Crelly put a hand over her mouth, took it away, picked up an old thought: here was her brother, needing help. She would have to be Christian.

By nightfall she had talked herself into a guilty hole. Her escape was to ask John for money. "John, Gene was here. He would like to borrow some money. I—I don't know how you feel about this."

"Borrow?" John looked at his papers. "How much does he need?"

"I—I don't know. Five thousand dollars."

"My God, Crelly!"

"For a store! He needs it, he has nothing!"

John hesitated. "I'd have to talk to my parents. Five thousand dollars is a lot."

"Poor but proud," said Crelly.

"What?"

"Worthy, but down on their luck. Give them a little boost. Why should we have so much and they so little? Especially since they are deserving."

"Crelly, are you all right?"

"No!"

She headed for the bedroom, slammed the door behind her, locked it.

There fell a silence. For a day, John and Crelly were each punctilious in their care not to disturb the other. Coals were fanned, however. Their glow pulsed upward through the ash.

When Gene buzzed again, in two days, Crelly opened the door without hesitation. "Yes, Gene?"

"Alice didn't even get up today," he said. "She's got nothing, Crelly. Nothing. You have to pity her."

"Have to?" Crelly's head came up. Her eyes hardened, her lips pulled in. "I'm not going to help you, Gene," she said. She wasn't sure where this cutting voice came from or why it spoke. "Get out. Now. I'm sick of you. I never want to see you again."

She tried to slam the door. Gene held it open with his arm. "Don't think you can stay away from me forever, Crelly," he said. His voice was dangerously quiet.

Crelly slammed the door, locked it. Three loud bangs shook the frame. Somehow she kept from crying out. There was silence.

She waited, unlocked the door, opened it a crack: no one.

Grabbing a coat she left the building, spent the day in the city. Everywhere she walked was ugly, everything she saw, askew. Dead people walked the streets, mannequins from the stores. It was late when she called a taxi. No one would want to walk alone in the dark.

The hallways at the Towers were deserted. Crelly was too overwrought to look around corners or care whom she might meet. She let herself into the apartment. John was sitting on the sofa.

"I guess you didn't miss me," she said.

"I thought you were at the theater." John saw by her expression that innocent words could be weapons. He tried again in his most reasonable voice. "Crelly, what do you think is going on here?"

"Gosh, I don't know. Why don't we measure it and find out?" Crelly dropped her coat on the floor. It lay like a dead animal. The coat had never been hers, anyway.

Her hand lingered over a little chair opposite the sofa, a chair so frail no one had ever dared sit upon it. The chair tipped. One of its high-backed knobs knocked into the etched glass shade of an expensive floor lamp beside it. The lamp rocked, the shade shattered on the floor in a skirl of sharp milky pieces.

John rose, alarmed. "Crelly, don't walk there. It's all broken glass."

"No." Crelly looked him in the eye. "I hate all this stuff," she said. "Don't you, really?"

John mouthed the only formula he had ever used. "My mother is generous."

"Is she?" Two red spots glowed on Crelly's cheeks. "What has she given away? Think now, John, what? Dishes?" She whirled, flew into the dining room. John followed her. She opened the breakfront, surveyed its contents. "Are these yours? Are they mine?"

She turned, disappeared. He caught up with her in the bathroom. "Three dozen orange towels," she muttered, tossing them into a fiery heap in the middle of the floor.

John thought she'd gone mad. "Crelly. Crelly, please."

Crelly heard him speak the words. She saw his approach, like a shaken black thing. She shoved at him claustrophobically and ran.

John fell, cracked an elbow, swore, found Crelly in the kitchen. She was pulling out pots and pans, tossing them onto the counters. "None of this is mine," she was saying. "What is mine? What, here, is for me?"

John lunged, Crelly pulled back. What she saw was a black marionette. The silverware tray in her hands flew upward. A shining silver cascade of forks and spoons, so many fish, poured upstream. The noise was terrific.

"Crelly!" John roared. "Stop it!"

She hadn't meant to throw the silver, but she wouldn't take any more orders, or any threats. She couldn't. "No!" she cried, found the heavy marble breadboard, swung it off the counter. "Don't touch me. Don't you ever touch me."

John roared again. "Don't you dare take anything more! Don't you dare, Crelly! It's selfish. So selfish. You never loved me. Only money, my money."

The breadboard flew out of Crelly's hands, narrowly missing his head. It gouged the side of the refrigerator, clattered to the floor in one immutable piece.

"I hate you! I'll kill you!" She tore at John, hit him with her fists again and again. John, in a voiceless rage, pulled back, slapped her once, hard, on the face.

His hands fell to his sides.

"Oh, no," he said. "Crelly, I'm so sorry. Are you all right?"

She had died, Crelly felt. She was dead; they were both gone. "Yes, I'm all right." Her eyes were piteously frightened. "Please."

The print of John's fingers was rising in a red bruise on her cheek. John's face was ashen, his lips white. "Crelly, I have never— in my life—" Words failed him.

Tears ran down Crelly's cheeks. "I want to go to Uncle Elder's," she said.

John nodded, made a hurt sound in his throat.

Crelly went to the bedroom, hauled out a suitcase, opened the drawers of the bureau. Underneath all the other things in there, the few articles of apparel she still thought of as hers made a small heap. The suitcase wasn't hers, either. She went back to the kitchen. Without a word to John she rummaged, found a paper bag.

It was late when they reached Edgar. Aunt Lois and Uncle Elder came to the door in their bathrobes. "Crelly? Are you all right?"

They crowded into the doorway, then back again so that Crelly and John could enter. Aunt Lois's face showed alarm, but she was ready to smile.

"I'm sorry," said Crelly. "I—I didn't know where else to go."

"You sit right down," said Aunt Lois. "Both of you. Have a cup of tea. Is everything all right?"

Uncle Elder's face grew hard. His eyes were on Crelly. As she stepped into the light, Aunt Lois saw the finger-shaped bruise on the side of her face.

"Crelly! What happened?"

Crelly opened her mouth to answer, closed it again. Uncle Elder's eye moved to John. "Did you do this?" he said.

Twice John tried to speak before he could. "Yes."

Uncle Elder drew in a breath. "You should go. Now."

Aunt Lois's look of disbelief hurt John more. He set his lips together, fighting for control. "Crelly—I—if you would ever think about coming back, I would come and get you, Crelly. Anytime." He left.

"Oh, Crelly." Aunt Lois led her to a chair. "What happened?"

Uncle Elder stood in the doorway, watching John's car rumble away. The white bristles of beard on his face were like salt on sand. "Crelly, John hit you?"

"Yes. But we've been fighting. Tonight I was so angry, I hit him. First. A lot of times." She raised her head, looked at Aunt Lois. "Is this me?"

"I don't understand, Crelly. I don't know what to say. You seemed so happy."

Tears rolled down Crelly's cheeks. "I'm so ashamed."

"If he hit you, Crelly"—Uncle Elder's voice was controlled—"he can go straight to hell."

"Elder." Aunt Lois closed her eyes.

"I don't care." He raised a fist, brought it down slowly and gently, rocked it on the door frame. "This is what divorce courts are for," he said. "So be it."

John felt himself enclosed in a tin canister, hurtling through the dark. He headed back to Portland, the sun sending a dribble of yellow across vertical lines of buildings. He got out of the car, realized the canister was not that enclosure but his head.

The condominium was a shambles. Chain-locking the door from the inside, he went first to the bathroom, saw the orange towels in various sizes strewn on the floor. His throat filled, made to swallow the whole terry mound. He stood at the toilet, squirted sourly. Crelly's shadow was on the wall, her face was in the mirror; at night she would reach for the toothpaste while he bent over the sink. He looked again. The only real sign of Crelly in this room had been Crelly herself, and she was gone.

Had she hated this place so much?

In the bedroom he caught sight of Dr. Brinkley's book on a night table; he picked it up, drop-kicked it into the living room. It landed in a corner. He went back, sat on the bed.

There was Crelly's suitcase, upside down on the floor, heavy with straps and buckles, nothing Crelly would have wanted in the first place.

The juices in his mouth tasted like tears. John lay back. Crelly had been in this bed; she was gone. Hard hurt sounds rose inside him. He would not let them out.

He could hear Crelly's voice. "What has she given away? Think now, John, what?"

For an undisclosed amount John's mother had bought him this condominium high over Portland Harbor. The garage space for the MG cost $30,000. "All in my name, John, a good investment. When you go to a real school, I'll sell it for a profit."

The rooms, decorated by his mother, had always made John chilly. He'd sat on the silver sofa, looked at all the mirrored surfaces. "This is nice," he'd said.

"Out on your own," his mother had said. "All grown up."

John gave her a peck on the cheek. Helen Werner had flushed scarlet, let herself out the door.

In the evenings before he met Crelly John had jogged, enjoying the long lovely fall dusk in Portland, watching the view of the ocean from the Promenade as he ran. The Promenade bloomed with fall colors. Wide lawns sloped past park benches down to the harbor. In the distance was the flat line of the Atlantic. A former governor, Baxter, had had foresight enough to set aside these stretches of ocean-facing land for public use in the city. People came to sit and talk, to stroll or jog, glancing out to sea.

One evening he nearly ran into a strange woman. He stopped to help her, apologizing. She was older than he, with a vivid face and a lot of dark hair. She was drunk.

"What's your name?" she said.

"John Werner. Are you hurt?"

She lurched forward, laid a hand on his collar. "May I call you John?"

"No," he said. "I think you should call me Mr. Werner."

A bus stopped; she ran for it.

A day later his doorbell rang. He opened it to a small dark woman of thirty. "John," she said. "John Werner, welcome to the building! Your mother said you were here. I'm Clydy McPherson. I live upstairs—at least I have for the last couple of months. The process of divorce, you know. Thought I'd stop and find out how you're doing. How do you like it here?"

"Fine, thank you," he managed to say. Clydy McPherson was the woman he had bumped into the day before.

"Good." She looked at him as if she were about to laugh. "I'm waiting for you to invite me in, John."

"Oh. Oh, please," he mumbled, "come in. Sorry for the mess, I'm in the midst of some work. Would you like something to—drink?" He had wine, but he was not going to give it to her. "Fruit juice, maybe?"

"That would be nice."

He brought her some orange juice, sat down. "I think I must have seen you the other night."

"Oh?" she said. "I don't remember."

She had a short, plumpish neck. As she talked on, she shook her brown curls back. With one finger she tapped the skin just below her jaw. Now and then she smoothed her full skirt down. His eyes moved from neck to bosom to skirt.

Usually John was too abstracted to feel any but the most profound urges, which he had learned to dispose of in private, then get on with real business. But sitting across from Clydy McPherson could make a man think thoughts.

"Well, I should go," she said. "But I'll check in again." In the doorway she turned. "John, it just occurred to me—would you like to meet for dinner tonight? If you came up I would cook, and we'd both have some company."

"I—"

"You'll love it. Come at six. Bring your appetite."

She left. Bemused, he shut the door.

He went back to his books, but he kept an eye on the clock. This was a tiny silver gadget his mother had chosen, with a chrome face and pointed black arms that stuck out beyond the face like whiskers on a cat. At five-thirty he could study no longer; he showered, changed, brushed his hair. He had fifteen minutes to go.

He didn't know which apartment was Clydy's. It would take some time to find it, perhaps the full fifteen minutes. He was nervous. To comfort himself he wondered: If he measured his steps, how many would he take to the half minute on the way to the directory in the downstairs hall?

Eight seconds to a floor. Twenty seconds to walk to the elevator, thirty-two seconds to the fourth floor. Five seconds for the door to open, four more to cross the threshold. He would have to walk down the hall. He would have to knock.

Standing by the directory in the deserted downstairs hall, John eyed his watch, lifted a hand, knocked on empty air. Three seconds.

Five minutes before the time he began his walk to the elevator. The door opened, closed on schedule. Thirty-two seconds up, forty across the threshold, one minute to the end of the hall; turn right, turn right again. Nine seconds from Clydy's door he stopped. Should he have brought a gift? His mother, on the occasions when he had accompanied his parents out to dinner, always took a gift.

John turned, ran back to the elevator door, leaped over the threshold, sprinted to his apartment, fumbled for his keys. The clock was the first thing he saw. He tangled the cord in its whiskers. The button, the door. Door, threshold, length of hall, right, right again. He knocked twice.

Clydy had put her hair on top of her head and dressed in something soft. It made a line at her breast, another below. "Well, John, come right in. Is this for me?"

"I thought, for a little gift," he said, breathing heavily. "Sorry I'm late."

"Are you? I hadn't noticed. Well, it's a clock! Why, thank you very much! But John, isn't this yours? What will you do for the time?"

He shook his head. "I always have it with me. The fourth dimension, you know."

She took him by the hand, led him into the living room. On the floor was a white rug with many raised patterns.

"You sit here on the sofa," she said. "Push some of those pillows aside, you're so tall. I can't think why I needed so many."

The pillows were ruffled. He laid them aside with clumsy care. A plainer one he stuffed behind his back.

"Do just make yourself at home. Glass of wine, John?" She already had a half-finished glass.

He sipped slowly while she talked. The effect of the wine tingled along his arms, down the back of his neck. Clydy seated herself on the white rug. When she looked down he could see the complexity of her curls. When she looked up her eyes swept along the rug, over his legs, across his body to his face. He tried to move on the sofa, but the pillows caught him in a vise of iron stuffing.

Ruffles, fabric, the perfumy smell in the air, made him overly warm. Skin riffled at his chest, down his back.

John finished his glass of wine. She poured him another. Then another.

"We should concentrate on the future, John. If I had a future, I wouldn't need to talk about the past, isn't that right?"

"Yes." This wasn't at all the kind of conversation he was used to carrying on.

John wished she would sit beside him, wished he could be out of there and gone off jogging down the sidewalk. She laughed, stood close to him. "Come on, dinner's all ready."

She held his arm against her. He could feel the slimness of her waist, the richness of her hip.

He sat at the table. His knees were shaking. He had to plant his feet firmly upon the rug.

In the center of the table a bouquet of small proportions allowed its blossoms to trail against the dark wood, a reflection in a pool. He could scarcely bear the sweetness of those tiny cupped buds. His hands were clammy as he managed his napkin into his lap.

Clydy said, "I do hope you like to begin with fruit."

Melon in a sauce that caressed his throat. "Delicious," he said.

"Glad you like it. An old recipe, a gorgeous beginning."

He watched her carry dishes back and forth from the kitchen. His hands felt stiff and heavy, two pieces of knurled wood. Clydy set before him a steaming dish. "I hope you like curry?" She stood beside him.

"Oh, yes."

"Good. One of the few dishes I know how to make well."

On the table were two tiny but heavy silver pieces up on little silver legs, a pepper shaker and a silver salt bowl; in the bowl was an even smaller silver spoon. It was a set similar to one his mother used at home. "I think your flowers are the most beautiful I have ever seen."

Clydy smiled. "When your mother was here, working on your place, I sometimes invited her up for a cup of tea. She, too, loved my flowers."

"My mother was here?"

"Yes. She's so charming. So wise about her son." Clydy moved closer. "A mature young man sometimes chooses an older woman, a mother figure, as a confidante."

John swallowed hard. He recognized those words. They weren't Clydy's or his mother's. They belonged to Dr. Brinkley. He looked from Clydy to the silver. His head hurt. He had to get out of there, run. "I'm not feeling well," he said.

Clydy frowned. "Oh, dear. John, come and lie down. Some aspirin? Some wine?"

If he waffled now he might have to deal with it again. "Clydy, this isn't going to work."

"Oh, now, here." Her lips pouted, coaxed. "Come sit in the living room. I hope it isn't my good curry that is making you feel bad."

"Clydy." Heat rose to John's eyes. "You are too old for me."

Her face slid momentarily into lines that were indeed old. "I know it may seem that way, John," she said.

"I'd better go."

"All right."

A little later he had let himself out into the night to jog, feeling the scrape and thud of each sole on cement. He wasn't aware of the places he ran to. Against streetlights, leaves shone in confusing colors and patterns. He stared out across the ocean, a black surface swept in the distance by lighthouse light. The night felt heavy, waiting for rain. Stars blinked out. The ground held firm as he ran. Only his own muscles gave until they ached.

John's head was heavy as he lay on his bed. His nose ran. The door shrieked, caught by the chain. "Crelly?"

"John, don't you ever shave?" His mother pushed past him into the room. "Please don't put the chain lock on when you know I come in every weekday morning."

"You do." Crelly had told him this. Now the awful reality of it struck him.

Slim, elegantly dressed, his mother stood in the middle of the room. "What in the world happened here? John, were you robbed?"

John suddenly disliked his mother. The feeling took him by surprise. "Crelly—" He stopped.

"She did this? My Copley lamp? I knew it! I knew she wouldn't fit in!" His mother collected pieces of the lampshade. "I wonder if these can be glued." She rose, went through the dining room to the kitchen. "My silver. Oh, my beautiful refrigerator!"

John didn't move.

"How could she do this?" Helen Werner strode back into the living room. "Something was wrong with that girl, John, very wrong. I knew it, but some things a young person must see for himself. You come right home with me. I'll ask the maid to clean up this mess." Helen Werner walked around the room, touching belongings. "Was she rational at all, John? Where is she now? I should call Dr. Brinkley right away. He'll know what to do for her."

"Crelly isn't here. I took her to stay with her aunt and uncle."

"Good place for her. She should get some help. Dr. Brinkley does this kind of counseling. Also, John, he's written a wonderful book, *The Healthy Divorce.*"

"Divorce?"

"It's a solution," said his mother. "Sometimes the only solution. What has she done?" Helen Werner went to a corner, picked up the volume of Dr. Brinkley, straightened out his pages, dusted him off. "John, pack your things." Her hair glinted in many careful rows.

"About the Dr. Brinkley," John said. "I did that."

"What?"

"I kicked it. One kick."

"John Werner!"

"Come with me." In the bedroom, he hauled open a drawer of Crelly's. "Look."

"That's orderly, at least," said his mother.

"Yes. Nothing has been touched. Of all these things." He rattled open his own drawer, pulled out a pair of undershorts.

"One dozen, the same time I bought a dozen for your father. So at least that's off my list."

"You have my underwear on a schedule?"

"John, what did she take with her? Perhaps we should check the jewelry? Some of those little things I gave her are worth quite a lot."

"Mother, I have a better idea. Here." John fished in his pocket, found the keys to the Towers. "Take these. I'm giving them back to you." Her pink nails closed over them. "All yours. See? You haven't lost anything, Mother. Not a thing. You can take it all back. But"—he paused, looked squarely at her—"know this. I don't come with it. Neither does Crelly."

He left, ended up at the university, sleeping through every class until Emil's. Emil took one look at him and announced, "Class is canceled. Everyone go home." Emil's students should have been used to him, but they weren't. Murmuring, they left. "John," Emil said, "we will go to see Gretta."

On the island John told Emil and Gretta as much of the story as he could. It was like undergoing a beating. His logical mind, turned inward, found a dark place, tomblike. On some walls, primitive pictures. Staggering with weariness and hurt, he left them sitting in the living room, went upstairs to sleep. Every step, every window and doorframe, reminded him of Crelly.

Downstairs Emil paced. His glasses were steamy. He took them off repeatedly, rubbed them. " 'A plague o' both your houses,' " he muttered to Gretta.

" 'A plague o' both your houses.' " Emil raised his arms, shook his fists, dropped them. "Mercutio says it. Would Crelly know that?"

"She must," said Gretta. "Crelly knows the whole play."

The Brunholtzes left for New York, regretfully, worried. "If there were something we could do," Gretta told Emil. He shook his head. "John doesn't know if we're here or not."

If I can be by myself, John thought. If I don't have to listen to anyone. He saw Emil and Gretta off, a smile on his face to mask his relief at their going. No one was fooled.

Alone, he turned to the one consolation he had always had, his work. But now, for the first time, numbers made no sense. He stared at his papers, his maps. They sifted through his fingers onto the floor. He and Emil were at an impasse anyway. Let the physicists have it. After all, what had they expected to do? John looked at the pages on the floor. Make a map of the infinite?

He remembered Kummer, a mathematician known for his work on a proof of Fermat's last theorem, an infinite number of primes. "When I attack a problem experimentally," Kummer had said, "it is proof that the problem is mathematically impregnable."

Mathematicians. In his studies John had found so many human beings full of passion, willing to fight for their particular notion of their science. Having subjected themselves and their own theories to the most rigorous kinds of proofs, they were ready to do battle when they had to. Sparks flew. Lifelong feuds erupted over the placement of a coefficient. Mathematicians stood up, they presented proofs, they published. They stood for things.

What did he believe? What did he stand for?

Wandering around on Emil's bitterly cold island, John found himself respecting most those mathematicians who had known who they were and what they wanted. He thought of Bell's description of the great mathematician Gauss: "A small study, a little work table with a green cover, a standing-desk, painted white, a narrow sofa and, after his seventieth year, an arm chair, a shaded lamp, an unheated bedroom, plain food, a dressing gown and a velvet cap." John thought of Kummer, surrounded by wife and children and happy to live retired in their company for the last few years of his life. What did he, John, want? What was worth fighting for? Suddenly, in Emil's quiet house, he knew. A peaceful home of his own. A warm kitchen where Crelly was making him an egg.

The next day he rode with Owen to Peaks Island to catch the ferry back to Portland.

Owen buttoned the cabin, hesitated before flipping the motor switch, stared out across iron-colored waves. "Not much to say today?"

"Not much," John replied.

"Cold old day." Owen reached for the switch, pulled back. "John, where is your wife?"

"She went back home to Edgar. We had a fight." John looked out over the ocean.

Owen considered all of his dials, switches. "Damn." At once, mercifully, he turned the motor on.

The floor of Gene's car was littered with cellophane wrappings of little pies, little cakes he had wolfed down and cans of soda he had emptied, crushed and tossed aside. He had followed Crelly all day. Lights went on in an upstairs room at the Leavitts', were gradually extinguished in the house except for the light over the kitchen sink. Lois Leavitt always kept it burning in case, she said, someone needed something in the night.

The Leavitt house slept. Gene turned his car quietly around, drove home.

The front of Alice's house sagged toward him. With the loss of any more support, it would fall in. A smell came from it, of wood smoke, decay. This is how your brother has had to live, Crelly, he thought. This is your fault.

Alice was up, sitting in her chair by the stove. Her head was back, her mouth open in sleep. She had few eyelashes, and her eyelids didn't quite close, leaving a band of white eyeball visible. She snored. Gene looked past her into the living room, where the Victorian lamp burnt, wooing. In the kitchen, the cupboard doors were open. So little to eat.

Gene took out his black-handled knife, pressed the button. The blade flicked open, glinting. He stared at it. Once Nick had told him a story about a man impaled on a meat hook, tortured with electric prods.

Gene shut his knife, opened it. Alice started at the sound, looked at him. "Good, you're home. The furnace needs wood, Gene. I've fed it floorboards all day."

This is the house that ate itself, Gene thought. Something in him separated, shredded. "Go get the wood yourself," he said.

Alice stood up. There was a magazine in her hand. "I knew you wouldn't get that money from Crelly."

The shriek of separation. Below that, the incessant, comfortless, closed-mouth hum of a child, crying. "Do as I say, Alice."

Her skin was sallow; she was probably hungry. "You were a good boy," she said. "You came along just beautiful. It was like being drunk, watching you."

Gene's lips barely moved. "Get up on the hill. Get your own wood, Alice."

"No. Now, I'm hungry, I'm cold. It's time you listened to me."

The light knifed the air, a reflection from his hand. Gene quivered.

"Everything your way lately," Alice said. "Off in all directions, out of control." Her voice rose. "Bib was smart, he knew kids. He and I went way back. I was fourteen when I first met Bib! He knew what to do."

"Watch it," said Gene. "Watch out."

"Oh, sure," said Alice. "Big man. Can't even manage his own sister."

Gene remembered walking down the beach. He remembered a man whose head blocked out the sun, and a black bird, swooping. "You don't know me." He slashed the air with his knife.

"Oh, yes," Alice said. "I know you. A skinny dirty kid who grew up to be a murderer. I made you. Don't forget that. I can break you."

Gene slashed, sliced the magazine in her hand. Half pages flapped, blanked faces loose. He slashed again.

Alice edged behind her chair, tripped on cups there that spilled, clattered, broke. "No, Gene." Her face was puzzled. "You don't want to do this."

"Yes!" Gene vibrated on a high frequency. "Come on! Come on, run up on that hill!"

Alice tipped the chair at him; he jumped back. She dodged out of her corner. "You don't know what you're doing! You've forgotten me!"

Gene grappled, caught her. "I haven't forgotten. I haven't forgotten anything, Alice. And I know what I'm doing. Oh, yes," he breathed. "Oh, yes, I know."

His knife sank into her, a popping, sucking sound. Alice cried out, sagged against the blade, her face skeletal with realization.

Gene pulled out the knife. A fuzzy-edged spot soaked into the front of her clothing. "Listen," she whispered. "Crelly will get you. You haven't got a chance." She fell to the floor. Her eyes closed partway.

"Crelly's next," said Gene. "You just sleep. Sleep, Alice!"

Free of Alice! Good. She had been a terrible weight.

Gene rummaged through the cupboard, took out the last of the food. This would be a long campaign, he would have to be ready. He rolled his car toward Elder's, drove into the woods.

Behind him, in the house that ate itself, Alice Herrick roused, dragged herself across the floor, leaned on the door, fell out onto the steps. Inch by inch she pulled herself forward over frost-etched ridges, rubble. Patches of blood painted the grass, gravel, as she moved. She hauled herself forward through saplings to two mounds of earth. "Bib?" She whispered, hummed, lay still, waited.

Crelly found herself in Aunt Lois's living room, paging through a family album, searching for whatever it was that had made her, her life long, so miserable.

Here in the album were people she didn't know, a stiff, unsmiling generation of ancestors. Here were Uncle Elder and Aunt Alice and Crelly's mother as children. Then came pictures of Crelly's mother and father together, of their marriage. Here was Uncle Elder, tall and thin with a full complement of hair, and here was Aunt Lois, young and pleasantly plump, in a light-colored dress and white shoes. Standing beside her were Aunt Alice and Uncle Bib, Aunt Alice taller by a head. Here was Uncle Bib in a sailor suit, lounging back against an old-time car. He looked at the camera crookedly.

Next came pictures of Crelly and Gene and Jimmy. Then there were no more pictures of Crelly's parents, Ann and Bill Kemp, but a few of Uncle Bib and Aunt Alice with the three Kemp children. Here was Uncle Bib, leaning against the store, mugging for the camera. Aunt Alice's hair was cut short; her face was older, she didn't smile. In another picture Uncle Bib turned to her, clinging to a door frame, as if he were asking for something.

Staring at that picture Crelly remembered the books she had tossed out the window at that store. What had that been about? She remembered the smell of chocolate.

Aunt Lois and Uncle Elder were in the room. "Think I'll go for a walk," she said. "I'm just trying to put it all together."

"We know," said Aunt Lois.

Shadows gathered. Crelly let herself out of the house. She was lonely. Losing John was hard. The hardness of God, she thought.

The lawn sloped to pastures, the river. On the other side of the driveway, up beyond the mailbox, rose the trees of her childhood, black against the setting sun. Crelly moved toward the woods. She'd go to a clear spot she knew, see the sunset.

October air. As she breathed it in, she found herself remembering a jump from a window. She remembered a feeling, that there was no place for her to escape to, nowhere on earth that would ever be safe. When she jumped, no one would catch her. As quickly as these memories came, they went. Somewhere was the piece of information that would make everything clear. What was it?

Up at the edge of the woods she paused. Inside them it was already dark. Pines grew close together. What was this extraordinary feeling she had, that the woods were alive?

She stumbled away from the trees, back toward the Leavitts'. It had always been a safe house. Now it shone, only a little light.

Back inside she went to stand by Uncle Elder's chair. "I need to go to the theater. Will you take me?"

Uncle Elder looked over at Aunt Lois, who nodded. Early the next morning they drove Crelly to Gorham.

John saw, as he came off the ferry, a flock of birds, rising. They presented their flat backs to him, banked, shifted. Their bodies were thin slats against the sky. Crelly is like that, he thought. The opening, the drawing up of blinds.

Gene drove to Gorham. He hadn't lost them; there was the pickup. He pulled into a side street in time to see Elder drive off and Crelly disappear.

Crelly opened the familiar back door of the theater. The smell was of cement block corridors and the paint used on canvas flats. Her eyes filled. She tried to walk softly past the office, but Marta called out, "Crelly? Is that you?"

"I—I just couldn't stay away." She faced Marta.

"No?"

"There's been an argument. John and I have separated."

"I'm sorry." Marta stared at the coffee cup on the desk in front of her. "I was married once." Every hair on Marta's head had been pulled severely into place, twisted into a bun, as into a bundle, one headful. "When he left, I couldn't believe it. A big hole opened. I fell in." She looked at Crelly.

"I know," Crelly said. "You say to yourself, what do I want? Who am I? And you don't know. I used to believe that all the—the sheep were counted, and the door of the fold safely closed at night. Now I don't know. I—I just came here."

"Pretend home." Marta rubbed her hands over her eyes. "Sitting in this office, Crelly, trying to recognize the footsteps. Hearing all the doors clang shut at night. Welcome home."

Later Crelly walked out on the stage. Between her and the seats in front was a gulf she had never seen. She thought, There is a pit between me, and me.

She tried to read, her thin, shaken voice stumbling along. Failing to get at the heart. She gave up, went down the stairs to the side of the stage.

Far in the back someone waited for her. Stood.

He was tall and blond, his thin face elegantly carved out of shadow. Crelly saw his pallor, the set of his jaw. His eyes were clouded, but the cloudiness passed away and all that was in them was love. There was nothing she knew, no play-acting on earth, that could match it. "John," she whispered.

She took his offered hand. John led her out. They walked down the sidewalk, hardly daring to look at each other.

"I love you," he said. "Let me learn to say it more often. Crelly, I love you."

"Oh, God," she prayed, muffled against his coat. "Don't let me be afraid anymore."

Gene followed them onto the wharf, to the ticket office. They looked warm. They had probably eaten.

"Two for Peaks," said John.

The ferries were small. Gene knew he would have to be careful.

"One for Peaks," he muttered inside his collar, then had to repeat it when the woman in the ticket office couldn't hear.

Crelly chose to sit below for the short ride to the island. "We'll get some warmer clothes once we're at Emil's." Gretta kept an array of parkas, leggings, boots, mittens and scarves in her entryway. She expected them to be used.

Gene watched Crelly and John go below. He hid on the deck, in the lee of the ferry cabin. His collar was up about his ears, but he was chilled. His hands, in cheap leather gloves, were cold in his pockets.

"Want some coffee?" a man asked him. "No charge. I bought some for a friend, but he couldn't come. There's doughnuts there, too. Help yourself." He gestured to a bench beside the cabin, where a cardboard container of food had been placed.

Maine friendliness. Good will, suspect anywhere but on a ferryboat headed to Peaks Island. This small winter colony had learned long ago how to get along.

Gene studied the man's face. "Thanks," he said. "Appreciate it."

The man nodded, moved away.

Gene hadn't slept the night before, he hadn't eaten this morning. His limbs were cramped, achy from his car. He wolfed down two doughnuts, drank the coffee more slowly, feeling it circulate, warm him.

The ferry pulled in to Peaks. Crelly and John got off first. Gene watched them walk, hand in hand, down a ramp to the landing. He lowered his head, followed them. There was no cover, but he managed to walk by without being seen. No one stopped him; no one spoke. He kept his distance, watching.

"Well," he heard a tall man say. "Glad to see you again, Crelly."

Crelly gave the man a smile, stepped aboard his lobster boat. Gene saw how she clung to John's hand. "Glad to be here again, Owen."

The boat chugged off. Gene hadn't the least idea of what to do next. Somebody would help him, somebody always did.

He gave the lobster boat a start, stood on the landing beside a couple of men in red and black checkerboard wool jackets. "Damn," he said. "Will you look at that? I missed them." He pointed to the lobster boat far out in the harbor.

"Owen?" said one of the men. "You missed Owen? Going out to Emil's, was he?"

"Yes," said Gene. He memorized the two names: Owen, going to Emil's. He looked helpless.

The man shook his head. He knew what it was like to be stranded on an island.

"Got here late." Gene paused, playing it for what it was worth. He waited.

"Hell," said the man, "you see that boat over there, the green moorin'? That's old Clarence Bower. He's goin' out that way, later on. He'd take you to Emil's, or I dunno but he will. Might not be for a while, though."

"That's all right," said Gene. "That might work. How do I get ahold of Mr. Bower?"

"Wait right here, I shouldn't think. He'll be down."

"Thanks."

The two men nodded.

Gene stood to one side of the landing, his arms clenched to the sides of his body. He had on work pants of dark poplin; the wind whipped through them.

An old man, bent at the shoulders, walked slowly and carefully to the shore beside the landing. Gene scrambled to meet him, introduced himself with a fake name. "Look," he said, "I missed Owen, going out to Emil's. Someone thought you might be going out that way."

Clarence Bower lifted one shoulder. He looked at Gene through square, wire-rimmed spectacles. "Well, I guess I could," he said. "You a relative, must be?"

"Yes," said Gene. "I am."

The old man bent over again, nodded him aboard. They putted off, pulling at last near three islands farther out than the rest.

"I'll be glad to pay you," said Gene. He hadn't a cent. He knew men like Clarence Bower.

"Don't mention it," said Clarence. "Glad to help." He held out his hand. Gene shook it. What Gene saw was a clean old man whose ears beneath their green wool cap were pink, whose handshake was firm, whose word had probably always been his bond. Gene leaped onto the landing, nodded his thanks, tore for the woods. Clarence Bower frowned. The bent shoulders bent a little more. The old man putted away.

There were certain things Gene knew he must do. Get into the entryway, out of the wind. Listen for voices. Slide inside the house. In a little utility room he crouched, waiting, one hand in his pocket, on his knife.

His heart beat wildly.

Voices approached. He moved quickly backward to the entry, out to the shed. It was chilly; collar up, his leather jacket wasn't much.

Arm in arm, John and Crelly came out, paused to tie scarves, pull on wool hats. They wore boots and red knitted wool leggings. They smiled at each other, moved in the direction of a small boathouse.

Gene followed, hiding himself. Crelly and John pulled out a rowboat, climbed into it. John rowed across. They dragged the boat up on the other side, entered a meadow on the island opposite, disappeared.

Gene crept inside the boathouse. Set high on the rafters was a canoe with its paddle. He hauled it out, set it in the water. He was an inlander, not much acquainted with any kind of boat, but he knew how to climb in. The canoe dampened at the bottom.

It took all the strength in his arms to pull across a span of water that looked smooth and still but that eddied just under the surface in snaking currents, over boulders. He tipped, nearly sagged over into the water, realized he shouldn't try to paddle, only to steer. Awkwardly he did so, cold water running down the back of his neck as he flipped the paddle through the air.

The tide was with him. He reached the other side, scrambled

out of the canoe, dragged it through the water toward the woods, where it wouldn't be seen. On one end was a rope, which he wrapped around a rock at the water's edge. Shaking with cold he prowled, obscured by trees, up to a building with a graveyard beside it.

Crelly and John emerged from the building, looked over the graveyard fence. John was laughing. "The tales Owen told me that day. Ever hear of a wolf dog?"

Gene skirted the building, climbed an embankment, listened, peered inside an empty church. Deserted.

He bolted back through the woods to the shore, spotted the rowboat, stumbled to it, dragged it down the sand, cast it adrift. It spun, twisted, seemed bound to float back in to shore.

Gene moaned. The current took a new direction. Like a leaf on a stream, the boat floated around the island.

Gene fled to the side to check his canoe, but water in frigid green gallons poured at him from the new direction. The rope of the canoe pulled loose. He lunged. The canoe changed direction, floated off. Madly Gene splashed after it. Cold gallons sawed, sucked at his legs. It was get out of the water or be pulled under.

On shore he shivered, fingered his knife. He would scout the island first, see where everything was.

Off he went. The land rose gradually at its edges in gullies and over treacherous mossy boulders to cliffs at the far end. Beyond the cliffs was a narrow, loudly crashing passage of ocean. Gene looked down into the chasm. Water swirled. There would be no escape from this middle island.

Crelly and John, making their way over a little path, went to stand quite near the edge of the cliff. One push, Gene thought. He stole toward them.

"Tide's going out," John was saying. "The angles are different. This is us, at the top of the head. These spruce trees are the buzz cut."

Crelly laughed.

"Down there, all that rock below us, that's the forehead. See that hollow?"

Crelly looked. Below twenty feet of vertical ridges the rock had been hollowed by glaciers into a succession of bowls. "Those are the eyes. Below that, cheekbones."

"Yes. That's the nose." John pointed to a long escarpment of stone. "Right now, just after high tide, the mouth is probably in the water."

Crelly clung to him. "John, let's go back."

They strolled toward the beach.

"Why don't we ask Emil," John was saying. "He might be able to do something, for the summer at least, if we wanted to camp out. Pretty lonely here, though."

"Quiet? No one to talk to?"

"We could use that."

"Yes. Look, we're going to have a sunset row home." They looked along the beach. The sun made a rippling orange path on the water. "Where did we leave the rowboat?"

"It was here." Crelly pointed to a long trough in the sand, the prints of heelmarks alongside. Alarmed, she met John's eyes. "Would—would someone have taken our rowboat?"

"They've pushed it into the water. The footprints—someone in leather shoes."

"Well, it has to be a joke," said Crelly. "They'll be back."

"Better go inside. See if we can make a fire. It might signal someone if they saw the smoke."

At the chapel John found some armfuls of wet wood underneath the ell of the church, and on a high shelf in the kitchen, a few matches wrapped in an ancient dusty plastic bag. Shelf paper and twigs in the stove started a blaze that sizzled fitfully, threatened to go out. "If we could just get some more coals," he said. "It's getting dark."

"When those people come back, whoever it is—" Crelly stopped. "John, someone could be on this island with us." She couldn't see his face. The only real light came from coals at a side grating of the stove.

At that moment three loud knocks shook the kitchen door on its hinges.

Crelly's face froze. "Oh, no," she whispered. "Oh, no."

The door flew open. Gene stood facing them, his knife in one hand. "That wind is a bitch," he said, slamming the door behind him. "My feet are frozen." He waved the knife at his shoes, stepped to the stove. "Now, nobody move. We'll get this over, real fast."

"Gene, what are you doing here? I don't understand."

"Don't move, Crelly." His knife quivered. "Crelly." He spoke in a strange wooing voice. "Crelly, please."

Crelly heard. Remembered. Suddenly she was a little girl, a

reader with a book on her lap, the blankets of her bed drawn about her. The place smelled of chocolate. Uncle Bib and Aunt Alice were downstairs. Uncle Bib was saying, "Alice, it's part of the plan."

What plan? Crelly knew. The plan was a trap for children.

Sometimes there was nothing in the house to eat, she remembered. When Aunt Alice and Uncle Bib left a room, you hunted wildly for treats, found them, found other things as well. Placed strategically beside the candy were pictures, books. Those, you had to pretend, didn't exist. You ate, wolfing down the chocolate you found until you heard someone coming. Then you hid everything again, just as you had found it. In the sofa, under a chair, behind a stack of boards.

Books and magazines, naked women or children on the covers. Once Crelly had opened one of the books, read. A brother wooed his sister, touched her private parts, had intercourse with her. Crelly had slammed that book shut, tried to forget it, but after reading it she was always afraid. Always. Of her brothers, but most of all of Aunt Alice and Uncle Bib, their plan. Night after night she had huddled in her bedroom, wished it had a door that could be shut tight, locked. The floor in her room was broken, light came through. There was one small window, without glass, covered with torn plastic sheeting. There was no door.

Gene had watched her. All the time. She was afraid. In some ways, as afraid for Gene as for herself. What had happened to her had surely happened to him. She tried to stay away from him, to protect him as well as herself.

One fall night Aunt Alice and Uncle Bib went to bed. Crelly, sitting awake, heard the drawer with that book in it open, close. She heard footsteps. Fifteen years old, Gene stood in the open doorway.

"Crelly," he said in a wooing voice. "Crelly, please."

She had moved like lightning from the bed, which she knew was of danger to her, to the middle of the room. That, too, was a mistake; her nightgown hooded the light, her legs were visible as shadows beneath. His eyes were on her. She felt skinny and naked. Gene came toward her, a black form, quivering.

"Gene!" she cried—somehow she had known enough to pitch her voice so it sounded like a child at play. "Watch this."

Her voice stopped him. She whirled, ran to the little window, pushed back the insubstantial plastic, and slipped out. She hung by the strings of her fingers and taut arms.

"Crelly!" he cried, and she had heard the loss in his voice. "Come back!"

His hands touched hers, a cold sandpaper touch. She let go, dropped ten feet from the tips of her toes to the ground. She had landed with some pain, but nothing had snapped, broken. She disappeared around the corner of the house, made her way, stumbling, crying quietly so as not to be heard, from one sharp, dark field to the next. Scared wordless by those hours alone in the black countryside, unsure if Gene had followed her or where he might be, she'd finally arrived at Uncle Elder's, where it was safest for a little girl, who might be thought to be making up stories, or exaggerating details, or maybe just plain crazy, to act as if nothing much had happened. A nightmare walk in the woods, maybe, but that was all. She could pretend that. She could work hard endearing herself so that a visit to these people could eventually become a lifetime pass. By pretending that everything was normal. As indeed she wished, always, that it could be.

At this moment Crelly saw Gene's slim knife cut arching flashes. She backed away slowly, separating herself from John. It was she Gene had come for, she knew. She saw the set of his shoulders, his profile against the orange light from the kitchen stove. The shoulders and neck were so much as she remembered them.

"John, I've been mistaken. I didn't know what was in my mind. I think when I looked at you I saw—"

"Shut up!" Gene snarled. "Don't move!" He was shaking.

The black marionette, Crelly thought. "Gene, please, we have to get you some help. Real help. Gene, this isn't your fault."

His knife slashed. She pulled back her outstretched hand, a sound in her teeth, the hissing intake of breath. He had sliced at her, not breaking the skin, but running the knife blade slickly through layers of her sleeve.

John erupted from his corner, in his hand a tin pot. "Crelly!" he roared. "Get out of here!"

Crelly disappeared. A door opened, shut. Bodies crashed to the floor, rolled. John groaned. Gene broke free.

"Crelly!" he cried, and tore out of the building after her.

Swiftly, silently, Crelly came from the sanctuary, where she'd hid, dragged a chair against each of the outside doors, flew to John. "Is it bad?"

"I need a towel."

She tied a towel about his leg. They pulled it as tight as they dared, but the flow of blood was not completely stopped.

"He'll be back." John looked at his watch. "After six. That means the tide is almost out. We have to get to Owen's."

"On those boulders? In the dark?"

"What else can we do?"

"I hear you talking in there!" Gene's voice rose beyond the door.

"Help me up," John said.

They waited, listening. The kitchen door splintered. Gene leapt in. Crelly and John fled into the dusk, closing the sanctuary door behind them.

"There's no place to hide in here," they heard Gene say. "This won't save you."

"A little to the left," John whispered.

Inside the chapel Gene swept his knife blade into every dark corner of the sanctuary. No one cried out. No one was there. It took him a few moments to be sure. Shivering, he swayed over the stove.

"They'll be back," he muttered. Either that or he would haul them, like logs for the furnace, out of the woods the following day. "Best thing to do is wait," he said aloud, turned, slunk out of the kitchen with its rusty glow, into the falling night.

Crelly and John felt their way to the edge of the cliff. Below them the water of the lessened tide thrummed like drums, rumbled under their feet. "We have to get down," John whispered.

"There isn't any path."

"No. Go one at a time. Remember, it looks like a face. Forehead first, bowls for eyes, cheekbones. Below that, I'm not sure."

"All right." Crelly helped John to kneel. They lowered themselves down. John's teeth ground as the rock bumped his wound.

In daylight it would have been difficult. At the top of the forehead, the rock ran in thin vertical ravines. By daylight they might have picked some kind of path, hitched from side to side. As it grew darker, however, there was only the thunder of water landing so loudly below that it seemed about to split the rock.

Crelly crawled first, pulling back in sick horror when she put out a hand and it landed nowhere at all, in air. The rock before her eyes was less dark as she grew used to it, but it was cold and slippery.

"Don't move! Hold on!" she cried out when her hand sank into nothing at the far edge of a switchback.

After a bad scare or two, however, she began to say "Okay, nothing here, time to change." John followed her as he could, not bothering to try to answer over the pain in his leg.

Slowly they progressed down the rock channels of the forehead and stood in the bowls of the eyes. John was figuring: half an hour to go twenty feet? It must have been about that. Half an hour to go over the cheekbones. The lower face? If it took more than forty-five minutes in all, they might not make it because of the tide.

Water sluiced into, but not yet over, the outside guardian caverns of lower rock, poured back into itself. The bowls of the eyes were several glacier-smoothed sockets, dead cold. For centuries, year round in their crevices, lay snow from some ancient winter.

"Over the cheekbones." John raised his voice to be heard above the thunder. "Take our chances."

Hands and feet scrabbling, Crelly turned, lowered herself down. John followed, worried by a traitorous blackness in his brain, the loss of blood from his leg.

The rocks were gritty with barnacles, sea growth. The front of Crelly's clothes was damp; her skin quaked from the constant embrace of cold and wet.

They made it to the cheekbone, but at its lower edge, they discovered, the rocks were steep, hollowed. Several times Crelly let herself over the edge only to pull back. "Nothing!" At last she did find a place.

There was little to grab but the strings of moss, which soaked through her gloves, came away in her hands. Water dripped in tiny, constant rivulets. The thunder was deafening. Did Gene follow them? She couldn't tell.

Standing on a tiny ledge Crelly turned her head, laid her face against the rock, tried to look down. It was dark. Desperately she searched for any gray ruffle, which might mean boulders, marking the water below.

"I don't know," she muttered. "This is too hard. I don't think we can do it."

At that moment the mossy shelf let go. Crelly shrieked, slid, scrabbled with hands and feet against the slippery face, cried out, fell into black air.

"Crelly?" John grabbed for her, missed, swung around the side of the jaw of rock. "Crelly!" He, too, found himself hanging by his hands in the dark. He seesawed for a toehold, realized that below the air at his feet was gravel—plain hard gravel. He let go.

"Crelly!" he roared, on his feet below the jaw. He thrashed forward, was immediately knee deep in water. "Crelly!"

Below a dripping overhang, careless of the wet, Crelly lay still. Nobody gets out of here, she was thinking idly.

When John found her, she was lying in a heap, barely conscious. "I fell in the water," she told him. "We should stay here."

"No, Crelly. The tide's dead low. Has to be. If we wait, the water will start pouring in, pull us down. A few more minutes, that's all we've got. We have to go."

Crelly saw how he swayed. "I don't even feel the cold," she said.

Without a word John leaned down, gathered her up, limped into the water. Crelly's arms closed about his neck.

John felt neither Crelly's weight nor his wound. His leggings had been sliced in strips, fluttered like wet rags about his knees, but he ignored this, clutched Crelly to him, set his mind on configurations he had seen earlier that day and with Owen, months earlier.

He could recall in detail what he had seen. Three big boulders lay somewhere in front of them. Two were round with peaked tops, but the third, farthest on, was flat, a table. Beyond that rock, shallow waves lapped against a black wall. John's eyes moved in the dark as along a sunlit corridor. He slogged forward, the water hip deep.

Skirting the two round boulders, he came to the third. Beyond, he could hear wavelets skirling against the farther lip of rock, the other island. There came into his head a space of black smoke. He knew he might faint.

He pushed Crelly up the side of the table rock. She clung, climbed, and, recovering some strength, managed to pull him up, too. Ten feet to the top of this, John thought. It would give them some time. Turning, fighting at the blackness in his head, he took Crelly's arm, pointing it so she could feel the direction.

"Small shelf, three feet up, the lip," he cried. "Another, the nose. Above that, some niches, the Indians—find the steps!" The dark swirled. He sagged. Crelly held him or he would have pitched forward, into the water.

"John!"

No answer. She settled him on the rock. In the mouths of skulls, she was thinking, was sea water. Queer creatures swam in it, white-horned, pale things, digesting the bodies that drowned.

Gene heard a cry from over the cliff. Did they know a path? He would find it. He descended, hanging on, scraping with his numbed feet for toeholds. He was cold, exhausted. He kept on until his hands would no longer grip, panicked, swung out into the air, landed against some rocks, one arm lame, severe pain in his side. Half immersed he flailed, slid, fell from rock to rock.

He scuttled over the stones. His jacket scraped barnacles, his fingers were in ribbons. His face was lacerated. Here were two boulders, huge, pointed. He stumbled, landed against another. Above, he heard a voice. He felt about. This rock would be easier to climb.

At the top Crelly lay, pressing John to her. It would be easier, she was thinking, to drop off to sleep as John had done, wake again in some better place.

Water was whispering in. Leaning down, she crooned to John, played a scene from memory. " 'We two alone will sing like birds i'th'cage.' "

A dark bird hovered. The fingers of its cold ragged wing felt along her face, knocked her head from one side to the other against the rock, fell away, reached for John.

"No!" Crelly cried. "Can't you see he's dead already?"

The hand paused, returned to close about her throat, shove her against the rock. Gene leaned over her. Crelly thrashed, battled for air, in a second of clarity realized: Juliet didn't want to live. With a control drilled into her months before by Marta, she allowed her oxygen-starved limbs to gather tension, heave until she knew Gene felt her doing it. A moment before she blacked out she let go. Her body relaxed. She fell back, dead.

The black hand lifted, hesitated, felt along John's body. Then Gene backed off the rock, slid into the water.

Crelly leaned against John, daring, once again, to breathe. John didn't moan or move. She would never let him go. She would never face the awful roar of mourning, the wide mouth of that roar, the realization that he was gone.

Together they lay, in some pleasant place. A warm breeze blew, blew again. Waves lapped somewhere, somewhere mourning thundered, but in this place a little breeze touched the skin of Crelly's face, warmed it. Then again. It was John's breath, against her cheek.

"Crelly?" He pulled her close. "Crelly, go," he whispered. "Try. An apron, steps." He spoke as if he could see it plainly. "You have to go."

"Gene is there."

"He's wearing leather shoes!" There were some other things John wanted to say, to set straight. There were things he wanted to apologize for. He didn't have the strength. He held her. "Friends?"

"Yes. Always." Crelly blinked back sudden tears. "Friends."

"Go. Please."

She nodded, settled him as comfortably as she could, lowered herself over the edge of the rock. "Ahh!" she cried out, stumbled forward. Bruised, soaked, she fell onto, rather than reached, the rock face of the other island, heard John's voice: "Small shelf, three feet up."

I can do this, Crelly thought. She reached up, searched along a surface polished by waves, found the lip, a shelf, hoisted herself up, landed where she could sit. Above she could make out a larger plateau. What had John said? An apron? A pine—the nose? Hugging the rock face she managed to stand, to turn.

But then a hand wrapped itself about her ankle. The fingers were cold as steel.

"John!" she cried.

"Dead!" came the answer.

"No!" Wrenching her leg free, Crelly hoisted herself up onto the apron above, crawled. Here was the pine tree as John had said; its slapping needles hurt her bruised face. Out of her head with fear, she thought, I can't do this. It's too hard. God, I can't. I'm not good enough, not strong enough. Let me die.

Below her was a rattle, gravel. Gene was coming. She stood, pressed her full length against the rock, reached. Nothing. "Oh, God," she sobbed. "Where are they?" The first step, a pockmark, tear shaped, was not high up, out of reach. It was at knee level. Crelly set her foot into it, reached. To the side, carved roughly into the rock, was a place for her hand. She raised her other foot. At knee level again was a second step, above it a second handhold. She began to climb.

Gene's arm was useless, thanks to his fall. He had lost his knife in the water, his clothes were in ribbons. He knew two things. Crelly mustn't get away from him and he didn't want to die. He would get her. He would get out of this. He would go away, he would live. He would be the spider in the middle of the web.

There was no sensation in his hands or feet, but when he realized that Crelly was out of his reach, he searched along the wall, kneed a teardrop niche, set his foot into it, reached, began to climb.

Crelly heard him. She pulled herself above the crag, which was the eye, reached, scrambled onto the forehead. Gene groaned close behind. The sound didn't frighten her. She pulled herself up over the ridge of the forehead, crawled a little distance at the top of the head, sank onto a flat, muddy place.

Below her, Gene pulled himself into the eye socket, then up the forehead, grabbing with his good arm, scrabbling with his feet, crawling on his belly until he reached the place where Crelly lay. With one hand he pawed at her body.

A puppet man, Crelly thought, too exhausted to move.

Gene wanted her to run. "Crelly," he gasped, "don't you know who I am?"

She lay still.

Kill her, Gene thought. Oh, little sister, I have you.

He gasped for air, lungs bursting. As he did a picture came to him, a little girl in a red plaid dress, white buckle shoes.

A little girl. A little girl in a white nightgown.

Crelly lay face down, waiting, her breathing so labored that it hardly mattered what happened to her. Let him, she thought. I've run long enough. All my life.

Gene stood, walked to the edge of the cliff. His mind worked. He was anyone. As good as. Pain. There must be some. Way out of this. Think it through again. Cold. Pain. But he was alive.

Then his shoes began to slip. They slid, went out from under him altogether. Gene fought the fall, smiled, let everything go.

Crelly heaved herself up. "No!" Black on black, a great one-winged bird rose into the air, disappeared. From below came the thunder of the sea, the tide. My brother, Crelly thought. Only my brother. Somewhere a dog barked. Turning, she saw at a distance a little square of light, Owen's window.

Owen heard the dogs bark. "One of those nights," he muttered, swung his legs over the side of the bed. Standing in longjohns, he turned on a light, reached for his shotgun. What were those dogs after this time? Owen might enjoy tall tales, but on this island animals would drag off his chickens if he let them.

He opened a large wedge of light, his front door. Couldn't see a thing. Dogs leashed, have to go unhitch them. Worth it? He hesitated. As he did, an apparition wavered out of the dark, causing him to raise his gun to his shoulder. "Stop right there," he said.

The figure stopped. For one horrified instant Owen thought: the ghost of Goose Island. But then he saw that the gore at the mouth and nose was plain, ordinary mud. "Crelly? Crelly Werner?"

"Yes." Crelly swayed. Owen caught her, helped her into the house.

"Lie here on the sofa, Crelly. I'll get some blankets, something hot. I left some soup on the stove."

She lay still. He wrapped her in blankets. "I haven't fainted," she said quite clearly, struggled up, gripped his arm. "John is still down there. Between the islands on the rocks. He hurt his leg, he's lost blood."

"You climbed down those cliffs? Of all the damn fool—"

"Listen. Please. John is trapped between this island and chapel island. A man—Gene, my brother—chased us, he took the dinghy. He had a knife. He's gone now. I think. Owen, the tide is coming in. We have to go down there, get John. Please."

In another instant Owen was on the phone. "Coast Guard, quick." He gave the details, made another call, put some more blankets on Crelly. "You stay here. Don't move. I've called the neighbors."

He took one look at her pale face, left the house.

"Rope ladder, in the barn," he muttered. "That outdoor lamp, the big one." In a few moments he was loping over the field, his arms full.

At the head of the cliff he trained his light straight down. On a flat rock below John lay still. Beside the rock a body floated, the water around it rimed with red.

The sides of the rope ladder Owen had brought were as thick as his fist, its rungs substantial, well woven. He set it securely into the rock face, wedging its metal hooks tightly. He piled loose rock on his light, to hold it, and climbed, at the foot of the ladder slogging into water shoulder deep. Reaching the rock, he pulled himself onto it. He hardly dared to touch John, but he did, rolling him over, holding him up by the shoulders.

"John? Are you all right?"

John didn't open his eyes. The white lips moved. "Yes. Owen?"

"Yes. Come on, now. They'll never get a boat in here. I have a ladder. We have to go. Ready?"

"Yes."

Owen helped John down the rock. They stumbled through the water, in and out of the beam of light Owen had wedged above. The cold was numbing. At last Owen managed to heave John safely onto the first rung. He wasn't just sure how he was going to get him up the ladder. Never be able to carry him. Water was rising.

"Owen?" said John. "How many?"

"How many what?"

"Rungs."

"Jesus, I don't know. Thirty, maybe. Head up, now. Hang on. It's going to begin to pour."

"I can climb," John said.

"Sure." Owen wedged one arm about John's chest, placed his own body behind John's. "Now when I say step," he hollered, "you step!"

John nodded. It took some concentration to connect with his feet.

Their progress was slow. When John blacked out, Owen held him up, swaying on the ladder, hollering, "Step! Step!" Slowly, one of John's feet would lift, slide, find the next rung.

"We're here!" Owen hollered at last. The two men hung, swaying. Another light appeared at the edge of the cliff, and another. In a moment there were more hands than anyone knew what to do with, of neighbors who had heard the call and come to help, to grasp John and pull him over the top, to hold on to Owen, whose face was green, pale.

"I'm all right," Owen kept saying. "Be careful how you handle him. There's another one, up at the house. Somebody call Maine Medical?"

"Already did," came a voice. "Take it easy now, we've got them."

"Owen?" John lifted his head as they carried him toward the boat on a stretcher.

"Yes, what?"

"Thirty-two, not thirty."

"What?"

"Rungs, Owen."

Out of his head, Owen thought.

"Each," John said, "for itself." He lay still.

EPILOGUE

In April, Owen, Crelly, John and the Leavitts gathered on the island with Gretta and Emil for a party honoring Owen's rescue. John's parents had been invited, but they declined. John spoke to his father on the phone.

"You have to pardon your mother," Jack Werner said. "She's in the process of giving up Dr. Brinkley. That in itself—" The man stopped, catching the nasty slippage of a side comment. There was a silence. "We're both going to this new guy, John. He says I'm part of the problem." Jack Werner tried to laugh. "What do you think of that?"

"Could be." John spoke as gently as he could.

It was a sunny afternoon. Lois Leavitt talked yarns with Gretta Brunholtz. Owen and Elder were conferring.

Elder Leavitt had been through horrors. First, Crelly and John in the hospital, then a trip up to see Alice, to follow her bloody trail onto the hill, find her dead. There'd been the sheriff, the state police, newspaper stories, the tracing of Bib and Jimmy, which led eventually back to the hill Alice had died on and to the digging up of the ghastly remains. And, of course, the unspeakable materials secreted everywhere in that wreck of a house.

"I should have known," Elder said in a low voice to Owen. "I should have asked, I should have taken steps." He shook his head. "Too busy building nice, straight houses."

"Look at those two." Owen pointed.

Crelly and John, hand in hand, smiled at each other. John's leg had healed with a scar. Crelly's forehead also bore some scars. "Enough to give an actress character," she said.

"Dear folks," Crelly called out. "I want to say some thank-yous to all of you. Thank you, first, to Aunt Lois and Uncle Elder." Uncle Elder shook his head, turned away. Aunt Lois laid a hand on his sleeve.

"From you," Crelly said, allowing her voice to bell out, to reach them, "I learned that all the sheep come down, all the possible sheep. They are counted, put into the fold. You know, I remember that, even when it doesn't seem to happen all the time."

John cleared his throat. "I want to thank you, Emil and Gretta. For all the things you have done for me, for us both."

"But we are here this evening," said Crelly, "to honor a courageous man. Owen, we give you our love and thanks."

Owen's eyes were on the water. "Hold on," he said. "Watch."

Close by, waves rippled. Farther inland, in the lee of the next islands, the water was like glass. In the distance a rowboat slim as a pencil turned on that smooth surface, moving without human help, until it lay still once again, pointing in the opposite direction. "The tide has turned," Owen said.